A Hometown Christmas
Hometown Hearts

Holly Jacobs

A HOMETOWN CHRISTMAS

Copyright 2021 by Holly Fuhrmann
ISBN: 978-1-948311-12-0
Ilex Books

Previously published as
A Valley Ridge Christmas
ISBN-13: 9781460323267

Copyright © 2013 by Holly Fuhrmann

Dear Reader,

My love of Christmas has nothing to do with my holidayish name. Many people think my birthday must be sometime during the festive season. It's not. It's in August. Mom liked the name Holly because she didn't see any potential nicknames in it. This is why I spent most of my life as Hall. To the point that I turned in papers in school as Hall. Move over Madonna and Cher.

So, the fact I've written seven Christmas books over the years doesn't have anything to do with a birthday, or my name. I just love the season. It's a special time. There's a spirit of giving and kindness that I'd love to see last throughout the year.

My heroine Maeve Buchanan carries that spirit with her year-round. As opposed to Aaron Holder, who's troubled by his past and future. Ultimately, he finds his place in the present next to Maeve—a place he never thought he'd find.

It was so much fun to return to my hometown series and meet up with the other couples from the wedding trilogy. It's at one of their weddings that Maeve and Aaron share a very special dance.

Thank you for sharing your holiday with me and Maeve and Aaron! I hope you enjoy A *Hometown Christmas.*

Holly Jacobs

Hometown Hearts

1. Crib Notes
2. A Special Kind of Different
3. Homecoming
4. Suddenly a Father

A Hometown Hearts Wedding

5. Something Borrowed
6. Something Blue
7. Something Perfect
8. A Hometown Christmas

A HOMETOWN CHRISTMAS
Hometown Hearts

Holly Jacobs

For Jack

And for librarians, who have made such a difference in so many people's lives...including mine. Special thanks to Miss Kitty here in Erie.

PROLOGUE

BOYD MYERS WANTED more than anything to glance over at his wife, Josie, but he didn't dare take his eyes off the road. Not that he could see much of the road beneath the white wall of snow.

"We need to pull off the interstate." His voice seemed very loud after listening to the wind buffet the RV for so long.

He white-knuckled the steering wheel and hunched forward, as if moving closer to the windshield would help him see some landmark. A guardrail. A sign. Another car. He hadn't seen headlights in what felt like forever. That didn't mean there was no one else on the road, only that the snow hid them—and that possibility scared him.

"There," Josie said, pointing to the right.

Boyd jumped and tightened his grip, thinking she'd spotted some other vehicle, but Josie simply said, "A town. Valley Ridge."

A small sign bearing the words, Valley Ridge, lit up for a split second under his headlights. There must have been other signs farther back that they'd missed because the turnoff was almost immediate. If he'd been going sixty-five miles an hour, he'd have shot right by the exit ramp. But because he was only going ten, maybe fifteen miles an hour, it was possible for him to ease the RV off the highway.

"Now I know how the shepherds felt," Josie murmured.

"Shepherds?" he asked.

"They had a star that lit the way to Bethlehem—all they had to do was follow it."

Despite the weather and his anxiety, he chuckled. "If there were stars tonight, we'd never see them through the snow. We'll have to be thankful for the street signs." The off-ramp ended and he brought the RV to a halt. "Which way?"

"All we have to do is follow the signs," she said, pointing.

There was another sign proclaiming Valley Ridge to the right.

Some of his anxiety eased—Josie always knew what to say. He put her through so much, but her optimistic attitude never wavered.

Boyd had never heard of Valley Ridge. He wasn't sure if they were in New York still or if they had crossed over into Pennsylvania—not that it mattered. Just as it didn't matter how small a town this Valley Ridge was. It would have some parking lot he could pull the RV into. And if not, pulling over to the side of the road there had to be a great deal safer than pulling over to the side of the interstate. Frankly, he hadn't been sure he could tell where the side of the interstate was.

He eased the RV onto the two-lane road and followed the sign that pointed to the right. It felt as if it took hours to enter the town proper, but he finally spotted a sign that read Valley Ridge Library. He couldn't see the building, but there were reflectors that marked what he assumed to be the driveway. He pulled the RV between them and parked. It was probably the middle of the unlit parking lot, but for tonight, that would suffice.

He turned off the engine and finally looked at his wife. "I wasn't sure we were going to make it."

"I never doubted you for a minute." Josie's arms were resting on her enormous stomach. "Carl slept through the whole thing."

He glanced at his two-year-old son, safely strapped into his car seat in the back.

"I've never driven in such a bad storm." And he never wanted to be out in weather like this again.

His fault. This was all his fault.

If the plastics plant he'd worked for hadn't closed. If he hadn't lost his job, they wouldn't have lost their tiny bungalow in Plattsburgh, Vermont. If they hadn't lost the house, he wouldn't have sold everything to buy a twenty-year-old RV that had seen better days and packed up his family, then headed off to North Dakota and the promise of work there.

As if she knew what he was thinking, Josie leaned over and kissed his unshaven cheek. "It will all come out in the wash, Boyd."

He smiled to hear her using her *grandmother's* saying. Her grandmother had been a crusty old woman who'd scared the heck out of him at first, but eventually became a grandmother to him, as well. When their families objected to them marrying at such a young age, she'd stood up for him and Josie.

"We're all here together, safe and warm," Josie said. "The storm can blow the rest of the night. It won't bother us."

"I should..." he started, trying to prioritize what needed to be done.

"You should go to sleep."

He nodded, knowing she'd worry if he didn't go to bed with her. "After I turn on the propane so we have heat." He pulled on his parka and opened the driver's side door. The snow was almost up to his knees and blowing so hard that he couldn't see the library or any other houses. He shut the door and felt small and alone, standing in the midst of the snowstorm. Then he looked back through the window and saw Josie kneeling by Carl. He took a deep breath. Josie didn't deserve the situation they were in. And somehow he'd find a way out of it.

For a moment, the wind stopped howling and rather than being pelted by flakes, the snow fell gently around him. He glanced up and caught the merest hint of light in the sky. A star. One small beacon in the sky, shining like a promise of better things.

He heard the thought and laughed at himself. Josie the eternal optimist, forever talking about signs, had turned his brain to mush. He was thankful he was alone and hadn't said the words out loud.

As if on cue, the wind picked up again and the small star disappeared behind the whirling snow.

Boyd turned on the propane and went back into the aging RV.

Josie had Carl unbuckled, and as Boyd picked him up, his son stayed asleep. "I'm sorry," he said softly as they walked toward the bed in the back of the RV.

"Boyd Myers, you've got nothing to be sorry about."

He gave voice to his thoughts this time. "If I hadn't lost my job, then we wouldn't have lost the house, and we wouldn't be out here in the middle of..."

"Snowmageddon," she supplied with a grin. "We could play 'what-if' all night, but that's not going to get us anywhere."

"We're going to spend the holidays in a RV. We're driving away from everything we know. We're driving across country, not knowing if there will really be a job waiting for me."

"We're going to spend the holidays with each other. With Carl. With the new baby." She patted her stomach. "We have a roof over our head, and we have each other. For Thanksgiving next week, I have a whole list of things I'm thankful for. You're at the top of it. You'll find a job," she finished with utter conviction and certainty. "Everything happens for a reason. Plattsburgh wasn't our real home. We're on our way to finding the town we belong to, but no matter what, we're already home as long as we have each other."

"My little optimist," he said as he shucked his jeans and sweatshirt and crawled under the covers.

Josie tucked the sleeping, pajama-clad Carl into the middle, then climbed into the bed on her own side.

"We're lucky, Boyd. We might not have much money..."

He snorted at the understatement.

Josie continued as if she hadn't heard him. "And you could make a long list of what we once had and were forced to sell, but we've got the RV. We've got Carl and soon we'll have this new baby. We have each other. Everything else will work out."

"You really believe that?" He reached over and stroked her fine, soft hair that lay spread on the pillow next to his.

"I really believe that. Life is funny. One moment, you think you've lost everything, the next you discover that you've found something even better."

The image of that lone star shining in the midst of the blizzard flitted through his head. He leaned across their sleeping son and kissed Josie's forehead.

She was right. He'd lost his job, but so had many other people in recent years.

He'd also lost the house because he couldn't afford the payments, but again, so had many others.

Even though he was in the same boat as all those other folks, he had one advantage. He had Josie. He'd loved her ever since meeting her on their first day of kindergarten.

She always denied that and insisted he'd never even noticed her until high school, but she was wrong. He'd noticed her all right. It had taken him the nine years between kindergarten and high school to work up the courage to approach her as anything more than a friend. But he'd known as a five-year-old that Josie Bentley was someone rare and special, just as he'd known she deserved someone so much better than him. But to his utter amazement, she loved him. She'd picked him.

They may have lost everything, but somehow, he'd find a way to get it all back—if for no other reason than because Josie believed in him. And that thought, like one lone star in the midst of a blizzard, burned bright as he closed his eyes. Somehow, he'd get it all back for Josie.

No matter what it took.

CHAPTER ONE

Maeve Buchanan woke up at precisely 5:00 a.m. She didn't need to look at a clock to know it was five. Maeve had an internal alarm that went off on its own every morning. Some people might find that annoying, but she liked mornings, so she didn't mind. She enjoyed being able to catch a breath before jumping into her day—her normally very busy day.

As she snuggled under the covers she realized how cold her exposed face was. It was colder than a typical November morning in Valley Ridge, New York. She glanced out the window and rather than being greeted by the big oak tree, all she saw was snow. The blizzard that the weatherman forecasted had obviously arrived.

She eased down the cover and realized that it wasn't simply cold...it was freezing.

She glanced at the alarm clock she never set, but no bright numbers lit up the room.

Darn. That meant the power was out. And no power meant the furnace wasn't working, so she not only had no light, she had no heat.

Like ripping off a bandage, some things were easier if you did them fast, so Maeve pushed back the covers and yipped as the frigid air assaulted her. She quickly put on her robe and slippers and when that didn't seem like enough, she pulled the throw from the bottom of the bed over her shoulders. She hurried down the narrow, steep steps into the kitchen and checked the window. Her view was reduced to almost nothing.

She kicked off her slippers and put on her UGGs, her barn coat and a hat. She looked down and couldn't help but smile. Her red-and-black checkered pajama pants looked absurd sandwiched between her burgundy barn coat, the edge of her robe and her tan boots, but there was no one around to notice as she nipped out the side door and marched along the house to the small shed at the end of the driveway where she stored her wood.

She piled as many logs as she could manage into her arms and hurried back inside. God bless Mrs. Anderson's sense of thriftiness and nostalgia. The former town librarian had done so much for her, and taught her a lot, as well. The woodstove still sat in the corner of the kitchen. Maeve dumped her load of wood in the wood box and opened the stove's door. She didn't use it often, but given the fact that she lost power at least once a winter, she'd had enough practice to make short work of starting a small fire inside it. She left a few of the logs for backup and took the rest to the basement where another wood burning stove was hooked up to the house's heating system. Her house was small enough that between the two stoves she'd stay warm.

It took two tries to get the basement stove's fire going, but she finally managed it. She went back upstairs and put the old percolator on the top of the stove in the kitchen, then went back outside to bring in more wood.

She'd made two more trips when the wind died down enough to allow her a bit of a view. Normally she looked out at some old oak trees that marked the edge of her property and, beyond them, a small stone wall, then the library parking lot and the library itself. Today, a ratty-looking RV blocked her view of the library.

The parking lot was a smart place to pull over. She listened and couldn't hear anything. She wondered if someone had abandoned the RV, or if the occupants were still inside. If they were inside, they might not have heat. She wasn't sure how the heating system on an RV worked. Even if they did have heat, how insulated could an ancient RV be? She'd barely asked herself the question before she made her decision.

She put her load of wood in the house, then went back outside and trudged across the parking lot.

She knew that Dylan, who was a friend—or at least friendly—and a cop, would give her a stern lecture about knocking on a stranger's door, but there was no way she was going to let someone freeze to death steps away from her house. The snow was even higher in the parking lot. It fell into her boots as she broke a path. Later, she'd clear the lot and her driveway, but for now, she continued on.

She knocked on the RV's door and a small boy dressed in a snowsuit toddled into view. A tall man with blond, thinning hair, wearing a coat came after him. He eyed her a moment, and then opened the door.

"Hi. You look like you could use some hot coffee and a warm place for your family." He didn't respond, so she smiled and said, "I'm Maeve Buchanan. I live in the house next door." He still made no response, so she added, "I have a woodstove going and the coffee's hot."

The man glanced over his shoulder and an equally bundled woman with a thick brown braid trailing under her hat came into view. "Excuse my husband. He doesn't function before seven, and even after that, manners aren't his strong suit. I'm Josie, he's Boyd and that little one is Carl, and we'd be very appreciative of someplace warm. The propane ran out about a half hour ago and it's starting to feel like an ice chest in here."

Maeve smiled. "Well, grab what you need and follow my path across the parking lot. I'll make some oatmeal." Maeve smiled one more time at them before turning and following her track back across the lot.

She could hear Josie telling her husband that she was going to see to it that Carl had more manners than his father.

Maeve didn't envy Boyd, because she doubted that the scolding had stopped, even when she couldn't hear it any longer. She hurried back inside, took off her coat and boots, and slipped on her fuzzy slippers.

She rarely greeted guests in her flannel pajama bottoms and robe, but she doubted the upstairs had warmed enough to make changing comfortable. She decided that given the circumstances, she wasn't changing yet.

Moments later, her guests arrived. Boyd had Carl in one arm and his free hand on Josie's elbow. Maeve hurried over and let them in. "Welcome. You can hang your coats out here. The kitchen's warming up nicely."

As Josie took off her coat, Maeve couldn't miss what the bulky winter coat had disguised. Not only was her guest pregnant, she was *very* pregnant. "Oh, my, you come right in and sit down."

She hurried into the living room and pulled Mrs. Anderson's rocker into the kitchen next to the stove. "Here you go. You sit here and warm up."

"Thank you for the invitation," Boyd said formally.

Maeve wanted to laugh because she was pretty sure that Josie had fed those words to her husband. But she simply smiled and said, "You're welcome. It's the least I can do."

"It's a lot more than most would," Josie said. "We were so thankful to find your town and the parking lot last night. It was the worst weather I've ever been out in. The little man—" she mussed her son's hair as he climbed up on her lap "—slept through the whole thing."

"We'll be out of your hair as soon as I can get out and buy more propane," Boyd hurried up and added.

"Really, it's fine. It's not as if I planned on doing anything but hibernate inside today," she said. "So, where are you all heading?"

The four of them sat down at the table, and Josie told their story over a breakfast of oatmeal and toast.

From that one question Maeve learned that the small family was heading to North Dakota, which was supposed to be experiencing a job boom. She learned that Boyd could do anything if he set his mind to it. He'd worked construction, and then worked at a plastic plant where he'd been a manager.

Maeve learned that Josie and Boyd had started dating in high school and married right after they'd graduated. Boyd had gone to work and Josie had gone to the state university campus in Plattsburgh. Josie had almost finished her degree when she had problems with her first pregnancy and had taken time off. She'd been heading back to school to finish her final term when she'd gotten pregnant with the new baby and, given her problems with Carl's pregnancy, she decided to wait until after the baby was born to go back to school and get her degree. "But I'm going to finish," she announced with such conviction that Maeve was sure she would.

The snow had eased up a bit, but the wind continued to blow fiercely. Maeve stood. "I'd better put some more wood in the stove in the basement."

"May I bring in more wood for you?" Boyd asked.

"That would be a huge help," Maeve said. "It's in the small shed at the back of the driveway."

He nodded, put on his coat and boots and headed out.

"Thank you for giving him something to do," Josie said as Boyd shut the door. "He hates feeling as if he's taking a handout."

"I'm pretty sure sharing a woodstove and some oatmeal doesn't constitute a handout. It's merely the neighborly thing to do. It's nothing."

"Not to you, but it means a lot to us. I was so worried about Carl. It was freezing in the RV. Let Boyd help. He'll feel better about taking advantage of you."

Maeve snorted. "Well, there was no advantage taken, but if I can get out of carrying in wood, I'm glad to oblige."

Josie laughed. "He's generally much friendlier. But between losing his job, then the house, and worrying about me, the new baby and Carl...it's taken a toll."

That explained why they were heading to North Dakota at the start of winter. The Lake Erie region was known for its harsh winters, but North Dakota was colder by far.

Maeve sensed that Boyd wouldn't have appreciated his wife sharing that part of things. "Well, when we're in the midst of a storm like this, the more the merrier is what I say."

After the stoves were both loaded, she left the family to themselves while she ran upstairs to dress. When she came back down, Boyd was bouncing Carl on his knee and smiling. But when he spotted her, the smile disappeared and his expression turned serious again.

Maeve handed a small pile of books to Josie. "I thought Carl might enjoy a story. I'm going to head out and start the snowblower."

"Let me," Boyd said.

Normally Maeve would bristle and inform him that she was more than capable of clearing her own driveway, but remembering Josie's words, she smiled instead. "I'm pretty sure there's enough snow out there for the both of us. And when we're done, if you move your RV to my side of the parking lot, you're welcome to hook up to my utilities. We'll have to give the plows a chance to clear the roads, but then we can head to the store and get you some propane. My truck's got four-wheel drive."

Boyd didn't say anything. For a moment, Maeve thought that he was going to refuse the hook up and the ride, but he looked past her at Josie, then said, "I'll pay you for the cost of the utilities and the gas."

"The drive is a couple blocks. Normally I'd walk, but I'm sure the sidewalks aren't cleared and I don't think we want to carry a propane container. As for the electricity, we'll work it out."

He nodded, bundled up and headed outside.

"Thank you," said Josie.

Maeve nodded as she put on her outdoor gear again. "Really, it's my pleasure."

She started for the door, but Josie stopped her. "You sort of live by your motto, don't you?" She pointed at Mrs. Anderson's cross-stitch. *I can't save the world, but I can try.*

"That was a friend's. She saved me in so many ways. This doesn't even begin to compare."

"It does to me, and despite his bearishness, it does to Boyd, too."

Maeve nodded. "I'm glad to help. You stay near the stove, but watch Carl. It gets hot and I wouldn't want him to be burned."

"Will do."

Maeve followed Boyd out into the snow, thankful to get away from Josie's studying gaze. The small woman had a look about her that said she saw more than Maeve wanted to share.

Maeve had never shared easily. She was a private person.

But sometimes, especially over the past year, as she watched Sophie, Lily and Mattie bond over the loss of a friend and then grow closer and become friends in their own right, she wished she had someone she could confide in like that. Oh, the three women were her friends. She went to their showers and weddings, but they only knew her on the surface. And Josie, a practical stranger, already looked at her as if she knew more than the surface bits Maeve felt comfortable sharing.

It was disturbing and tantalizing at the same time.

Maeve guessed she could afford to be a bit more relaxed around Josie. After all, when the weather cleared, she'd be heading to North Dakota with her family.

So for today, and maybe even tomorrow, Maeve would let Josie be the friend she'd always hoped for.

* * *

AARON HOLDER BUNDLED into a pair of Carhartt overalls and a coat. The thick layers of cloth were constrictive and stiff. He felt like Ralphie's little brother in *A Christmas Story*. If he fell onto his back, he suspected he'd give a very turtlelike impression as he tried to right himself.

He'd been in Valley Ridge less than a week and already wished he was back in Florida. If he was, he'd take his coffee onto his back porch—a lanai in local parlance—fire up his laptop and work there in shorts.

He stuffed his feet into a pair of boots. In his Florida fantasy, he was barefoot.

Sure, Orlando got some colder weather, but not in November. And when an occasional cold day hit, he might need to wear jeans and a sweatshirt, but he'd never woken up to snow that was measured in feet. Many feet.

He loved his uncle Jerry, but he wished he'd said no when he'd asked Aaron to spend a few months in Valley Ridge in order to mind the store. His uncle had pointed out that Aaron could do his work anywhere, and that the employees at Valley Ridge Farm and House Supplies took care of most of what needed to be done at the store. All Aaron would have to do was keep an eye on things. Uncle Jerry wanted someone from the family at the business's helm because, as he said, "I have the best employees, but family is family, and blood is thicker than water."

And because Aaron had grown up with the Holder family motto, Family is Family, he found it impossible to say no. His family's near obsessive drive to support each other was why he was bundled up and heading out to plow the Valley Ridge Farm and House Supplies' lot on a post-blizzard November morning. The store would open, albeit late. But from the looks of the quiet main street of Valley Ridge, all the businesses in the area would be opening late today—if they opened at all.

He hoped his uncle's arthritis was benefiting from the warm dry heat of Arizona.

Aaron opened the garage door and a foot of snow tumbled in. He cursed under his breath as he climbed into his uncle's truck. He'd made two passes when another truck pulled up in front of the store, leaving tire imprints in the six inches of snow that had fallen since the snowplow had last gone by.

A woman got out. She was bundled up almost as much as he was. Red hair stuck out wildly from under her hat. A man got out of the passenger side and pulled a propane tank out of the bed of the truck.

"Can you fill the tank?" the woman asked.

"I could. I think the question you want to ask is if I *would*." Aaron felt immediately apologetic. He shouldn't take the fact that he hated the snow out on customers.

He was about to say as much and apologize for being snippy when the redhead asked, "Where's Jerry?" Her tone suggested she wanted to find his uncle and tattle on him.

Aaron had grown up with three younger sisters who liked nothing better than running to their parents with stories of his abuses—some real, some imagined. Maybe that was why he bristled, or maybe it was simply something about this woman that inherently annoyed him. "Jerry's in Arizona, basking in the warmth, so if you want to tattle, you'll have to call him to do it. I can give you his number."

Despite her layers of clothing, he could see her back straighten to the point of breaking. Her words came out measured, as if she was struggling to hold her tongue. "I would prefer it, sir, if you simply filled the tank, then we'll let you get back to your plowing."

"Anything you say, Red." He smiled, hoping she'd read the apology behind his words. But then realized she might find being called *Red* insulting.

"Sorry," he said, hoping that a spoken apology at this point could cover his multitude of failings with this particular customer.

She didn't acknowledge his apology. The now silent woman and the always silent man followed him as he filled the tank. "That's—"

The redhead cut him off. "Can you simply put it on my account? I've got to come back later and get some salt for the library steps."

"And your account is?"

"Maeve. Maeve Buchanan. Or maybe your uncle has it filed under the Valley Ridge Library. Either way, that's me."

He nodded. "Fine, Maeve Buchanan of the Valley Ridge Library. I'll do that."

"That's much better than Red," she muttered as she turned around and waded back to her truck. Once there, the man started arguing with her about something.

Now, that was an odd romance, Aaron thought as he got back into his truck. Maeve. Maeve Buchanan. She was a bristly thing. The town librarian, from the sound of things. He'd have to do a better job apologizing when she came back later for her salt. Aaron had promised his uncle he'd look after the place and he didn't think chasing away customers would qualify as doing a good job of it.

Maeve.

Maeve Buchanan.

He'd remember her name.

* * *

"YOU SEEM RILED," the hitherto silent Boyd said as Maeve pulled back into her now clear driveway.

"You think?" she snapped and immediately felt sorry. The fact that the stranger at the store was awful didn't mean she needed to be, as well. "Sorry."

Boyd nodded. "Being called Red seems to have set you off."

"Humph." Maeve remembered when Mrs. Anderson first introduced her to L. M. Montgomery. *Anne with an "e"* was one of her favorite characters, and Maeve had definitely commiserated with Anne when she broke a slate over Gilbert Blythe's head because he called her *Carrots.*

Maeve was pretty sure that being called Red was as bad as being called Carrots. It was lucky for the man who was filling in for Jerry that she didn't carry a slate around, otherwise she'd have been tempted to follow Anne Shirley's example.

"If you don't mind," Boyd started hesitantly as if talking to anyone other than Josie was a strain, "I thought I'd take your snowblower out and help some of your neighbors. Looks like some of them are slow getting cleared out."

"A lot of them are elderly," she told him. "I was going to go out and do that myself."

He silently studied her a moment, then nodded. "Yeah, I can see you doing that. But if you don't mind, I could do it this once."

"If you'll have dinner with me without snapping your spine telling me you don't need my charity, I'll graciously accept your offer to help out my neighbors," she said.

"Snapping my spine?" he asked, and for the first time, Maeve thought she saw a hint of a smile in his expression.

"I think you and I both have our fair doses of pride, but I think for Josie's sake, you need to put some of yours aside and let me help."

He mulled her statement over for a moment and nodded. "I'll try."

"Then I'll put some of my pride away and let you help out my neighbors while I go in and check on Josie and Carl. I'll have some soup on for lunch when you come in."

"About noon?" he asked.

Maeve nodded. "Sounds good."

She stomped her boots off before she went back into the house. Carl was sitting at the table, playing with some plastic measuring cups and dry cornmeal.

"I hope you don't mind," Josie said quickly. "I'll clean up any mess he makes."

"I definitely don't mind. What's a bit of cornmeal?"

Josie went to stand, and then grimaced.

Maeve hurried to her side. "Josie?"

Josie was silent and her expression grew more serious. Slowly she relaxed and looked at Maeve. "I had a twinge about an hour ago, and now this one."

Maeve had been a bookworm her whole life, which meant she knew a little about a lot of things, but other than understanding the basic mechanics of birth, she knew very little about the process. "Could you be in labor?"

"No." Josie seemed panicked at the thought. "It's too soon. He has at least another month to go. I'm sure it's only Braxton Hicks contractions."

Maeve didn't know Braxton Hicks from Adam, but she knew that she did not like the situation. And she was equally sure that Boyd wouldn't like it, either. "Sit down and let me make a call. I have a friend who's a nurse. I'll see if she can come over."

"In this weather?" Josie asked.

"The snow's stopped and your husband's out there personally clearing my half of Valley Ridge, as well. Plus, Lily lives close enough to walk if need be."

Josie shook her head. "I won't have anyone walking—"

"Shh," Maeve interrupted. "Don't argue or I'll think you're as stubborn as your husband."

Josie laughed, which had been Maeve's intent.

"You tell your friend it's not an emergency," Josie warned her. "I don't want her hurrying over here and inconveniencing herself more than she already will have to."

"I'll tell her that we don't think it's anything, but want to be sure." Maeve got her cell phone from the window ledge. Thank goodness it still had a charge. She went out to the front room and dialed Lily's number.

"Hello?" the almost–Mrs. Bennington answered.

"Getting pre-wedding jitters yet?" Maeve asked by way of a greeting, though she already knew the answer.

"As long as Sophie's Tori doesn't speak up at my wedding, there's nothing to worry about. I have everything planned to the nth degree," Lily assured her.

Their friend Sophie had been about to marry this summer when a stranger stood up and objected. The entire community was shocked to discover the girl, Tori, was Sophie's biological daughter.

"How's Mattie handling everything?" Maeve had listened to Mattie complain about Lily's bridal ways in the past. The two friends couldn't be more different. Mattie would have gotten married in jeans if Lily hadn't pitched a fit. While Lily had definite ideas on what a wedding should entail and jeans weren't in the picture.

Maeve wished she had friends who were as close as family.

She had friends, but nothing like them.

"Mattie's calling me Bridezilla now. That's an upgrade from Bridesmaidzilla." Lily had been a bridesmaid in Sophie's wedding, as well as Mattie's. "And Sophie keeps joking that if the baby gets any bigger, she's renting a scooter to ride down the aisle."

"Speaking of pregnant women," Maeve said, "that's why I'm calling."

"I didn't know you were seeing anyone," Lily said slowly.

Maeve chuckled. "I know it's the season for immaculate conceptions, but no, not me. I've got a pregnant woman in my kitchen. And I hate to ask, but I'm hoping you'll run over and check on her.

She's got about a month until she's due. She's had a couple pains. She had a name for them and tried to tell me they're nothing to worry about, but I'm worried."

"Braxton Hicks?" Lily asked.

"Yes, that's what she said."

"She's probably right, but I'll come over and check her out."

Maeve released a breath she hadn't realized she'd been holding. "Thanks, Lily. Her family spent last night camped out in an RV that ran out of propane this morning. I'm worried. Can you get out, because if not, I can come get you."

"That's not necessary. I have four-wheel drive for work and you're only a few blocks away."

"I hate to make you—"

"You're not making me do anything. I told Sebastian I'd give him a hand at the diner this morning and I have a few house calls to make this afternoon, so I have to go out, anyway."

Maeve felt a flood of relief. "Thanks, Lily."

"See you soon."

Maeve hung up and walked back into the kitchen. Carl dumped a cup full of cornmeal into a bigger cup, while Josie sat, eyes closed, in the rocker, her hands over her protruding stomach.

Maeve glanced at Mrs. Anderson's cross-stitch.

No, she couldn't save the world, but she was going to do her best to help this one small family.

CHAPTER TWO

MAEVE HAD ALWAYS wanted dark, mysterious looks like Lily Paul's. Lily tended to wear a lot of Bohemian clothes that would be considered suspect by the locals if anyone other than Lily wore them. Lily had a fondness for a lot of clunky jewelry and bold colors.

None of that was evident today as she came into the kitchen bundled up in a hat, parka and knee-high boots. Her scarf was wrapped around her face so many times, only her eyes were visible.

"Come in, Lily," Maeve said, and then teased, "I mean, I'm assuming you're Lily. It's hard to tell under all those clothes."

Lily began unwinding the scarf and shucked off most of the layers. "Seriously," she grumbled, "Sebastian had some very firm opinions on what I should wear today. Most of the time, he doesn't say a word about my clothing choices."

"He probably wanted to be sure you stayed warm," Maeve said. She wouldn't say it out loud, but it was endearing. No one worried about her dressing warmly enough except her mother. That thought made her feel lonely, despite the fact that her house was currently overflowing with people.

"Yeah. Sebastian also wanted to drive me. I put my foot down on that notion. However, he insisted I wear two pairs of socks inside my boots, so there was no satisfying stomp when I put my foot down, only a very wimpy smooshing. Still, he got the picture." Lily turned and smiled at Josie. "Hi, I'm Lily. And this handsome man is?"

"Carl. And I'm Josie. Thank you so much for coming out in this mess. I'm sure I'm fine and I hate to be a bother."

"I'll tell you what. Why don't we let Carl sit with Maeve, and you and I will borrow her bedroom for a quick checkup."

Josie hesitated long enough to make Maeve wonder if she'd agree, but Lily said, "I did come all the way over here in the snow. The very deep, frigid snow."

"Wow, way to lay on the guilt." Maeve laughed.

Lily laughed, too. "I have to wheedle a certain feisty patient on a regular basis. Guilt is a first foray. I do have a trump card I can pull out and use if necessary."

"A quick game of one-handed basketball?" Maeve asked. Everyone in town had talked about Lily and Sebastian's one-handed basketball game this past summer. If talk were to be believed, half the town had witnessed the game. That's how things went in Valley Ridge. People told stories so often that after a while they felt as if they were there, even if they weren't.

Josie smiled. "More guilt won't be necessary. Plus, I'm not sure what one-handed basketball is, but I'm sure I'm not up for it. You're right. My husband will feel much better about everything if I can tell him I got checked out."

Maeve took Carl as the other two women left. "What do you say we start some water for tea?" she said.

She held the boy on her hip as she filled the kettle.

As they passed the fridge, Carl reached for a postcard that the Langley kids had sent her from Disney World. When Mattie and Finn had gotten married in August, they'd taken the kids—his nieces and nephew—on a family honeymoon to the Magic Kingdom. Abbey, the youngest, was still telling anyone who would listen about *her* honeymoon.

Carl reached for the card and said, *"Mickey."*

She let him grab the postcard. "Yes, that's Mickey Mouse. Let me put the kettle on the woodstove. I think I have a Disney book that we can read together."

She carried the toddler into the front room where she had some books waiting to go to the library. "I think I saw..." she muttered as she dug one-handed through the pile. "There." She pulled out the Mickey Mouse storybook and carried both Carl and the book back into the warmth of the kitchen. They'd read the first few pages when Lily and Josie rejoined them.

"Everything all right?" she asked them both.

"I think so, but I want Josie to come in and see the doctor. No one's at the office yet. To be honest, I don't think any stores or offices are open except Jerry's and the grocery store, but I'm sure Neil will be in soon. After I've talked to him, I'll call you with a time today or tomorrow."

"Really, we can't afford a doctor's visit," Josie protested.

"Of all the things you need to worry about, that's not it," Lily said gently but firmly. "Neil owes me."

"But..." Josie looked as if she was trying to find an argument.

Lily put her hand on top of Josie's. "One of the things I love about Neil's practice is that we see everyone regardless of insurance or means. He could have practiced anywhere. He had offers and to be honest, still occasionally gets offers from bigger towns. He chose a small town because he wanted to make a difference. He's not in this for the money."

"Boyd is very proud," Josie said softly. "He won't accept charity."

Maeve might not have known him long, but she knew that was the absolute truth. "He's paying me back for some oatmeal and an electric outlet by single-handedly clearing half of Valley Ridge's sidewalks and driveways."

Lily thought a moment. "Okay, Josie, I'll tell you what. You come in for a visit, and if Boyd is willing he can help us out with a couple of projects around the office."

"He can do anything. I mean, absolutely anything. I've never met a job Boyd couldn't do," Josie gushed.

"Well, then, it's settled." Lily reached out for the toddler. "May I?"

Josie nodded and Maeve handed him over. "He's adorable." Carl reached up and wrapped his hand in a clump of Lily's hair. She gently unwound his chubby fist.

"That's why I go with a braid or ponytail most days. We call him the hair monster. Boyd likes to quip that his hair is thinning out of self-preservation."

Maeve had a hard time imagining Boyd joking. But people could hide things behind their public faces. She knew this from experience.

When Carl was unwound, he held his hands out for his mother and Lily passed him over to Josie. As she cuddled the toddler, Josie said, "Thank you so much, Lily. First Maeve, now you. I think that snowstorm stranding us in Valley Ridge was the first bit of good luck we've had in a long time."

"You wouldn't be the first person to find yourself coming to Valley Ridge for a quick visit, then falling in love and staying," Lily said. "I came here for a nursing assignment. When it was over—" Lily's voice caught on the word *over,* then she continued "—I stayed. I'd made friends here and fallen in love with the town itself."

Maeve remembered when Lily came to town. She'd watched as Lily bonded with Mattie and Sophie as they all cared for Bridget Langley. It was true that most of the community had pitched in to help the sick mother of three, but Lily, Mattie and Sophie had shouldered the bulk of Bridget's care. As Bridget got sicker, the three of them had become so close. When Bridget had passed, their friendship had buoyed them.

Maeve envied their friendship. She wasn't jealous. At least she didn't think she was. She tried not to be, but she couldn't help feeling as if she'd spent her whole life on the outside looking in. She'd watched each of the three friends fall in love. Mattie and Sophie were married, and Lily was on her way to the altar. Maeve wasn't jealous of that, either. At least most days she wasn't.

She rarely shared too much about herself, but this once, she forced herself to say, "I grew up here, but I left home for college and didn't think I'd be back. Yet here I am. Once Valley Ridge gets its hooks in you, it's hard to tear yourself away."

"So far, it seems like a lovely place," Josie said wistfully. "Not that I've seen much more than Maeve's house and the library parking lot. But the company here has left a very good impression on us."

"Where are you all headed?" Lily asked.

"North Dakota. Boyd read an article that said jobs were to be had there, so we sold pretty much everything we owned, bought the RV and are going to see for ourselves. The article also mentioned a housing shortage, and Boyd thought we could live in the RV until we got settled."

"Traveling in your condition must be hard." Maeve knew what it was like to call someplace with four wheels home. Granted, she hadn't had an entire RV, but she remembered how awful it was.

She hadn't thought about those times in a while. It didn't take a psychologist to see why her subconscious was making a connection between Josie's circumstances and her own back in the day.

Josie answered, "No, it's not hard. I'm sitting in the front passenger seat, and that's not any worse than sitting in a recliner at home. Frankly, the RV is so small that cleaning is a breeze. And..." Josie continued to entertain them with all her happy reasons why living in an RV had some huge advantages over living in a house. Lily was laughing, but Maeve couldn't join in. She made tea and served everyone and pretended to laugh along with Lily at the appropriate places in Josie's soliloquy, but Maeve knew deep in her heart that no matter how nice a spin Josie put on the situation, being homeless was no laughing matter.

Lily checked her watch. "I've got to run. I need to get to the diner because a few of our employees are snowed in. Then I have a couple of home visits that can't be put off until later. But I'll call you soon with a time for your appointment."

"Thank you again," Josie said.

Lily smiled. "It was no problem at all."

Carl's head was nodding against his mother's shoulder. "Josie, if you want, he can have a nap in my bedroom. The whole house has warmed up quite nicely, so he should be fine."

"Thank you, Maeve." Josie hefted herself to her feet.

"Do you want me to carry him up for you?" Maeve asked.

41

"No, I'm fine," Josie assured her.

"The stairs are a bit steep and narrow."

"Are you saying I can't fit up a narrow staircase?" Josie asked.

Maeve felt utterly embarrassed. "No, honestly, Josie. That's not what I meant at all. I would—"

Josie held up her hand, interrupting Maeve's apologies. "I was just kidding. Honest. Boyd tells me all the time that my sense of humor is warped. I'm afraid he's right." She picked up the toddler and went through the living room to the stairs.

Maeve turned to Lily. "Thank you so much for helping. I've just met Boyd and Josie, but I know they'd pitch a fit if I offered to pay for her visit, but maybe we could work it out on the sly."

"No need for that," Lily assured her as she started to put on her layers. "I meant what I said. I don't even have to ask Neil to know that he'll work something out with them. Last spring he got paid in chickens for a home visit. I used to watch stuff like that on TV when I was younger, but really, I didn't imagine it ever working in this day and age.

"Neil insists he didn't go into medicine to be rich. Plus, we've got honey-do jobs galore at the practice. Neil is a very gifted doctor, but he's hopeless when it comes to a paintbrush or screwdriver. Ask me sometime about the time he decided to change a washer in the bathroom faucet." Lily shivered as if to say the project hadn't gone well.

Maeve didn't know what else to mention. That was part of her problem when it came to making friends. She was no good at the easy give and take, but she did ask, "How are the wedding plans?"

"Everything's in order. Mattie keeps teasing me, but I don't see what's wrong with being well prepared. Look at last night's blizzard. I know Valley Ridge gets snow in November, but normally not this much all at once. I have a bunch of friends with plows on standby in case we get another storm and..." She let the sentence fade. "Short of some unexpected volcanic eruption, I've planned for every contingency I could think of."

Maeve was impressed. "Well, if you need something, you only have to holler."

"All I need is you there," Lily assured her. "Of course, if you need a date..."

Maeve could see it coming from a mile away.

"...I know someone," Lily finished. "One of my patient's grandsons moved into her house to help her out. He's a very nice guy."

Maeve sighed. "If I decide I need a date, I'll let you know." She wasn't sure what happened to turn half of Valley Ridge's minds toward fixing her up, but it had been bad ever since Mattie and Finn, and Sophie and Colton were married.

She took that back. She knew exactly what had happened.

Tori Allen—her summertime volunteer at the library and Sophie's rediscovered daughter—that's what happened. Or rather *who* happened.

Tori had decided that Maeve needed to get out more and she'd not so subtly tried to fix her up whenever she could. And for someone who lived in

Ohio and only came in to Valley Ridge for visits, she managed quite a bit. She'd tried to convince Maeve to date the town's bachelor cop, Dylan. But she was pretty sure she'd dissuaded Tori from making that particular match. Dylan was a nice enough man, but he wasn't what Maeve was looking for.

To be honest, Maeve wasn't exactly sure what she was looking for in a man. But she was certain that when she found him, she'd know. Immediately. That's how it had happened when her mom met her dad. And after her father passed away, her mother had fallen head over heels for Herman Lorei, a new farmer in town. It was good to see her mom happy again.

Yes, someday Maeve would meet the man for her. Until then, she'd wait. She wasn't willing to settle.

"Well, if you change your mind..." Lily let the offer hang there a moment. "My client's grandson is cute."

Maeve grinned. "Thanks, Lily. I'll let you know." *But don't hold your breath.* "Thanks for everything." Maeve saw Lily out and hoped that she'd dissuaded her friend from playing matchmaker. After all, she had Tori, the teenage yenta matchmaker-wannabe, on the job.

Maeve was comfortable. And she was busy. Between her paid job at the winery in Ripley and her volunteering at the library, there weren't enough hours in the day. She wasn't actively looking for a relationship. She was content to wait until she found him, or he found her. And if it never happened? She'd be okay. Ms. Mac, the school principal, had never married but seemed perfectly happy with her full, productive life. She'd made such a difference in Maeve's life.

There were fates much worse than being single.

She glanced at the clock.

Since Maeve's boss, Gabriel, had called and said not to even try to get to Ripley today, she could cross the now-clear parking lot to the library and catalog a few of her new books.

She hadn't heard a peep from upstairs, so she left Josie a note on the table with her whereabouts and cell phone number, and took a pile of books with her.

She doubted anyone would be out today and even if they were, she doubted they'd be in desperate need of a library book, but still, as was her practice, she went to turn on the small neon open sign in the library window—before she remembered there was no power.

Well, that was that. Maeve would leave the books to be cataloged some other day.

As long as she was dressed for it, she decided she'd walk the few blocks to the grocery store and buy some more milk. She had some meat in the fridge and could easily put together a stew for herself and her unexpected guests. She should probably think about moving the contents of the refrigerator outside if the power didn't come back on soon.

And while she was out, she might as well stop at Valley Ridge Farm and House Supplies for the salt and some more lamp oil, just in case the power wasn't restored by nightfall.

She hadn't exaggerated this morning when she told Boyd that she normally went on foot to the shops in Valley Ridge. She rarely drove anywhere other than to work. If Valley Ridge ever approved a budget that would pay her for her work at the library, then she would probably be able to give up driving all together. Well, mostly. She crossed over the bridge that spanned Cooper's Creek, then past the schools. She continued up Park Street, past the familiar shops. As she approached the grocery store, she found that a number of Valley Ridge residents were already there. The owner had a generator that kept the freezers and refrigerators running. Her shopping done, she headed back toward home. The Farm and House Supplies store was on the way.

The store took up most of the block of Park Street right before the schools. The parking lot and outdoor yard comprised a great deal of it. Jerry carried mulch, stones, some bricks and other basic items he stored outside. She looked past the empty lot and saw the top of the old Culpepper place.

She walked around the block to get to the residential street where the Culpepper house was located. From Park Street there wasn't much to see apart from the roof. Standing in front of it now, she recalled how people said that it had good bones. The bones of the Culpepper place were becoming better disguised with every passing day as neglect etched itself onto the facade. The stonework was covered with ivy that was dead and brown given the cold. As for the yard, she knew there was no lawn under the snow, but rather a collection of weeds that the neighbors occasionally mowed. Most of the windows were boarded over, and the corner of the porch had begun to sag in a way that gave the impression the entire porch would someday completely slide off the house.

There was nothing sadder than a deserted house, Maeve mused. Once, a family had lived there. She had a vague recollection from her childhood of Mr. and Mrs. Culpepper. They'd seemed ancient then. The house had been vacant since Maeve had moved back to town.

Even the layer of snow that covered it couldn't erase the lonely look of the place. For some reason, it made Maeve ache. She remembered a time when she would have been thrilled to call even that sorry neglected house her home.

She forced herself to ignore the wave of unpleasant nostalgia that had been biting at the edge of her memories since she met the Myers family.

She cut through the back of the property, went around the dilapidated fence and arrived back at the store. She went inside and was relieved when she practically bumped into Sophie McCray. Sophie was one of those eternally sunny people, around whom it was impossible to stay glum.

"Maeve," Sophie cried out as she teetered toward her on high-heeled boots. Sophie was petite and as such, rarely seen without some kind of heel on her footwear. But given that she was only weeks away from giving birth, Maeve thought maybe her friend should consider trying out some more sensible shoes. Sophie's stomach protruded so far out that she couldn't zip her coat, sensible shoes made even more sense. But Sophie didn't seem to care as she ran over and embraced Maeve.

"What are you doing out?" Maeve asked. "Colton should have tethered you to the farm in this weather."

"He tried, but I don't tether well. Besides, we needed a few things and he's helping Sebastian and Finn dig out some neighbors. I'm on my way to the diner to meet Mattie and Lily."

"Lily will probably run late and I'll be the one at fault," Maeve admitted. "I have company and she came to help me out."

Sophie nodded knowingly. "I heard."

"The Valley Ridge message boards—I should have guessed. Social media doesn't have anything on our grapevine, does it?"

Sophie laughed. "So how is your pregnant visitor?"

"Her name's Josie. She's passing through Valley Ridge with her husband, Boyd, and son, Carl. She's fine for now. Lily's going to set up an appointment with Neil before they move on. I'll feel better after he checks her out."

"If you don't mind more unexpected company, maybe I'll stop by later and say hi. Us pregnant women need to stick together."

"I'm sure Josie would enjoy that." Maeve rarely had anyone over to her house. Instantly she'd gone from no guests to overflowing with guests.

"Is it true they lost their house?" Sophie asked.

With some people, Maeve would have bristled at the question, assuming they were only looking for some juicy gossip. But this was Sophie, and there was concern in her eyes. Maeve didn't want to give up Josie's confidences, but felt safe confiding in Sophie. "They're headed to North Dakota to look for work."

"I wish I knew about some job in Valley Ridge," Sophie said. "But times have been tight here like everywhere else."

"I know." Maeve jostled the grocery bag from one arm to the other. "But as soon as the storm's aftermath is cleared, it sounds like they'll be on their way."

"Well, I'm glad I'll meet her before they leave. I'll stop in after lunch, if that's okay?"

"That would be fine."

Maeve wasn't sure why she didn't like to open her home to anyone, but that was the truth of it. She had never been someone who could have friends over after school, or after work. Her home now was her private sanctuary. She hadn't thought twice about having Josie and her family come over, but with more people crowding into her modest house it made her feel...anxious.

She pushed the feeling aside and went looking for the first thing on her list. She rounded a corner in the home section and spotted an employee with his back to her. He was wearing a T-shirt that had a large logo of the store. "Excuse me. Can you tell me where the lamp oil is?"

"Can I? Certainly, I can. The question you wanted to ask was, *Will I?*" the employee muttered as he turned around.

"You," was Maeve's response. Not that she was surprised. The minute the words left the man's mouth she'd known he was the snarly guy from this morning. Despite his surliness, Maeve couldn't avoid liking his voice.

Maeve hadn't realized until this very moment how much she loved a good voice. The rich, low gravelly type was her favorite. Put a voice like that on one of her audiobooks, and she could listen to the phone book being read.

And this man's voice was deep, commanding, intoxicating.

"Listen, I don't want to start another debate with you. You're Jerry's employee and even if he's not here, he has standards. So, I'd appreciate it if you would help me find the lamp oil without any more of your sarcasm."

He tipped an imaginary hat. "Anything for you, Red."

"Maeve. Remember?"

He chuckled. "I'm not likely to forget. Maeve Buchanan, the librarian."

"Well, then, if you haven't forgotten my name, I'd appreciate it if you'd use it." That was polite, not that this guy deserved polite.

"Follow me and I'd be happy to show you to the lamp oil, *Maeve*."

She wasn't the only one he was testy with. That much was evident as he led her through the aisles, ignoring everyone as they passed.

"So is your mood an everyday occurrence, or is it specific to today?" she asked.

He gave her a quizzical look.

"You are less than salesman-nice."

"You're right. I find the snow and the power outage unbelievably annoying. And I feel sort of naked without my computer..."

At the word *naked* Maeve got a very vivid image of the man with the good voice in far less clothing than he was wearing. She immediately tried to push the unwelcome image away.

Pretty is as pretty does, or so the saying went. So far, judging by his attitude, he wasn't very pretty at all.

"...I guess it shows in my manners. Sorry." He stopped at a shelf and pointed.

"Oh, you have manners? I hadn't noticed." Now she was the one being snippy. She felt a little guilty—but only a little. After all, it wasn't his fault that she'd had crazy images of him in her head. She coughed. "Thank you for showing me to the proper aisle."

"Would you like to have dinner sometime?" His look of surprise matched how she felt.

Maeve couldn't have been more taken aback if the man had asked her whether the moon was flat, or if it was summer. "No, I don't think so. To be honest, not if you were the last man on earth." She said it as nicely as she could, but she wanted to be clear. Her mother would have scolded her for being so blunt, but this man set her teeth on edge and didn't seem to realize how off-putting he was. "But thanks for asking and for your assistance."

She practically sprinted toward the cashier, anxious to get away from this man, who she suspected was still staring after her.

"I'm Aaron, by the way, Maeve the Librarian. Aaron Holder," he called.

She didn't turn around, but did wave a hand to acknowledge him. Aaron. Nice name. Nice voice. But other than those two things, she could find very little that was nice about Mr. Aaron Holder.

* * *

AARON WATCHED RED dash for the register with her lamp oil and grocery bag in hand. She certainly had the temper of a redhead. He wasn't one to believe in stereotypes, but this one seemed to apply.

He acknowledged he'd been less than pleasant both times they met. When he was younger, his mother used to say that the world had best watch out when he was in a mood—especially when it involved his sisters. Recently, his mother informed him that he'd been in a mood for the past two years.

Today's exercise in wireless living only exacerbated his general level of frustration. He hadn't lied when he said not having power ticked him off. He felt disconnected. He was a man who made his living on the computer. So, not only could he not work on his new program today, his only access to the internet was via his phone, and answering clients' questions on its minuscule screen was a pain because he was pretty sure he needed glasses. Constantly increasing and decreasing the size of the screen and font only fueled his frustration. Added to that, he was here in snowy Valley Ridge, New York, rather than sitting in the sun, enjoying life in Florida. But for some reason, Red had perked him up.

His family would say he took perverse delight in being annoying.

He'd disagree. He never intended to be annoying. He merely liked to understand things. And he counted people as things that he liked to understand.

They were so complicated.

Give him complex ideas to code into a computer and he could puzzle through any of them. But people? There was no algorithm for understanding them. You could input data to your heart's content, but they still surprised you. You thought you knew everything about them and then when you least expected it, they'd spring something new on you.

Sometimes, they'd spring something on you that shook you to your core.

Okay, he knew where this line of thinking would lead and frankly he didn't have time for that today. He'd already annoyed one customer. He owed it to his uncle to not annoy any more.

He wished Maeve the librarian had said yes to his dinner invitation. Maybe he should have assured her that he wasn't asking her on a date. He wasn't interested in dating anyone. But he could do with a friend here in town. Or at least an acquaintance. And because Maeve the librarian seemed to be able to hold her own with him, she seemed like a good candidate.

He didn't have more time to think about *Red.* He had a store to see to. Aaron spotted a man whose uniform proclaimed that he was the local cop. "Do you need help, Officer?"

"You're new here," the cop stated. "Even if I didn't know almost every soul in Valley Ridge, I'd have known because you're the first person to call me *Officer* in weeks."

"What do most people call you?" Aaron asked with interest. He was curious. This guy's pants and shirtsleeves were creased. Anything metal, from badges to the grip on his weapon, gleamed. Everything about him screamed, *my job is my identity.*

"Sheriff." There was significant annoyance in his voice as he spit out the word. Sort of like Maeve bristling every time he called her *Red.*

"Doesn't matter how many times I explain that there are differences between a police officer and a sheriff," the cop grumbled, "certain people here in town still persist in using the wrong term. And they've polluted the populace to the extent that most of them use it, as well. The other cops all get officer, but not me. Sheriff?" He looked fierce. "But don't worry, I know the origins of my sheriffing—so I know where the blame lies—and someday, Colton will get his. I'm Dylan, by the way."

"Did I hear my name?" A man wearing a cowboy hat rounded the corner. "I'm trying to find my wife and I am sure I heard my name." He smiled at the cop. "Sheriff."

Aaron had heard a lot of men refer to their wives, but never with so much love put into the term. He knew without probing any further that this was Colton and that torturing the cop was part of his fun.

The man in the cowboy hat extended his hand. "Colton. Colton McCray."

"Aaron Holder."

"So, you're the nephew who got in last week," Colton said.

"Whose nephew?" Dylan asked.

"Jerry's," Colton and Aaron said in unison.

"Oh, you're the one spending the winter with us. Sorry it started with a bang. I mean, we definitely get snow here, but for the most part not this much this early," Dylan offered.

"You know what they say about jumping into the deep end," Aaron said. "You sink or swim. I'm not sure I'm doing either right now. It's more treading water, but at least I'm not drowning."

"Well, welcome to Valley Ridge," the cop-not-sheriff said.

"Dylan, this is my friendly reminder. You haven't RSVP'd to Lily's wedding yet. It has been the subject of discussion. Much discussion," Colton added ominously.

"Oh, crap," the cop said, looking nervous. "I could have not RSVP'd to Sophie's or Mattie's weddings with little repercussion, but this is Lily." He started rummaging in his pocket and produced a phone.

"Yeah, it's Lily," Colton agreed.

Dylan punched in a number on his phone, made a hang-on-a-minute gesture and walked down the aisle. "Lily..."

"What's the problem with this Lily?" Aaron asked as Dylan took his conversation out of earshot.

"Nothing. She's marrying one of my best friends and is one of the sweetest women in the world. But she has some—" he hesitated as if trying to think of the right words to describe this sweet woman who made cops cower "—uh, very definite ideas about how weddings, engagements, even showers should work. RSVP'ing by the date indicated on the card is in her must-do column."

"Oh, I see." But he didn't. Dylan, a man who carried a gun for a living, had looked truly nervous.

He came back to them, clearly relieved. "Okay, I'm out of the doghouse. I think. I offered to direct traffic out of the church's parking lot for her."

Colton chuckled. "Sucker."

"Hey, they don't call me an officer of the peace for nothing."

"No, they call you Sheriff." Colton laughed at his own joke and Dylan growled.

"I'd better get back to work," Aaron said. "It was nice to meet you both."

"Nice to meet you, too. I'm sure Sophie's going to stop in and invite you to dinner sometime. She's fond of Jerry. I know he asked her to keep an eye on you and make sure you get introduced around."

Aaron groaned. Socializing had never been his strong suit. "I'm awful busy between my own work and taking care of things here for Uncle Jerry."

"I get it," Colton said. "Dinner with strangers is nobody's idea of a good time."

"But you can't resist," Dylan told Aaron. "Honestly. You can try to tell Sophie no, but it's not going to happen. When you meet her you'll know almost immediately you've met your match."

"I'd like to take offense, but he's right," Colton said. "My wife doesn't know the meaning of the word *no.*"

"We'll see," Aaron said. "Do you guys know the redheaded librarian?"

"Maeve?" they answered as one.

"Yes."

"What do you want to know?" Dylan asked.

Aaron shrugged. The better question was what didn't he want to know. "We had a bit of a run-in."

"That sounds more like the old Maeve than the new one," Colton said.

"Old Maeve?" Aaron asked.

"I went to school with her. When we were younger, she spent a lot of time in the principal's office. Called there almost daily. All sorts of rumors about her and what she might have done to warrant so many trips to see the principal. To be honest, I never noticed much of a wild side to her.

What I remember most about Maeve growing up was that she always had her nose in a book. She spent most afternoons at the library with Mrs. Anderson. Maeve was...quiet."

"And since that's the longest string of words I've ever heard Colton say, as he's usually so quiet himself...to have him call *her* quiet says a lot," Dylan continued. "If I had to use one word to describe her, it would be *busy*. She's always busy. Always in motion. She volunteered to reopen the library practically on her own and when she's not at her day job, she's generally there. A lot of kids head to the library after school to wait for their parents to pick them up. I know a few kids who say Maeve helps them with homework. And little Abbey Langley assures me that Maeve is the best storyteller ever, though according to her, Tori, Maeve's assistant, is a close second."

"Where does she work?" Aaron asked. Then he clarified, "Her day job."

"A winery in Ripley," Colton said. "My partner, Rich, and I have talked about trying to hire her away from them when we have more cash flow. Right now, Mrs. Nies is handling everything at my winery, but if things continue to pick up, she'll need the help."

"Colton here owns a winery and a farm," Dylan told him.

"Who was the guy she was with this morning?" Aaron hadn't meant to ask that. But the thought of her and that guy had bothered him.

"Guy?" both men asked.

"Not old, but average height, roughly our age. He was bundled up, so I can't tell you much more about him other than he needed propane and she drove him over here to get it."

Dylan went from looking like one of the guys to looking like a cop in the blink of an eye. "I don't know. It doesn't sound like anyone she hangs out with."

"That's because she doesn't hang out with anyone," Colton said.

"I'll find out," Dylan promised.

Aaron told them goodbye and turned to help other customers. He had a nagging feeling that he'd broken a confidence by talking to the men about Maeve. That was ridiculous. She'd made no secret of the man—she'd brought him to the store after all. But still, the feeling persisted.

Colton and the *sheriff* had given him a lot of information to process.

And as the rest of the busy day flew by, he couldn't help thinking about Red. Bad girl, bookworm, librarian, winery employee, spitfire.

She was a puzzle, and there was nothing Aaron liked better than a good puzzle.

* * *

THE POWER CAME on at three in the afternoon. Maeve could have moved the stew to the stove, but she left it on the woodstove instead. For some reason the sight of it bubbling away in her cast-iron Dutch oven was cheery.

It didn't just lift her spirits—Boyd seemed less taciturn than earlier. He'd taken the news that Josie had experienced some Braxton Hicks contractions better than Maeve thought he would. He'd even thanked her for calling Lily.

He hadn't exactly regaled them with tales of his day, but he told them about the people he'd met as he helped clear driveways all over town. "This one older lady came out with cookies and hot chocolate for me. She said she had her fireplace going. I offered to carry in some wood for her. She didn't look as if she should be doing it."

"Who was it?" Maeve asked.

"A Mrs. Esterly."

"She's a lovely lady. That was nice of you to—" She was interrupted by a knock on the door. She wasn't sure where she'd put anyone else. Her small kitchen was already crowded with her current company.

She opened the door and saw not only Sophie, who was obviously making good on her promise to visit, but also Colton and Dylan.

Maeve smiled, already predicting Dylan's first comment. "You're in luck. The power came on a few minutes ago."

Sophie and Colton went in, but Dylan stayed on the stairs. "I heard you had a strange family staying with you?"

"They're not strange, though I haven't known them long, and they're not staying with me." She pointed to the RV. "Before you give me the lecture I heard in my head this morning before I even knocked on their door, I'll let you know that not only have they been perfectly polite, honest and forthright, but Boyd even wanted to pay me back for allowing them to come in and warm up and eat some oatmeal. Really, Dylan? A man who feels he has to repay someone for oatmeal? They're perfectly safe."

Dylan sighed. "I'd prefer meeting them myself, but I just got a call about an accident off I-90. I'll check back in with you later. Colton will keep an eye out for me in the meantime."

"Honestly, I'm an adult," she reminded him.

"Yeah? And I'm the cop. Making sure people are safe is what I do."

She stuck out her tongue, which made him grin. "Just don't make a habit of taking in strangers."

"I can promise that, if you can promise not to make a habit of checking up on me," she countered.

"I can't make that promise," he said with sincerity, "but I'll take you up on yours."

She went into the kitchen and found Sophie talking to Boyd and Josie as if they were old friends, while Colton sat back, evidently assessing the couple for Dylan.

Living in a small town could be challenging at times. She pasted a smile on her face and said, "I guess you all managed to introduce yourselves?"

She sat down to the two pregnant women's assurances and joined in their conversation while Boyd and Colton continued to size each other up.

This was not how she'd imagined her day going.

CHAPTER THREE

THE NEXT DAY, Josie had a doctor's appointment. Rather than have her and Boyd drive their RV to Dr. Marshall's office, Maeve had Boyd drive her to work, then insisted he and Josie keep her car for Josie's appointment.

Boyd was in the parking lot on time, waiting for her, just as she'd known he would be.

Maeve expected Boyd to tell her the young family would be leaving soon. It shouldn't have bothered her, but if she was honest with herself, she had to admit she liked having them around. She steeled herself for the news.

"How are Josie and the baby?" she asked as she climbed into the passenger seat. It was a treat to have someone else drive her for a change. Not that she couldn't drive, or even minded driving, but sometimes it was nice to sit in the passenger seat and watch the scenery.

Boyd didn't start the car. He shook his head. "It's not good. She had a horrible time with her pregnancy with Carl and given her history, the doctor wants to be very cautious. She's on bed rest. She tried to convince him she'd stay in the bed in the RV, but he said travel might be risky. Especially since we don't know exactly where we're headed and how close we'll be to medical care."

Boyd turned to her. He looked worn and defeated. "I hate to do it, but I have to ask for more help. Maybe we could keep the RV parked where it is a few more weeks? At least until the baby comes?"

Maeve realized that every word cost him. Boyd was a proud man and he was humbling himself for Josie's benefit and the baby's. If it was possible, Maeve liked him even more. "Boyd, that's no problem. No problem at all."

"We liquidated everything we owned. I have some money—"

"Please, don't." She frowned. "Really, it's not necessary to explain."

He raked his fingers through what was left of his hair. He appeared as if he'd give up fighting his bad luck if he was fighting for only himself. But underneath that weariness was a firm resolve. She'd just met him, but Maeve knew Boyd was a man who would do anything for his family.

"I don't understand why you're helping us."

"I'd like to say it's what people do...but that's not necessarily true. Not all people." She remembered so many who had turned away from her and her mother when they were in the same kind of trouble as Boyd was now. "But some people do. Once, a long time ago, my mom and I needed help. Three people—for no reason at all and no personal gain I could ever see—stepped up. Ms. Mac, my school principal. Hank, who owns the diner. And Mrs. Anderson, the librarian. They all threw my mom and me a lifeline."

Maeve had spent her adult life trying to prove herself worthy of their help. To give back in a way that would make them proud. "Most afternoons I stayed at the library. Mrs. Anderson kept giving me new books to read. And over the years, she became more than a librarian to me—she was a friend. When she moved into a retirement home, she sold me her house at a ridiculously low price. That's where I live now, and I'm sure she'd have liked the idea of your family finding shelter there. She was never someone who did anything big and flashy, or that made anyone notice her. She lived her life quietly giving to others in countless ways."

Giving her help. Giving her time. Giving her heart.

Maeve had asked Mrs. Anderson to stay on at the house, but she'd insisted she was excited to move to the retirement home. Maeve had visited weekly, until two years ago when Mrs. Anderson had passed away.

"During the worst period in my life, she pointed me toward books that were filled with hope and optimism. Mrs. Anderson left me that cross-stitch in my kitchen. *I can't save the world, but I can try.* She lived by those words and I'm working at following in her footsteps. You've heard of paying it forward? Well, I'm paying it back. We won't be talking about money. The amount of electricity or water you'll use is minimal." He seemed as if he was about to protest, but she held up a hand. "And you can pay me back for it by helping someone else someday."

He still looked as if he was going to refuse, so she added, "And helping me with a few projects."

He eyed her suspiciously. "Busywork or things you really need done?"

She laughed. "I'm a single woman who is at home in a library or a winery. I'm competent in my sphere. Projects at home are always a challenge."

She pulled out the big guns. "And you'd be doing it for Josie."

"You and Josie," he muttered.

"Me and Josie what?"

"Know what to say to get your way." The quiet man offered her a small smile, and Maeve got a glimpse of what Josie had seen in him. "My father always warned me about women like you two."

She laughed. "Dangerous. Yeah, that's me. But dangerous or not, there are days I think I'd forget my head if it wasn't attached to my neck. Do you mind waiting another moment before we go home? I have to run back into the store for something."

"Sure," he said. "I can manage that all right."

She hurried into the winery. Its unique fruity scent was always welcoming, she thought. The shelves were filled with wine bottles and grape-inspired paraphernalia and were as familiar to her as the shelves in her library. True, there was no Dewey decimal system here, but she could find everything and anything in a moment's notice.

Gabriel must have heard her because he popped his head out of the office. "Oh, it's you. Did you forget something?"

Asking for help wasn't something Maeve was accustomed to any more than Boyd was. But this was for someone else after all. She looked her boss in the eye. "No, I didn't forget anything, even though I just lied to someone and said I did. I wanted to ask if you know anyone who is still looking for some short-term, seasonal help."

"Not offhand. Why?"

"I have a family, a young family, who's staying with me. Well, near me. They were on their way to North Dakota to look for work, but now they're stuck here for a while. Josie, the mom, is pregnant and the doctor's put her on bed rest. Her husband, Boyd, won't accept charity, and he needs something to do until they can leave..." She let the sentence fade, realizing she was rambling.

Gabriel looked as angelic as his name. He had dark hair, which wanted badly to curl. He kept it cut short, but if he was even a couple days late in trimming it, the curl took hold. He also had piercing blue eyes that didn't miss anything. Sometimes Maeve thought he saw more to her than she did herself.

"Well, that's more personal information than you've ever shared, Maeve. We worked together all day and you didn't mention you had guests."

She shrugged. She liked Gabriel. Liked him a lot. When she started here, he'd tried to engage her in small talk, but she wasn't very good at it. They'd found common ground discussing work, wine and customers, and he seemed to accept those

67

parameters. But he'd obviously noticed that she didn't reveal much about herself.

"I wondered if you have any odd jobs going, no matter how small, or if there's anyone else who needs someone." She knew that Gabriel didn't have a permanent, salaried position open, but from time to time there were small things that needed to be done.

"I can't think of when you've ever asked me for anything," he mused.

"Donations for the library," she reminded him.

He laughed. "Yes, you've hit up everyone in Valley Ridge for that. But this is different. I wish I had an opening, or had heard of someone who did. But I'll ask around."

"Thanks, Gabriel." She felt a bit awkward for having asked. "I'll see you tomorrow."

Okay, that was a good try. She'd ask Mattie. Maybe one of the shops in town was hiring, and if so, Mattie would know. Working at the coffee shop, Mattie heard about things like that.

"Wait," Gabriel called.

Maeve turned around.

"It's not a real job, but I could use someone to organize the garage out back. Clean it, put things away..."

"You're making up work," she accused.

"Maybe." He shot her a quick smile. "But are you going to tell him about the offer?"

"I will. Thanks, Gabriel."

"I wish it was more."

"It's a start." She returned to Boyd and tried to think how to word the job offer.

"Boyd, I double-checked with my boss since he's been complaining forever about the awful state of the garage, and he said you're welcome to the job. It's only cleaning and organizing the space, but..."

Boyd studied her in a way that made her feel he saw as much as Gabriel did. "Do you know what Josie told me last night?"

"No."

"We were in our bed, the RV was warm and she said, 'I told you so, Boyd.'" He paused. "When I got laid off, and then when we lost it all, she told me not to worry. She told me that she believed that angels were everywhere and that things would turn out all right for us. So, last night, she said, 'I told you so, Boyd. We've found our first angel.' I didn't argue.

"I can never argue with Josie. She listens to me, lets all my arguments bash themselves against her smile. Truthfully, though, this time, I wasn't sure I believed her. But maybe I'm starting to."

"Don't," Maeve told him. "I'm no angel by anyone's definition. Letting someone park an RV next to my house, or mentioning a job...that's nothing."

"You're wrong. Josie knew it right away and I'm beginning to believe it, as well."

Boyd put the car in Reverse, backed out of the parking lot and headed for the highway. He didn't say anything else. That was fine with Maeve. She was embarrassed by his praise. She knew that what she'd done wasn't enough. It wasn't nearly enough.

It wasn't long before Boyd pulled into her driveway and there was a light on in the RV. "Josie's resting in bed. I'd better go rescue her from Carl. When I left, he'd had a bunch of books for her to read to him. She'll be hoarse before she finishes."

"You're all welcome to stay in the house," Maeve offered. It had to be difficult for Josie, being bedridden in the RV. "We can make over the living room." She'd never wished for a bigger house until this morning. The small one-bedroom cottage was perfect for a single woman, but there wasn't a lot of room for overnight guests.

"I'd like to say I'm shocked that a practical stranger would make that offer, but nothing you do shocks me anymore. Thank you, but we'll stay in the RV. To be honest, I think it's as big as your house." He laughed then, and Maeve caught yet another glimpse of the man Josie had fallen in love with.

"I think there's a chance you're teasing me," she teased back.

He pretended to consider her statement, there was a definite twinkle in his eye. "There's always a chance," he said. "And again, about today, I really appreciate it."

"The garage thing is only short-term. A day or two at best."

"It's something. And it's not only a job, it's...hope. I haven't felt hope in a long time."

Since he was smiling, she decided to press her luck. "Will you let me help with Josie? Maybe make a meal, or mind Carl? If the doctor has her on bed rest, I can't imagine taking care of a toddler is easy."

He took a deep breath. "Yes. That would be great."

"Fine. I've got book club tonight, but tomorrow, after work, I'll come get Carl and he can visit with me at the library. That will give you both a break."

Boyd nodded, then got out of the car and walked toward the RV while Maeve went into her house.

He'd called her an angel. She snorted. She took off her coat and boots and sat at her dining table without turning on a light. She didn't need one to know that Mrs. Anderson's cross-stitch was on the wall.

Maeve had helped, but surely there was something more she could do.

When she was young, she'd needed help. Her mother had needed help. And now that she thought about it, like Boyd, they'd lost hope. Admittedly, she still found it difficult to talk about those times. She should have told Boyd. Should have explained. Maybe he'd feel better about accepting her aid if he knew how Hank Bennington had given them a hand. Mrs. Anderson at the library and her principal, Ms. Mac, had helped, too. Not one of them had asked for anything in return, either.

Not one of them had saved the world when they'd helped her, but they'd certainly saved Maeve and her mom.

She'd done things to try to repay their generosity over the years. Volunteering at the library was one of those things, but there had been others.

Though none of it seemed like enough.

* * *

AARON NAVIGATED A SLIPPERY PATH to the library. It seemed ridiculous to drive the short distance from his uncle's apartment above the supply store, but he wished he had. It was warming up and the snow was turning to slush. To make matters worse, Aaron hadn't put on his boots because he knew that the sidewalks had all been cleared. He'd worn his sneakers, which were now soaked through.

Wet sneakers did nothing to improve his mood.

He wasn't in Florida anymore.

He wasn't sure why he was in such a funk. His family would say it was par for the course. He had been working pretty hard around the store. But he liked working so that wasn't the cause of his bad mood. He just didn't have time for frivolous endeavors.

And going to the library tonight was one of the frivolous endeavors he should have avoided. He should have stayed at home and ordered an ebook. It would have been delivered instantly to any number of the devices that he could read it on. But there was something about holding a printed book.

But it was too late to turn around and go back. He could see the library from over the bridge, and he was closer to it than his uncle's apartment, so he kept on slogging through the slush.

He passed the small cottage that bordered the library. There were a few trees and a small stone wall that separated the cottage from the library's parking lot. He knew it was Maeve's house. There was a big old RV parked in front of it. When Uncle Jerry had called earlier that day, Aaron casually mentioned having met Maeve. Uncle Jerry told him the same thing Dylan had—that Maeve had almost single-handedly reopened the library, which had closed about a decade ago. And every customer who came into the supply store had been talking about the family Maeve had taken in.

"They're not staying in a barn behind the inn, but an RV in a driveway is close enough," he'd overheard Mrs. Dedionisio say to Mrs. Keith.

The two women had gone on and on about the young homeless couple who were expecting a baby at Christmas, as he set up a snowbrush display and eavesdropped.

He'd wished the conversation would turn to Maeve.

Aaron didn't know what to make of the fiery redhead who volunteered her time at a library and took in homeless families.

She had to have an angle. He wasn't sure what it was, but he'd learned the hard way that everyone had one.

To listen to his uncle and the customers, she was too good to be true. And Aaron knew that if something seemed too good to be true, it generally was.

Maybe it was his curiosity about her, more than some burning need to borrow a book that had driven him from his warm house tonight. He wanted to see Maeve again, and, according to his uncle, she was at the library most evenings.

There were roughly half a dozen cars in the parking lot and a neon sign in the window read Open. He stomped up the marble stairs. Someone had tossed sand on them to prevent people from slipping.

He opened the door and was greeted not only by heat, but noise.

He spotted Maeve immediately. Even if her hair had been a more sedate color, she would have still stood out. She sat on one of the wooden chairs arranged in a circle in front of the checkout counter. She was laughing at what someone had said. It struck him that there were a lot of people making a lot of racket and this librarian was not shushing a soul.

When she saw him, her laughter died. So did her smile. She turned to an older woman, said something, and then approached him. "May I help you?"

"I came in to browse," he said.

"Fine. Help yourself. If you find something you want to borrow, we'll set you up with a file."

"Not a card?"

"This is a small library. I just started a database and whenever someone borrows a book, I mark it in their file. When they return it, I take it off. It saves people losing cards and the library the expense of reissuing them."

He nodded. "Is there a time limit?"

"Time limit?" she asked.

"A deadline the book has to be returned by?"

"When you finish?" She made the statement sound like a question. She was looking at him as if he was nuts.

Aaron couldn't help it if he liked things spelled out. He pressed on. "But what if someone else is waiting to borrow it?"

Maeve sighed and the movement caused her hair to flutter. He wasn't sure what else to call it. Her hair moved.

Maeve smoothed it back, she'd noticed its movement, too. "If someone else is waiting to borrow it and you've had it a long time, then I'll send you an email and tell you that. Most people are polite enough to hurry and finish it, or bring it back and sign it out again when they have more time and there's no waiting list."

"Maeve?" an older gentleman in the midst of the gathering called out.

Maeve held up a finger indicating she'd be right with him, and then turned to Aaron. "If you have any problems, holler. We're in the middle of book club."

"What is the book club reading?" Aaron asked.

She sighed again. Sometimes Aaron felt he wasn't very good at reading people, but he had no problem understanding that Maeve was finding him frustrating.

"We finished Jim Butcher's first Harry Dresden novel and we're starting *The Hobbit* next. The English department at the high school wanted a book that was universal. Something both older and younger readers would enjoy. They've assigned the book to their classes over winter break. The kids get extra credit if they show up for our competition next week."

"I never heard of a book club competition."

"This is a first for me, too. But the teachers and I came up with it as a way to engage students and adults in the club. We're having a riddle competition. The kids get bonus marks for attending. And those who show up for our regular January meeting will get extra credit if they join in the discussion."

"Riddles?"

"Have you ever read the book?" Maeve countered.

Aaron frowned.

"Watched the movies?"

Again he frowned.

Maeve studied him carefully. "So, what you're saying is, you live under a rock when you're not filling in for your uncle."

"Can anyone join? I could check out a copy and read it." He wasn't sure why he said that. He read. But his tastes leaned toward nonfiction. Biographies lately.

"Sorry. The library's copies are all signed out. The school bought copies for the students." She paused and looked as if she was trying to decide something. "But you can borrow my personal copy if you want."

"You're sure it's okay if I borrow it and join your book club?" That seemed highly unlikely as she continued to look at him with an expression somewhere between exasperation and annoyance.

"The book club is open to all Valley Ridge residents," was her prim response. "You might be a temporary resident, but you qualify."

"Maeve," the old guy hollered again.

"I really have to go. If you want the book, let me know. You can pick it up at my house after I've closed here, or I can drop it off at the store tomorrow."

She rushed back to her circle, her hair bobbing as she crossed the room. She smiled at something the old man said.

Aaron walked over to the bookshelves, but he couldn't help taking note of the people who made up the book club. There were a wide range of ages, male and female. There had to be about twenty people crammed into the limited space.

After a few minutes, Maeve stood. "I want to thank everyone for being here tonight. Don't forget, we'll still have our regular meeting in January to discuss *The Hobbit,* but instead of a December meeting, we'll have our Riddlefest next week before the holiday activities begin in earnest. We're hoping to get a lot of young people from the school joining us."

She stopped and spoke to a few individuals as she made her way to the counter and began checking out books. A man with three kids in tow—a boy and two girls—put a large number of books on the counter. "Stamp 'em, Miss Maeve, stamp 'em," the youngest girl commanded.

Maeve pulled out an old library stamp and thumped it against the card at the back of each book. It made a satisfying *ka-thunk*. Aaron had never given it any thought before, but he liked the sound.

He remembered his once-a-week visits to the school library where the librarian had used the same kind of date stamp. It was a nostalgic sound and reminded him of those carefree days.

"Last one's for you, Mica," Maeve said, passing the stamp to the little girl. The boy picked her up and held her while she stamped the card with far more energy than required.

"See you next week," Maeve said to the family.

Slowly, the line of people shrank. Maeve spent a long time talking to a tall man Aaron didn't recognize. He'd visited his uncle on occasion and knew a few people here in town, but not this guy.

When the man smiled and nodded, Maeve walked around the counter and gave him an enthusiastic hug.

Aaron realized he'd been staring at Maeve rather than looking at books, so he grabbed the closest book to him and took it to her.

Maeve asked for all his pertinent information, including an email address. "I'll give you a shout if someone else asks for this title, but I think you're safe keeping it as long as you need to. I don't get a lot of requests for Julia Child. Are you cooking for someone special?"

Aaron glanced down and realized he had picked up a cookbook. A very old cookbook. "No. No one special."

Maeve nodded and looked at him expectantly. "Was there anything else?"

"Yes. If you meant what you said earlier, can I borrow your copy of *The Hobbit?*" he asked.

"I'm sure you can, but you also *may,*" she responded with a grin.

"Funny," he said, which made her smile wider. "I'm not known for my social skills, but my mother taught me better than that."

"Give me a minute to turn out all the lights and make sure everything's locked," Maeve said.

He waited at the door as Maeve walked through the library.

A few minutes went by before she grabbed a coat from behind the counter, slipped it on and joined him. "I'm only next door."

After Maeve switched off the sign in the window, and locked the door behind them, she and Aaron carefully made it through the snow-covered parking lot and past the RV to her door. His sneakers had begun to dry out in the library, but were now soaked again.

Maeve paused for a mere second and said, "You might as well come in."

They entered a tiny mudroom, and when she opened the second door, they walked into a small kitchen. There was a table, a woodstove and cabinets that looked as if they were original to the house, a circa 1960s laminate counter and basic white appliances that seemed ancient.

There were glowing embers behind the glass in the door of the stove. She flipped on a light and said, "It will only take me a moment."

She went through the archway and turned on another light, this time illuminating a cozy living room. A living room where every wall was in actuality a floor-to-ceiling bookshelf. The only breaks in the shelves were for doors and windows. And each shelf was bursting with books. It was easy to see that there were double rows of books on many of them.

"Wow," he said.

She gave him her first genuine smile of the night. "I'm out of room again. My stepfather is giving me another wall of shelves for Christmas."

There were no more walls available anywhere that he could see. Even in the kitchen, the walls were lined with cabinets. "Where will you put them?"

"My bedroom. Two of the walls are slanted from the roof line, but there are flat walls on either side. He's building the shelf around the windows and my bed. I can't wait."

"What will you do for shelves after you fill those?" he asked because he was absolutely sure she'd fill them, too.

Maeve dragged the footstool from in front of the rocker over to the shelf that framed the front door and climbed up on it. She pulled out a large book. When she came closer, he could see that it was green leather and in a slipcase. "When I run out of shelves, I'll think of something else."

"You could start reading ebooks," he said.

He waited for her to laugh at the suggestion, as he recognized the expensive book in his hand.

But she didn't laugh. Instead, she sighed. "I already read ebooks. But my first love will always be printed books. A bound book is a work of art in itself. Speaking of which, hang on while I get a bag for you. I'd rather this one didn't get waterlogged if it starts to snow or sleet again."

The slipcase of the green leather book read *The Hobbit* and the spine was embossed with gold and red lines and decorative squiggles. "I can't borrow this. I thought you were offering me a paperback. You're right. A book like this is a work of art."

She reached out and ran a finger over the leather binding, obviously savoring the feel. "I know. I found it while I was browsing through the bookstore when I was in college. I didn't have any money to spare. I took a job as a housekeeper full-time at a hotel, did work study on campus and still had classes. No time, no money. I didn't *want* this book, I needed it. I ate peanut butter and crackers for weeks to save enough money to pay for it. But it was worth it. What a wonderful way to read the book the first time round. Don't get me wrong, I have plenty of paperbacks, but there's something about a leather-bound book. The heft of it. The smell. There's even the sound. That creak as you open the cover. It tells you that the book was stitched together, not simply glued. A book like this is meant to be enjoyed. Savored even."

"I'll be very careful with it."

She took the book, tucked it into a plastic grocery bag, along with his cookbook, and handed them back. "There you go. And when you finish it, ask me to borrow my copy of *The Lord of The Rings.* It's in red leather and equally beautiful."

"More peanut butter and crackers?" he asked.

"No. I got that one later. I was past my peanut butter years then." She glanced at the clock and said, "Speaking of late—"

It was a hint. A not so subtle hint that she was ready for him to leave. But he wasn't ready to leave her. He stood there, with his plastic bag of books and his coat on and he didn't want to go. Not yet. He struggled to find a conversational gambit. "So, you worked all day at the winery in Ripley—"

She gave him a sharp look. "How did you know that?"

It wasn't the reaction he'd been looking for. He should probably face it—he didn't know how to talk to women anymore. "This is Valley Ridge. I bet I could find out your birthday and who you took to homecoming when you were in high school by next week's Riddlefest."

That look of suspicion was replaced by a smile. "The sad truth of it is you probably could."

He tried again. "So, now that you're done working and volunteering for the day, what do you do with your time?"

She glanced at the clock again. "I'm going to watch *A Christmas Carol.* It's on at eight."

"It's not Christmas yet."

"I know. I thought about recording it, but there's something about watching it live on TV that I like. There are so many versions of that movie. I'm planning to catch as many of them as I can, and then I'll reread the book."

She looked so pleased with her idea. He was confused. "Why watch them all?"

"I found ten television and movie versions. I want to see how each director's vision of the story differed, what parts are universal to all the films."

She seemed to sense his confusion and sighed. "Here's the thing, if you told a story and I told the same story, there would be differences. Things that stood out for you might not be the parts that stood out for me. A few years ago, Harlequin—"

He must have looked confused because she clarified, "They publish romance books. One of the biggest publishers in the world. Anyway, they asked a group of authors to participate in a storytelling adventure. The authors started with the same paragraph, and then each had to write the rest of the story. Every author came at it from his or her individual perspective. One was humorous, one was historical... They were all different, despite the fact they all started at the same place. I thought that watching the same movie as envisioned by different directors and acted by different actors would be interesting, so—" She shrugged. "Why am I telling you this? Go read *The Hobbit* and let me get to my movie."

"You could invite me to watch it with you. It might be fun having someone to discuss it with. Sort of like a book club, but with a movie."

He thought for sure she was going to say no. But instead of telling him to leave, she nodded. "Okay, but be quiet during the movie."

"Any chance you've got some popcorn?"

"And an air popper."

"Phew. I don't count the microwave kind as real popcorn."

She laughed.

* * *

"So, what did you think?" Maeve asked as she clicked off the television once the movie had ended, a little less than two hours later. She had to admit that Aaron was a good movie companion. He didn't eat all the popcorn and he hadn't tried to start a conversation while the movie was on.

"It's not going to supplant my favorite version," Aaron said diplomatically.

She turned sideways and faced him. "You have a favorite version?"

He looked at her with mock sternness. "Promise not to laugh?"

She crossed her fingers solemnly over her heart. "The Muppets."

She smothered a giggle.

"Are you laughing at me?"

She was afraid if she answered, she wouldn't be able to smother it, so she just shook her head. He grinned. "There is some very real cinematic value in the Muppets' version."

That did it. If he was going to talk about cinematic value he couldn't blame her for laughing.

"Women," he said to no one in particular. "They undervalue the Muppets."

"Hey, it's on my list, too," she said when she was able to talk. "And in between watching all the Christmas Carols, I've got a bunch of other Christmas movies lined up."

"I thought you'd be reading Christmas books."

"Most of the year, all I do is read. I'm reading a great book now for our romance book club called *The Secret Santa Club*. But as far as movies go, I love Christmas classics, and..." She let the sentence fade.

"And?" he prompted.

"Zombies," she admitted as if confessing to a horrible vice. "A good zombie apocalypse makes me happy."

He studied her for a moment, and shook his head. "You are an odd woman."

Maeve nodded. "Yes, I'm afraid that's the truth." She glanced at the clock. "I don't want to be rude, but I work tomorrow."

"Right, I'd better go." Aaron picked up his bag of books on the way to the door. "Thanks again."

"See you next Tuesday. Don't forget to bring a riddle."

"I'll be there."

Maeve closed the door and locked it. That was totally unexpected. She didn't like Aaron. After all, he'd been rude to her and then he'd called her Red. But tonight he'd been perfectly charming. She glanced at Mrs. Anderson's cross-stitch. *I can't save the world, but I can try.*

She switched off the kitchen light and noticed there was still a light on in the RV. She hoped everyone inside was okay. She worried about them, even though it had warmed up—warmth being a relative thing. The temperature was now in the upper thirties, which wasn't too bad for Valley Ridge in November.

Then the light blinked out and the RV was dark.

Josie thought that she, Maeve, was an angel and that everything happened for a reason.

I can't save the world, but I can try.

What more could she do for the nice family? She'd given them a place to park their RV, helped Boyd find a temporary job and offered to help with Carl.

She'd done what she could.

An image of Aaron, on his way back to Jerry's, popped into her head. And from there, her mind flashed to the old Culpepper place.

It was a home without a family.

She thought of Scrooge, buying that Christmas goose and embracing the true meaning of the holiday.

Round and round her mind went. Old Christmas movies, the romance novel she was reading, homeless people, peopleless homes...

It occurred to her that she'd read something about the Culpepper place going up for sale next week to pay for back taxes.

How much money did it cost to buy a run-down property to cover back taxes?

Probably more than she had.

She hadn't checked her bank account lately, but it had to be pretty sizable. At least, for an average person it was. She lived very frugally and Gabriel paid her a good salary, most of which she put into her savings account.

Not that she could spend that. That money was her safety net. If her mother had had money put away, they might have been able to hold on to their house all those years ago.

Everything happens for a reason.

I can't save the world, but I can try.

She thought of the movie and Scrooge buying gifts and dinners for people.

How much could the Culpepper place cost? And how on earth did someone buy a house that was meant to cover back taxes?

And even if she could make something like that happen, there wouldn't be any way to make it happen in time for Josie and Boyd.

It was a pipe dream.

She looked beyond the RV to the library. Reopening it had been a pipe dream. She'd been sitting in her kitchen on a night much like this, looking at the deserted building and suddenly knew that she had to do something about it.

Convincing the town council to give her permission had been a battle. They'd talked about insurance premiums and liabilities. Told her that soliciting donations for books would be next to impossible in these tough economic times. Yet she'd done it. There it was. Tonight it had been full of people who loved to read.

"I can't save the world, but I can try."

Upstairs in her bedroom, she pushed the crazy idea and picked up her current book. Reading had always been her means of coping. She could get lost in a good book and life's problems faded.

The Secret Santa Club. It was a book of loosely connected short stories. Sweet romances. Exactly what she needed.

Maeve turned to Ava's story.

Christmas might be a season of giving, but all it was giving Ava Jones this year was a headache.

Maeve slammed the book shut. She was giving herself a headache. She couldn't stop thinking about the down-on-their-luck family in her driveway.

Even if she bought the house, Boyd would never accept it if she tried to give it to the family. And he'd never be able to afford it if she bought it, fixed it up and sold it to them.

But what if he could afford it? What if the mortgage payments were set on a sliding scale?

Then again, Boyd couldn't afford even a minimal payment, unless he had a job.

What if the house wasn't from her?

What if it was from a foundation? A foundation that took old houses with good bones, renovated them and sold them back to low income families, with a low interest rate and a sliding scale mortgage? Money would go back into the foundation in order to buy more houses.

Those were a lot of what-ifs and a lot of opportunities for Boyd to say no. But what if the house was a gift from a Secret Santa? Who could say no to Santa?

Still, it could all go wrong.

Maeve opened the book again, not to escape this time, but rather, to be inspired.

* * *

AARON WALKED ACROSS the bridge and down Park Street, hugging his bag of books to his chest.

What an unusual woman. She cared about her books almost as if they were living things. He found himself fantasizing about her, caught himself and shut down the thought.

He had not come to Valley Ridge to start a relationship with anyone. He wasn't ready to be in a relationship with anyone. And even if he was, it wouldn't be in Valley Ridge. As soon as the weather warmed up his uncle would come home and Aaron would be on the first plane to Florida.

He trudged on through the slush, wishing for the umpteenth time that he'd worn boots. As soon as he got home he was going to take a hot shower and hope that he hadn't caught pneumonia.

He was cold, but he had actually enjoyed himself tonight.

Maeve was an enigma.

She took in homeless families. She single-handedly opened a library, and then volunteered her free time to keep it open.

No one could be as pure of heart as she seemed to be. She had to have some agenda he couldn't see.

What made a woman like her tick?

He shivered and hugged the books tighter to his chest.

He never had to worry about pneumonia in Florida. Heatstroke in the summer, maybe, but not blizzards before Thanksgiving.

Thanksgiving.

His whole family would be at his mom and dad's in Key West. Everyone except him. He'd skipped out on family holidays for the past couple of years. Not that he didn't like his family—he did. He liked them more than he liked anyone else.

Family was family—they stood by you no matter what. No, he'd stayed away because he couldn't stand their sympathetic looks. He couldn't stand to have them ask questions he couldn't answer.

Worse than their concerned looks and awkward questions were his younger sisters picking on him and driving him crazy. The last time he'd seen them they'd been so...nice. Sweet, even.

Miri had gone so far as to embrace him and tell him that she loved him.

He knew his family loved each other. He loved his sisters and they loved him, but he didn't go around telling Helen, Miri or Nan as much.

Likewise they never said the words to him.

Until two years ago.

And then he'd stopped going to family events.

He'd made up excuses. Plausible, possible excuses.

He'd thought several months ago that maybe he'd be safe to go to the Fourth of July picnic, but his sisters had been kind to the point of making him sick.

He couldn't stand the thought that he'd made them worry about him. Even after they'd stopped asking questions he stayed away because he knew that even though they hid it well, they still worried about him.

This year, he had an excellent excuse. Family is Family—that was the Holders' motto. Well, everyone in his family would understand that he couldn't be there for the holidays since he was helping his uncle.

Maybe next year he'd make an appearance.

CHAPTER FOUR

THE WEEKEND FLEW by. In addition to her regular commitments, Maeve had found time to see Valley Ridge's mayor, Ray Keith. She didn't know him well. He was Mattie's little brother, not that there was anything little about him. Maeve wasn't especially short, but she needed to crane her neck to look up at him.

The mayor not only liked her idea, he'd called everyone on the town council and explained what she was proposing. They'd all agreed to help.

She felt excited, and a bit sick at the thought of draining her savings.

I can't save the world, but I can try.

She kept coming back to that saying as a touchstone. She could save more money. She could rebuild her account. Even if she lost her job or her house, she had her mother and Herm...they would support her until she was back on her feet again.

She was lucky. Some people didn't have anyone to turn to.

The Culpepper place would go on the auction block tomorrow. The day before Thanksgiving. Ray had managed to get the paper to run a notice on Saturday in order to comply with the town's public notice ordinance.

One more day. In one more day she'd know if it was hers. Ray didn't think she'd have any competition. No one else had expressed an interest.

Once she won—assuming she did—there would be work. And she'd have to find donations of furniture and housewares. Donations of paint and whatever other things the house needed. The porch was an issue, but hopefully she'd have enough left over in her savings to buy new wood for that.

She'd didn't mind doing the work. A few weekends of painting and other touch-ups, and the house should be ready before Christmas.

If Jerry were in town, she knew she could go to him for paint. She wasn't so sure she'd be able to convince Aaron to help. Well, she'd figure out something.

In the meantime, she had to get the library ready for tonight's Riddlefest. It seemed odd to prepare for book club on a Tuesday. Maeve's weeks had a certain rhythm to them, but Thanksgiving was throwing her off. And worrying about Wednesday was making it worse.

She arrived home from work, made herself a quick PB&J for dinner and dashed out the door.

Josie poked her head out of the RV as Maeve approached and asked, "Are we still on for tonight?"

"I'm on my way to the library now. I've got to set up the chairs and start the coffee. Mattie's bringing Zoe and she's got treats from the coffee shop."

"I'll be over as soon as Boyd gets here," Josie said, looking thrilled at the prospect of getting out of the RV.

"As long as you understand that I've got strict orders that you're to keep your feet up the whole time. You know Boyd's welcome to come with Carl. There are going to be a ton of kids at this one."

"If the discussion was going to be about a murder mystery or biography, I might have been able to convince him, but he assured me that he doesn't do hobbits or riddles."

"He doesn't know what he's missing. Now, you should put your feet up, or Boyd's not going to let you come out."

Josie laughed. "Okay. See you in a bit." She shut the door.

The doctor had said as long as Josie rested a lot, she could handle Riddlefest and Thanksgiving at Maeve's. Normally her family had dinner at Maeve's mom and stepfather's house because it was bigger. But this year, they would have it in her house even though it was smaller, so that the Myers family could join them.

Her mom had been over the moon at the prospect of more people to cook for. Maeve wondered if her mom missed working at the diner. Renie Lorei loved to cook, but more than that, she loved to feed people. Maybe it came from all the years of worrying whether or not she would be able to put food on the table for the two of them.

Thinking about those times depressed Maeve, so she pushed the thoughts aside.

There was so much to be excited about. The riddle contest tonight. Thanksgiving was in two days.

And then there was tomorrow.

Tomorrow would be the beginning of her paying back to the community what she owed the people who'd helped her out in the past. The big opportunity she'd been looking for was finally here.... A car pulled into the parking lot as Maeve unlocked the door to the library.

Aaron Holder.

She tingled with excitement. She'd enjoyed their evening together. But when Aaron looked over at her, he frowned. As if he'd forgotten she'd be there, or maybe he simply regretted watching the movie with her the other night. He waved and called out, "Hey, Red."

The flame of excitement sputtered out, replaced by annoyance. "It's Maeve," she said as he approached.

"Sorry," he said innocently. "The hair's a sore point?"

"Having a nickname based on something you do, well that's one thing, but I was born with this hair." She picked up a hunk and let it fall. "It always made me stand out."

"And you don't want to stand out?" he asked.

She shook her head. "No, not most of the time. Not ever, to be honest."

He studied her, and then nodded.

She went into the library and switched on the lights. "What brings you out so early?"

"I saw Lily at the diner. She was on her way over here to help you set up, but she got a call from a patient. So I volunteered."

"There's not much to do," she said. "We have one book club or another almost every week, so I'm well practiced at moving a few chairs," she added.

"Then it won't take us long, will it?" he said, and offered up a smile.

His calling her Red was still too fresh in her mind for her to smile back. "Okay, fine. I was going to take the couch out of stacks and bring it up here. Josie's still on bed rest and I promised her husband I'd make sure she doesn't overdo it." She added, "Her husband's the guy who came with me to get the propane after the storm."

"Oh." Aaron seemed pleased at the news. "I thought he might be a boyfriend."

Maeve looked at Aaron. She realized that he'd been wondering who Boyd was to her, and for some reason, her initial annoyance faded away and she felt...pleased.

Boyd was a good guy. On Friday and Saturday he'd been working at Gabriel's while Josie and Carl had spent time with her. Despite the fact they'd recently met, Maeve felt closer to Josie than she'd felt to anyone in a long time.

Maeve wished she'd faced her own adversity with the same sense of optimism and wonder as Josie. She knew she hadn't. She was also aware that meeting her was no compensation for Josie and for what she'd lost.

Maeve led Aaron into the stacks.

"Is this the couch?" Aaron asked.

Maeve pushed aside her thoughts and nodded. "Yeah, this is the one."

It wasn't very heavy and she managed her end just fine.

"So, I was thinking about our movie," Aaron said, "and—"

He was interrupted when the door to the library opened. As much as Maeve wondered what he had been about to say, she was happy to see Josie walk in, holding on to Boyd's free arm. The other arm was holding Carl.

"I'll walk her home, if that's okay," Maeve offered.

"I'm not an invalid," Josie huffed.

"You are, however, sitting down on the couch and not moving until after book club or I'll call Boyd," Maeve said.

Boyd smiled at her mock bossy tone and said, "Thanks." At the same time Josie said, "Snitch."

People started to arrive for the meeting. Generally, it was a small group who came to the general fiction club. The romance club was always the most popular one. But tonight was jammed. It helped that the high school kids were obligated to attend in order to get their bonus marks.

If this kept up, the library wouldn't be big enough to host the book club anymore. Maybe she could talk to Ray about finding some space at city hall, or maybe one of the schools would let them meet in their cafeteria. That actually sounded like a viable plan. If she could keep the younger generation interested in reading and attendance kept growing, then after the holidays, she'd investigate the idea further. Of course, she'd already asked Ray for a lot.

Gabriel had given her tomorrow and Thursday off for Thanksgiving. She couldn't wait.

But right now, she had book club.

She smiled at Josie. "Make yourself comfortable and if you need anything, I'll get it for you."

Aaron was already ahead of her. He walked over with a cup of coffee. "Decaf," he told Josie with a grin. "I might not know a lot about pregnant women, but I know it's a caffeine-free condition."

He pulled up a chair and entertained Josie as Maeve finished setting up.

She was about to start the meeting when Sophie's daughter, Tori, came running up to her, squealing her name. The teenager gave Maeve a hug. "We're in town for Thanksgiving," she said. "Joe told me what the book was. I read it years ago, but I decided to reread it even though he said tonight was more about the riddle scene than the rest of the book. Anyway, I'm good to go."

"I'm so glad you're in town," Maeve said, hugging the girl back. Tori had stolen her parents' car and driven from Ohio to Valley Ridge last summer, looking for her birth mother. She'd found Sophie and introduced herself in a dramatic way. Maeve and the rest of the Valley Ridge would be telling the story of that introduction for years to come.

The driving underage was how Maeve and Tori had become close. Tori had been almost fifteen and

Dylan had agreed with her parents that Tori's punishment would be best served volunteering at the library. When Maeve had first met Tori, she'd been an angry, blue-haired girl. Now, she had Sophie's blond hair, with a much more subtle blue streak and seemed as cheerful as her biological mother.

"We're having Thanksgiving with Sophie. My grandparents are even coming in for it. Sophie's all flustered. It's the first holiday she's hosted at the farm. Mom and Dad said they wished they could have come to the library with me tonight, but they're pitching in to help Sophie since she's about ready to pop. Seriously, she's so tiny and I don't think there's much more room for the baby to grow. Lily told her that she had to wait until after the wedding to have the baby, but, Maeve, I'm not sure she's going to make it." Without pausing for a breath, she asked, "What are you doing for the holiday?"

"I was having dinner at Mom and Herm's, but they're moving it to my place because I have guests—"

"Yeah, I heard all about them from Joe before I even got here. Then I heard from JoAnn. And from Marilee and Vivienne. Half the town is looking for jobs for Boyd."

"Well, news does travel fast here." She loved that about Valley Ridge, except when it was about her. Which was why she'd always done her utmost to stay under the town's radar.

"Anyway, you've probably heard then that Josie is on bed rest. She had to persuade her husband that she should come out tonight. I thought it would be easier to convince him that they should join us for dinner if they didn't have to go too far, which is why Thanksgiving is at my house this year. Come with me, I'll introduce you."

* * *

AARON WATCHED AS Maeve led a young girl over to him. And then he realized he'd been flattering himself—she was leading the kid to Josie.

As they got closer, he noticed the girl was older than he'd thought. Midteens at least. Her blond hair was cropped short in the back and longer on the side and sported a blue streak.

"Josie, this is Tori, the best library assistant I ever had. Tori, this is Josie, a new friend."

Aaron cleared his throat and Maeve added, "Oh, and this is Aaron. He's working at the Farm and House Supply, filling in for his uncle this winter. But I don't think he's meant for the business, since remembering people's proper names is so difficult for him."

"Nice to meet you, Tori," Josie said. "Maeve told me how much you did at the library over the summer." Josie patted the couch next to her and Tori sat down. A young boy came in and sat on the chair next to the couch. Tori introduced him as her friend Joe, and the two of them proceeded to regale

Josie with stories of their summer and Joe's two younger sisters.

"They wanted to come tonight," he said, "but Dad said no. I promised to remember some of the riddles to tell them."

"Speaking of riddles..." Maeve said.

Aaron noticed how quickly the room quieted as Maeve stood and welcomed everyone. She gave a bit of history about Tolkien, his writing group with C. S. Lewis and others, as well as the origins of *The Hobbit.* He noted she was careful not to reveal anything about the story, other than the fact that there was a riddle scene. She read a bit of the section out loud, and then encouraged people to stand up and tell their own riddles.

The riddles were silly and he'd heard many of them before, but Aaron couldn't remember when he'd laughed so much. When it was his turn, he was ready. "What do computer geeks snack on?"

No one answered.

"*Micro*chips." It took a minute, but soon the entire room was laughing.

He'd spent more time than he should have coming up with riddles for tonight and he felt a sense of satisfaction that the first one was well received. "I have another one. What is a computer geek's favorite fruit?"

"*Apples,*" Tori shouted out.

He grinned. "Yes. And what do you call a swearing computer geek?"

No one answered and he was delighted that he'd stumped them. "A cursor."

Even Maeve laughed. "Did you work on those all week?"

He nodded.

"I know you're only filling in for your uncle, and that managing a store isn't your primary job. Let me guess, do you do something with computers?" Maeve asked.

"Guilty. I'm a programmer."

Maeve didn't look the least bit annoyed or exasperated with him. She was laughing, and he liked her looking at him that way.

The riddle competition continued. Aaron had initially been embarrassed by the lameness of his riddles, but there were others that were equally lame and everyone seemed to find all of them as funny as he did.

"Okay, it's time for our Riddlefest awards," Maeve announced. "It's safe to say our winner in the work-related category is...Aaron Holder." She gave him a quick nod and everyone clapped.

After Maeve had announced the rest of the winners and wished everyone a happy Thanksgiving, people started getting up.

Aaron continued to sit by Josie and half listened as she talked with Tori and the boy, Joe, but he mainly watched Maeve.

She smiled and chatted with everyone. Young and old. She laughed a lot, and people around her did, as well.

"Mr. Holder," someone said loudly. He turned and realized Tori was standing in front of him.

"Sorry. I was just thinking."

"Yeah, I can guess what you were thinking about." She glanced over her shoulder at Maeve, then faced him and grinned.

"So, I know you're a computer geek," she said. "But how long are you in town for?"

Something told him that Tori was quite mature for her age. "Until my uncle comes back. He's in Arizona. The Valley Ridge winters are getting too hard for him, so I'll probably be here until it warms up."

His uncle had been decidedly less than forthcoming on a specific date when he'd be back. He felt that Aaron's ability to work from anywhere meant he didn't have a life to get back to. And though he'd never say so, there really wasn't much waiting for Aaron in Florida, other than the sunshine and the heat.

"Where are you from?" she asked.

"Orlando, Florida." He missed the warmth. Missed his house. Missed his easy, simple life there. He'd been able to work when he wanted. Sleep when he wanted.

Here, he had to be at the store to oversee things, which made it more difficult for him to work on his own stuff.

There, he'd gone days without having anybody visit but the mailman.

Here, he interacted with people daily.

"Seeing anyone?" Tori asked.

He didn't like the direction of this conversation. "Not now." That was the truth. Not the whole truth, but all a stranger had to know, especially when the stranger was a teenage interrogator.

"Are you going home for Thanksgiving?" the girl asked.

He shook his head.

"Oh," was all she said.

Maeve joined their group. She actually gave him a half smile. "Your riddles were the hit of the evening."

"I got into the spirit of it. I'm only a few chapters away from finishing the book, by the way. You're right, reading a beautifully bound book does enhance the experience. I appreciate your loaning it to me."

Tori looked surprised and interrupted them. "Wait a minute." She turned to Maeve. "You lent him your copy of *The Hobbit?* The peanut-butter-for-weeks one?"

Maeve seemed embarrassed. "He wanted to join the book club and the library didn't have any copies left."

Tori grinned. "That was nice of you. *Very* nice of you." To Aaron she said, "You'd better guard it with your life. She loves that book. Well, all books. But that one specifically."

He made a cross over his heart.

But Tori had already moved on to another subject. "Did you know Aaron doesn't have anywhere to go for Thanksgiving? His family's in Florida and he's stuck here at the supply store. All alone. On a holiday."

Aaron knew where this tricky young girl was going. She verified his suspicions by winking at him.

Yes, she was definitely mature for her age.

"It's okay, Tori," he said, playing along. "I bought a microwavable turkey dinner." As Tori made an over-the-top gasping noise, he innocently and hastily added, "It's a step up from last year's Thanksgiving dinner. I had a turkey sub for that."

"I'm so sorry, Aaron," Tori said, her voice dripping with sympathy, though her eyes sparkled with mischief. "I mean, if we were having dinner at my house, I'd tell Mom to invite you. But we're staying at JoAnn's Bed and Breakfast and eating at Sophie's. And though Sophie adores me, I think it's rude to invite someone when it's not your house. And, given her condition, more work isn't what she needs. She's pregnant, you know. Very pregnant with my baby brother."

She referred to her mom and dad, and then referred to Sophie carrying her brother. He'd met the Sophie in question, but he didn't know anything about Tori's relationship with her. He didn't ask, though he was curious. "It's no problem, really. I'm used to microwave meals. I eat them most nights."

Tori was staring expectantly at Maeve. And Josie, who'd been quiet, looked at Maeve, as well.

Aaron could see that Maeve knew what was going on. He didn't blame her for not immediately inviting him. He'd been a bit of a jerk when they'd first met, but he thought their impromptu movie night had smoothed things over. Although, calling her Red again this evening had been a mistake.

Maeve sighed the sigh of the defeated. "Aaron, why don't you come over to my house on Thursday? My mom and my stepfather and Josie and her family will be there. Mom's making the turkey at her place and bringing it over to mine, so the food's bound to be good."

Her invitation was polite enough, but though she tried to disguise it, he could see the reluctance in her expression. He should be chivalrous and decline. To be honest, most of the time, it was easy for him to turn down opportunities where he would be forced to socialize. The past couple of years, he'd pretty much lived the life of a hermit. But he found himself saying, "Thank you, Maeve. I'd be delighted. It was kind of you to ask."

Maeve's face said she was anything but delighted at the prospect of dining with him, but he ignored it and when she left to see to other patrons, he turned to Tori. "Thanks."

"I'm not sure why I helped you, other than you seem to rattle Maeve, and she needs to be a bit rattled sometimes. But be on your best behavior," the girl warned. "Maeve's special."

Josie nodded. "Maeve is very special."

Aaron wasn't sure why they would think he'd be anything less than well behaved, but he wasn't about to start an argument. "I promise."

He hung around and helped clean up the chairs in the hopes of spending more time with Maeve. But after she closed up the library, she helped Josie to the RV and went inside with her, giving him a brief wave good-night.

Well, he had an invitation to Thanksgiving dinner, so he knew he'd see her then, if not before.

* * *

THE NEXT MORNING Maeve woke with a sense of excitement warring with anxiety. It was Wednesday. And she wasn't thinking about all the things she had to do before Thanksgiving dinner tomorrow.

She was thinking about the Culpepper place.

She'd been saving money her entire adult life. She wanted a cushion, something to fall back on if tough times hit. She didn't simply *want* to be prepared for any unexpected financial difficulties, she *needed* to be. She'd thought about dipping into her savings in the past and had felt anxious to the point of nearly having a panic attack.

She was still nervous, but she was energized, too. She could come up with all kinds of rational reasons why it was okay to do this. She knew her mother and Herm would always be there for her, and she had a college degree and work experience. She owned her home outright, so no bank could call in her mortgage. And she could always rebuild her savings. She was still young enough that she had plenty of years to plan for retirement.

Even if Josie and Boyd weren't interested in her proposal, someone else would benefit from this.

She'd gone to the bank and checked on her available funds. She knew what she had down to the penny.

She then talked Ray into starting the bidding at a reasonable amount. He had to make enough on the Culpepper place to justify bumping up the sale date to the town council, but he knew she had only limited personal funds and they'd agreed to stay within that amount.

She told him her half-baked plan and he'd offered to help. He'd also promised to work with her when it came to transferring the deed.

The deed to the house.

Though it wasn't just any house. No, not if she had her way. With any luck, the old Culpepper place would be a home for Boyd and Josie. They'd raise Carl and their new baby there. They'd build a lifetime of memories in that house.

Maeve flew through her morning routine. She took two insulated mugs of herbal tea over to Josie since Boyd had already left for work. He'd finished fixing up the garage for Gabriel, and had been hired by a local farmer to replace some fencing. She'd volunteered to see that Carl was dressed and fed. She found she enjoyed starting her day visiting with Josie.

Josie longed for roots, for *neighbors* in the truest sense of the word. People who looked out for you. And she wanted a garden in the spring.

Josie was convinced that everything happened for a reason, and the reason they were going through this upheaval was to find their true home.

And Maeve fervently hoped it would be here in Valley Ridge.

After saying goodbye to Josie and Carl, she began the walk toward the mayor's office. On her way there, she paused at the parking lot of the supply store and gazed at the broken, weathered house that stood beyond it. It had a good sized backyard. A backyard that definitely had enough room for a garden. She could see the Myers family there. Sitting on the porch in the summer, waving hi to the neighbors. Celebrating birthdays, anniversaries, holidays.

With the beautiful fantasy still unfolding in her mind's eye, Maeve continued down Park Street, stopping in at the coffee shop for two coffees—one for her and one for Ray—before continuing on to Ray's office.

Maeve patted her coat pocket and felt reassured when she felt her checkbook.

It was time.

She entered the office and Ray was waiting. He glanced at the clock, then back at her and smiled. "Five minutes," he announced by way of a greeting. "You're the only one so far."

She handed him the coffee. "Your sister said this was your favorite. And to be clear, it's not a bribe."

He laughed. "I wasn't worried. And thanks." He took a sip and his smile was replaced by a look of concern. "You're sure about this? Even at this price, it's a lot of money for you to put up."

A wave of nervousness swept through her again.

Her mind harked back to the words embroidered on Mrs. Anderson's cross-stitch, and the nerves faded. They were replaced by a sense of purpose. "I'm sure," she said. "The formal paperwork will take more time, but like we agreed, I'll buy the place and put the deed in my name, and then as soon as the charity's papers are finalized, I'll donate it."

Ray smiled. "I wasn't worried about that."

"No, but I want to be sure everything's aboveboard. I'll see an attorney to make sure it's all legal. One thing I will need is a board of directors to oversee the foundation. Frankly, the idea of dealing with the money end of things gives me fits. I was thinking about asking Sebastian if he'd like to be on the board. I hope you'll consider serving, as well."

"You know I will. It's a great idea. I really like that it's starting local and staying local. This can make a huge difference to the town. It will give us a chance to deal with vacant properties and turn them into assets." He glanced at the clock and said, "It's time." He stood. "The bidding will begin at the amount owed in back taxes. Do I have an offer?"

Maeve raised her hand.

"Then, since there's only one offer on the table—"

Before Ray could finish his sentence, the door flew open. "Am I in time?" Aaron Holder looked worried. "I'd have been here sooner, but my uncle's manager, Tom, was late again. Though he hasn't said anything, I think he must have found another job because he's been very lax around the store lately."

He spotted Maeve and smiled. "I didn't think I'd see you again this soon." His smile faded as he looked at her and then at Ray.

Maeve didn't know what was going on in his mind, but she knew what was on the forefront of hers. "On time for what?"

"For the auction."

Her heart sank at his words. Ray shot her a sympathetic look, then said, "No, you're not too late. We just started. We have an offer on the table."

When Aaron heard the price, he grinned and upped her bid by five hundred dollars.

Maeve felt sick as she countered his bid.

She knew there were only so times she could afford to do so. Not if she was to have any money left over for renovations. Even with donations, she would still need to put money into the place. The house had been empty for so long she that was sure there would be a few issues.

Minutes later, Aaron had officially won the bidding war.

Ray mouthed the words, *I'm sorry.*

She nodded and got up to leave.

"No hard feelings?" Aaron asked, grinning. "Maybe I can treat you to dinner tonight..."

Maeve glared at him.

She would have liked to take the high road and tell him of course there were no hard feelings, but she didn't feel particularly generous or forgiving at the moment, so she simply turned and walked out of the room.

* * *

AARON WAS CONFUSED. "What was that about?" he asked the mayor.

For a second, it seemed as if Ray was going to say something, but in the end, the mayor just shrugged and handed Aaron a bunch of papers.

As Aaron filled out all the paperwork, he wondered what he'd done now. Obviously, Maeve had wanted the house, but she had a house already.

As he wrote out the check, it finally occurred to him that if she had a house, she must have wanted this one for something else.

"You're sure you won't tell me what she planned on doing with this place?"

The mayor shook his head. "Ask Maeve." He paused and asked, "What are you going to do with it?"

"The house is a wreck. I don't need to be a contractor to know that it's a money pit. And, it's an eyesore. I thought I'd be doing a public service by pulling it down and using the lot to expand the store's storage facilities."

Something in the mayor's expression told him that Maeve's reason for bidding on the house had nothing to do with tearing down the building.

Well, he had an invitation to dinner tomorrow. He'd find out more then.

Maeve Buchanan intrigued him. It had been a long time since a person had managed that.

When his uncle suggested he come here to look after the store, the notion had come to him that maybe a change of scenery would help motivate him. Ever since he sold the rights to the computer program he developed, he'd been searching for a new project that would excite him. His program had been a revelation. After he'd attended a lecture by a professor who was using a voice synthesizer, Aaron became convinced that he could convert some of his basic AI software into a more human-sounding instrument. The concept had been brewing in the back of his mind for a year. Every morning, he'd take his laptop out to the lanai, sit down with a cup of coffee, try to code for a bit, and then call it a day.

As it turned out Valley Ridge wasn't the answer to his getting down to more serious work because the only thing here that seemed to hold his attention was Maeve Buchanan.

He wasn't sure why spending time with Maeve meant so much to him, especially when he annoyed her so easily.

He should probably bow out of joining her and her family for Thanksgiving, but he knew he wouldn't.

CHAPTER FIVE

Normally, Maeve loved Thanksgiving. She loved spending the day on the farm with her mom and Herm. She loved the smell of turkey and pumpkin pie. She loved the sense of family as the three of them worked together to put dinner on the table. She loved the parades. She even loved when Herm put on his football game. She and her mom would play an epic game of Scrabble, and then she would curl up with a book for the rest of the afternoon.

She loved Thanksgiving because it was the holiday that represented home and family to her.

This year, things would be radically different. Since her eat-in kitchen was too tiny to accommodate even such a small group of guests, she spent the morning moving furniture around and setting up the table in the living room. There was a bit more room in there, but not much.

She'd waited all night, hoping that Aaron would phone and tell her he couldn't come to dinner after all.

The phone never rang.

That wasn't a shock to her. Aaron Holder didn't seem to worry about what other people thought of him. She'd let her guard down after finding out they shared an appreciation for books, movies and riddles, but her first impression had been right—he was annoying and she didn't like him.

Since he didn't call and cancel, she at least hoped he'd be the last to arrive. He seemed to get along well enough with Josie. Maybe she'd seat him beside her new friend and he would eat and then leave immediately after dinner.

Again, she wasn't the least bit surprised when he was the first one to show up. "I came early so I could help." He offered her a grin, as if nothing was wrong.

"I don't need any help from you," she said and regretted how curt it sounded. While he might be rude and abrasive, it didn't mean she had to be. Her mother had raised her right.

She tried to soften the statement to something her mother would approve of. "I have everything ready."

"May I come in?"

She realized he was still standing outside and reluctantly opened the door to allow him to enter. But to be sure he was clear on where things stood between them, she sighed. "Yes. You can put your coat on the hook and have a seat. I'm finishing up the potatoes."

"I could help," he offered as he took off his coat.

She wanted to say, *Sure you could help, but we both know you won't.* Though she knew she wasn't being fair to him. He didn't know why she was bidding on the house. And it did border his uncle's property.

Ray had called her after Aaron left his office. He told her Aaron had bought the property in order to add the lot to Jerry's business. That made sense.

She shouldn't blame him, but she couldn't seem to stop herself.

Ray told her to tell Aaron why she wanted the building. Maybe he'd let her buy it from him. But she wasn't going to bother. He'd jacked up the auction price so high, she couldn't afford to buy it and still fix it up.

She was glad she preferred hand-mashed potatoes to those that were done with a mixer because it gave her an outlet to vent. She slammed the masher into the poor potatoes with far more force than was needed.

Aaron pulled her red stool up to the counter and took a seat. After watching her in silence for a few minutes, he said, "Okay, so explain to me about yesterday. I asked the mayor, but he wouldn't tell me anything."

"What's to explain?" She slammed the masher. "There was an auction." Slam. "You won." Slam. Slam. "I lost." Slam.

"I can't figure you out," he said softly.

That was fine because Maeve wouldn't have known how to explain herself to him, anyway. She kept silent as she continued mashing the potatoes.

"Why was buying this house so important to you? You have a house. Did you want something bigger?"

"My house is plenty big enough." Well, it was plenty big enough for a single woman, but it wasn't quite as comfortable for a large family dinner with friends at Thanksgiving. "And anyway, it wasn't for me."

"Then who?" he asked.

She had mashed the potatoes within an inch of their lives. She spooned them into a serving bowl, covered them and put them in the oven.

"Who?" Aaron pressed.

"It's a long story," she said, not wanting to explain her failed idea to the man who'd derailed it.

"I'm still the only one here, so we have a while."

She wanted to snap that he was the only one there because he was the only one rude enough to show up early. Instead, she answered his question. "I wanted that house to be the first one my new foundation bought and renovated."

"What foundation?" he asked.

She didn't say anything right away, but that didn't seem to bother Aaron. He sat quietly, watching her as he waited.

"Valley Ridge Homes, or something like that." She realized she'd jumped into this so fast, she didn't even have a name for the charity. "We'd take old, abandoned homes and fix them up, then allow low-income families to buy them. They'd be getting the equivalent of a low interest mortgage from the foundation and we'd have the ability to adjust their payments on a sliding scale, according to what they earned. The money they paid toward their mortgage would be put toward purchasing other homes. After a few years, it would be nice to have it be a self-sustaining venture."

"I'm sure there are other homes around town," Aaron said.

"I know there are other deserted homes in Valley Ridge. But there are all sorts of governmental hoops to jump through before the town can deal with them. I'm not sure what it entails, but Ray says there's nothing else that's even close to available right now. And trying to buy a foreclosed home takes longer than buying an abandoned place, plus the cost is way out of my league. This house was my only option if I wanted to get started right away. Ray bumped up the auction by a couple of weeks to help me out."

"So wait until something else comes up," Aaron said.

"I can't wait. I wanted to get the house ready for Christmas." She pulled the cranberry bread out of the refrigerator and placed it on a serving plate. She took a deep breath and said, "It was probably a dumb idea, anyway. You probably saved me from myself. I mean, I've never renovated a home, but I'm sure that doing it in four weeks takes more man power and money than I could've mustered."

She cut the delicate bread into thin slices.

"Why by Christmas?"

She glanced out the kitchen window at the RV parked next to her house. "Josie and Boyd are here until the baby's born. And the baby's due after Christmas. If the house was habitable and ready, they'd have the option of staying. Boyd's been picking up odd jobs all over town. Josie's right, he can do just about anything. If a full-time job came up and there was a house for them here, why go somewhere else. Without the house?" She shrugged. "Like I said, it was a pipe dream. Even if I had gotten the house, full-time jobs are hard to come by in a community as small as Valley Ridge."

It had started to snow, and the ratty RV looked even rattier than usual. She hated thinking of Josie moving to a strange town and trying to take care of a new baby in that old thing. But the idea of taking an equally ratty house and making it livable in a month was absurd.

"Yes, you probably saved me from myself," she repeated. "I tend to have grandiose ideas and not really think them through. I mean, even if I could get volunteers together and organize donations, having the house done by Christmas would take a miracle. And I know from personal experience that those are few and far between."

"Is that what happened with the library? Was that a grandiose idea that you didn't think through?"

She nodded and smiled, despite how dejected she felt. "That might have been one of my better ideas. It didn't cost much money."

"No, it just costs you your time." Aaron paused, then he added, "I guess I don't understand why you'd be so gung ho about buying a house for someone else."

Maeve pulled out a container of olives from the fridge and, her back to him, answered, "Because they need one."

"But they want to move to North Dakota."

She turned around and set the olives on the counter. "They don't *want* to move there. Boyd feels he *has to.* But can you imagine what it will be like for them? A young mom with a newborn and a toddler stuck in that RV all day while he's at work...if he finds work." What if he couldn't find work? What if their money ran out far from home, far from new friends?

"Again, those are reasons why it would be good for them. But why does it matter to you so much?" Aaron asked again.

There were many things about herself she didn't understand, but this one thing, she understood completely. Why did it matter to her? She never spoke of it. At first, it had been a source of embarrassment. Later? It just wasn't something that came up in conversation often.

She looked at Aaron, so genuinely puzzled.

"Because I was homeless once." The words exploded from her, as if she'd had to push them past some inner barrier to get them out. "Because I know what it's like to live out of something that sits on four wheels. And it was only me and Mom. I can't imagine what it would be like for a whole family to live like that."

* * *

AARON COULD SENSE how hard that admission had been for Maeve. He felt...

Hell, he simply felt.

For two years he'd cut himself off from friends and family. He'd hid himself away and buried himself in his work...well, not really work. He buried himself in the appearance of work. He still had ideas. He simply didn't have the drive.

Now he was in Valley Ridge, running a store and listening to some crazy redhead...and he *felt*.

"I've spent my entire adult life squirreling money away in order to be sure I never lost my home again," she said quietly. "I live simply. Count every penny. But the other night, when we watched *A Christmas Carol*, I realized that money that sits in a bank is all well and good, but I could take that money and use it for something even better. For me it's all about the security. Something I can fall back on if something catastrophic happened. But if I gambled and risked it, that money could be something more. It could be a home for someone who doesn't have one. It could be the start of a new foundation—a foundation that helps many families find homes. It could be hope. I think the easiest way to kill someone's soul is to take away their hope."

Aaron studied her. No one could be that generous. No one could take all their hard-earned money and just decide to give it away.

"You see that cross-stitch?" Maeve pointed to the wall. "*I can't save the world, but I can try.* I can try. Maybe that's the real answer to your question. That's why. I understand what Josie and Boyd are going through. I can't save the world, but I can help this one family. And if they still decide to go to North Dakota, then I can save one other family. I can start this foundation and work with the mayor and maybe help other folks in Valley Ridge. What more do you need to know?"

That was the question. Aaron should be satisfied. She'd answered him. She'd experienced hardship in her past and now she wanted to make a change for someone else. Okay. He got it.

Well, he mostly got it.

And doubt crept into his thoughts. She had to have an angle. No one bought a house for people they had only recently met, even if it was cheap. There had to be something that Maeve would get out of it. Being homeless once and understanding what the family was going through wasn't enough of a reason.

Everyone had an angle.

Everyone looked out for number one.

He wanted to figure out what Maeve was after. He needed to understand her.

The last time he'd felt like this was when he'd started to work on his artificial intelligence program. He'd known what he wanted it to do, but he wasn't sure how to make it work. He became obsessed with figuring it out. He dropped out of college and spent more than five years focusing on it to the point that he put the rest of his life on the back burner.

Maeve seemed too good to be believed. And he knew from past experience that *too good to be believed* was never as good as it seemed.

"Forget it," Maeve stated. "Like I said, it was an unrealistic dream. You did the right thing. It was going to take every cent I've saved to make it happen. And even at that, there probably wouldn't be enough time to get it done before they left for North Dakota."

Someone knocked at her door and she turned toward the sound. She looked a bit panicked. "Please, don't mention this to anyone. If it had worked out I would have kept it a secret from Boyd and Josie anyway, until the house was ready. But since it didn't, I'd prefer to not say anything at all."

"Let me help with dinner and I'll keep my mouth shut," he offered.

"Do you always have to bargain?" she asked.

He'd never thought about it, but as he did now, he admitted that he could trust in a bargain because he knew what someone got out of it. "I guess."

"Fine." She opened the door and Josie, Boyd and Carl walked in. "Welcome," she exclaimed with far more enthusiasm than when he'd arrived. "Josie, you met Aaron at book club. Aaron, I'm not sure if you've officially met Boyd yet. Boyd, this is Aaron. We met him when we went for propane after the storm. And this is Carl. Why don't you all give Aaron your coats. He came early to help out. And Josie, I left the couch against the wall in the living room. You make yourself comfortable and keep your feet up so that you can join us at the table for dinner later."

"Between you and Boyd, I don't have a choice but to listen to the doctor's instructions, do I?" Josie groused.

"No, you don't. If the doctor hadn't allowed you to come over here today, I was going to find a way to have Thanksgiving in the RV if it killed me."

Aaron believed she would have. It wouldn't have been much harder fitting everyone into the RV than it would be fitting all of them in her small house.

He looked around the cottage. He could see through the archway into the living room. There was a fire blazing in the fireplace and the couch they'd watched the movie on the other night had been pushed against the far wall. He wasn't sure how she'd managed the table. Then he noticed that underneath the fancy tablecloth there were what appeared to be sawhorse legs.

Maeve must have seen him looking. "Necessity is the mother of invention. And some plywood and nails don't hurt. Voilà—a table big enough for Thanksgiving dinner."

Josie sat down and held her hands out for her son. "Maeve's bossy, but Boyd's even worse," she quipped. To her husband, she added, "I can handle Carl without getting up, I promise."

"Bossy, bossy, bossy," the toddler parroted, then took his mother's long braid in one hand, and curled up next to her.

"It's almost nap time," Josie said. "I'm hoping he can make it until after dinner."

A few minutes later, Maeve's parents arrived. Aaron watched her mother as she bustled around the kitchen, helping Maeve. Renie, as he was instructed to call her, had shoulder-length white hair with a few streaks of soft reddish-brown color. It made for a striking contrast. He suspected that back in her day, her hair had been as red as Maeve's.

Her husband, Maeve's stepfather, Herm, was a relaxed, easygoing guy in blue jeans and a flannel shirt.

Aaron noticed everyone was in jeans or other comfortable clothes. He was definitely overdressed. He unknotted his tie, slid it from around his neck and stuffed it in his coat pocket.

He turned and saw that Maeve was watching him. He smiled and shrugged.

She didn't smile in return, but as she carried the bread basket toward the living room, she leaned over and said, "You looked very dapper."

To the best of his knowledge, no one had ever described him like that. He undid the top button of his shirt, too—and hoped he didn't look any less dapper to Maeve.

Food lined the counter. He helped Maeve and her mother carry things to the table. When everything was arranged to Maeve's liking, she said, "Well, I guess we're ready."

He took the seat that Maeve pointed to. It was at her right.

"Normally, it's only my mom, Herm and me for holidays. We're happy to have so many friends with us at our table this year. Before we start, our family tradition is to go around the table and say what we're thankful for. Mom is the first to remind me that even when things are tough, there's always something for which we can give thanks."

Maeve looked to her left, and Josie went first. "I'm thankful for my family. For new friends. And for a sign that appeared in the middle of a blizzard and pointed the way to Valley Ridge."

Boyd spoke next. "I'm thankful for Josie, Carl, the new baby and for new friends here in Valley Ridge, and for enough work to keep us going."

They gave Carl a free pass and skipped to Maeve's stepfather, Herm. "I'm thankful that when I finally stopped looking for love, it fell into my lap. I didn't just find my Renie, but her daughter, too. And I'm thankful that Queenie's mastitis has cleared up."

Maeve leaned over and whispered, "His prize milker."

Renie said, "I am so thankful that Maeve's new friends were able to join us. I know how hard it is to feel as if you've lost everything, but a few years from now, you might find some hidden blessings in the experience." She took her husband's hand. "I know I did. And I'm thankful for...well, every moment of every day."

It was Aaron's turn. He'd avoided family holidays for the past two years. Heck, he'd avoided people in general.

He was pretty sure that his family's concern for him was the reason he was in Valley Ridge to help his uncle Jerry. He hadn't been able to find a way to say no, but he'd resented their interference. Still, sitting here with Maeve, her parents and friends, he felt a bit grateful.

"I feel very lucky to not be eating a TV dinner and watching the game by myself."

He tried to laugh it off, but Maeve shot him a look that told him that he was a disappointment. He could ignore it, instead, he found himself saying, "And I'm grateful to be sharing the day with new friends."

He turned to Maeve, anxious to hear what his reluctant hostess was grateful for.

She hesitated, as if trying to remember a long list. "There are so many things in my life that I'm thankful for. My family. New friends. For having work I love. That we live in a real community—a place where people care about others. I'm thankful for all the weddings this past year, for Lily's wedding coming up and for all the new babies who will be joining us soon. I'm—"

She stopped and looked away. "I could go on and on, but let me simply say that I'm thankful. And now, let's eat."

The platters, plates and bowls were passed around Maeve's makeshift table.

Carl seemed to find the evergreen boughs that Maeve had used as part of her centerpiece particularly fun. Josie tried to keep him from grabbing them, but Maeve laughed and told her to let him be.

Everyone talked and laughed, and Aaron was struck with a keen case of homesickness. He missed his pain in the butt younger sisters. He missed his father's advice and his mother's worried looks.

He joined in the conversation when asked, but mainly he observed. There weren't as many people here as there would be at his parents' home, but it felt like one of his family's get-togethers.

As he was helping Maeve clear the table after dinner, his cell phone rang. Maeve looked at him. "My mom," he said.

"You can go upstairs and take it in my room. It'll be quieter there."

"Thanks." He pressed the talk button. "Hi, Mom. Happy Thanksgiving. Hold on a second."

He climbed up the narrow stairway to the bedroom at the top of the stairs. There was no girly, froufrou decor in Maeve's room like there'd been in his sisters' rooms growing up. There wasn't anything pink in sight. The bed was covered with a predominantly red quilt, with pillows laid neatly at the top. There were two dressers. Both long and low enough to fit under the slanted ceiling. And a door to what had to be the closet. There were two nightstands, and both, not surprisingly, were piled with books. He couldn't help but notice the title of the top book: *The Secret Santa Club.* A bookmark was placed midway through the book.

Secret Santa? Wasn't that, in essence, what Maeve had wanted to be for Boyd and Josie? Only she hadn't wanted to get them a small gift, she'd planned on giving them a house.

"Aaron?" his mom said, drawing his attention.

"Sorry. There aren't many of us here at my friend's, but it's a small house, so not many feels like a lot. It was noisy downstairs. I can talk up here. How is everyone?"

His mother launched into updates on his sisters and his dad. She also told him how she'd just gotten back from dropping off her special potato casserole for some elderly neighbors. "I wish I could feed everyone, but this is the best I can do," she said, reminding him of the thing on the wall that Maeve had pointed out.

Maybe that's what fascinated him about Maeve—she seemed to share his family's need to help people without anything in it for herself. His mother would love her.

He couldn't see his mom's smile, but he knew his mom well enough to be able to hear it in her voice over the phone. He also heard her get more serious as she commanded, "So, tell me who you're having dinner with."

"That librarian I mentioned. Her parents, another couple and their son."

"I'm glad you're having dinner with someone, but I wish you were home."

He thought about Maeve's Thanksgiving table. He was thankful for his family and for the first time in a long time, he wished he were there, too. He realized that this was the second year he'd left his father on his own, surrounded by women.

He hadn't understood how much he missed them until tonight's dinner.

"Will you be home for Christmas?" his mother asked.

"I'm not sure. I don't think Uncle Jerry's coming back until spring, which means I'm kind of stuck here. And I might not have much background in retail, but I'm pretty sure that's the busiest time even for a local hardware store. But I promise, I'll come home soon for a visit."

"I'll hold you to it."

"Mom, I want to tell you that while I was giving thanks today, I realized how lucky I am that you all are my family."

He heard what sounded like a sniffle on the other end of the line. "Aaron, you almost sound like your old self."

"I don't know if I can ever go back to being my old self, but maybe I can learn to be someone as likable."

"Did you talk to—"

He knew what the next word was. He knew *who* his mother was going to ask about, and he didn't want to talk about her. He was in a good place and he didn't want to ruin that.

"I've got to run, Mom. Pumpkin pie is being served and you know that's my favorite. I'll call in a couple of days, I promise."

"Love you, Aaron."

"Love you, too, Mom. Tell everyone else I love them. Well, never mind. Don't tell the girls that. It'll give them ideas."

His mother was chuckling as he hung up.

Aaron hadn't heard his mom laugh at something he said in a long while. He hadn't found anything funny in a long while.

What do you call a computer nerd who no longer laughs? A *memory stick-in-the-mud.*

He groaned and was glad he hadn't tried that one at the library. He wouldn't have won his award.

He sat on the edge of Maeve's bed and picked up *The Secret Santa Club.* He thought it might be a kids' book, something for the library. But it wasn't. It was a romance.

Maeve Buchanan read romance. She watched sappy Christmas movies. She liked zombie movies. She bought homes for people in need.

His thoughts ping-ponged. His mom was cooking for others. His father was spending the day in a house full of women and probably missing having Aaron there to back him up. He was trapped in Valley Ridge until spring. He was bored. He hadn't been seriously engrossed in a project for a while, despite coming up with ideas. It felt like forever since he'd had something to occupy his curiosity.

Maeve Buchanan was a mystery. She was too good to be true.

When he'd sold his program, he ensured he'd have enough money to buy whatever houses or toys he wanted for the rest of his life.

Whereas Maeve would have sacrificed to do what she was planning on doing.

There had to be another reason. No one gave away their savings to help someone else. Even if she knew what it was like to be homeless, people didn't really go around buying houses for other people.

Maybe she wasn't going to get anything material out of doing it, but she was going to get something. But what? And how else would he understand her if he never knew?

This need to spend time with Maeve was troubling. She kept intruding on his thoughts. Interrupting his dreams.

He put the book back on the pile and went down the narrow stairs. The table had been cleared and the pie served. A large piece had been cut for him. Maeve must have heard him come down the stairs. "I poured you coffee, but I can get you something else if you prefer."

"No, that's fine. Thanks." He took his seat.

"How is your family?" Josie asked.

"Fine. Thanks," he said again.

Carl must have decided utensils were not a necessary component of pie eating. The kid had pumpkin everywhere, but no one seemed to mind. Maeve had lined the toddler's seat with a piece of clear plastic and Josie had placed a giant bib on him.

Carl reminded Aaron of his little sisters back in the day. As Aaron watched the toddler play with the pumpkin puree on his tray table, Carl's head started to tilt to one side.

"I think he's almost down for the count," Aaron said softly.

Boyd managed to catch Carl's head before it hit the pie.

"Let me clean him up and find somewhere to let him sleep," Josie said.

"You're still on bed rest," Boyd said. "I've got him."

Josie looked as if she was about to protest, but Boyd leaned over and kissed her forehead, silencing her. Then Boyd carried the toddler into the kitchen.

Josie watched the two of them go, and Aaron could see the love in her eyes. She turned to him and smiled. "He's a good man," she said.

"How did you meet?" Maeve's mom asked. "I met Herm at the diner where I worked. I always tell people he married me for my chocolate shakes."

Herm nodded. "That was definitely part of it. Finding a woman who can scramble an egg isn't so hard, but a good chocolate shake? That's a rare gift."

Josie still looked toward the kitchen where her husband and son had disappeared. "I've known Boyd practically all my life. I started kindergarten with him and we were in the same class every year until high school."

"When did you start to date?" Maeve asked.

"According to him, he had a crush on me from early on. He stole cookies from the snack tray for me, and had to sit in time-out. I gave him a kiss after that, and the way he tells it, that's when he knew I was the one. We started dating our freshman year and were married three months after graduation. He got a job at the plant. Within two years, he was the third shift manager. I started college, and then Carl came along. We had so many problems when I was pregnant with him. This pregnancy has been so much easier, until now." She patted her stomach.

Aaron looked at Maeve. She was teary eyed. "Why don't I go get more coffee." She sprang up from her chair.

"Do that and I'll start to load the dishwasher. You did say I could help," Aaron added.

"The dishwasher's broken."

"Boyd could have a look at it. He can fix anything," Josie said.

Maeve smiled and hurried to leave.

Aaron knew she needed a moment. Josie's story had really touched her.

She returned and poured a drop of coffee into her cup. "Anyone else want their cup warmed?"

Boyd came back into the room and sat down with Carl asleep in his arms.

"I told Maeve that you can fix anything," Josie said.

"Maybe not anything, but I'm good with mechanical things. Something not working right?"

"Her dishwasher. She was planning to do the dishes by hand," Josie said, sounding like one of Aaron's sisters when they told on him.

"I can take a look." Boyd started to get up, as if he was going to take a look right away.

"How about tomorrow?" Maeve asked, waving her hand, indicating that Boyd should sit back down. "Finish your pie. Most of the dishes are china and can't go in the dishwasher, anyway. I'll do them by hand, and if you can fix it soon that would be great. If not, I'll call a repairman."

"I'll be over first thing," Boyd promised.

Aaron was surprised to hear himself asking Boyd, "Are you still planning to stay in Valley Ridge for a while?"

"We can't leave until Josie's had the baby." As he said the words, Boyd's forehead furrowed, making him seem years older.

"Why don't you come over to the store tomorrow, when you're done here? I might have some work for you." Aaron wasn't sure precisely what job he'd find, but there was plenty to do around the store. He loved his uncle Jerry, but he'd let the place coast into the new millennium. Nothing was computerized, for instance, and fixing that was right up Aaron's alley. But there were other areas to update, too.

Boyd grinned. "I will. I'll come over here first and go straight there. Thank you, sir."

"Aaron," he corrected. "Once we've shared a Thanksgiving turkey, first names are fine."

Josie shot him a look and he saw gratitude in her eyes.

It made him uncomfortable. After all, he'd practically stolen a house from her. Granted, she didn't know about that, but he did, and it made him feel guilty.

Once everyone had finished their dessert, Aaron helped Maeve's mother bring the dishes to the kitchen, and Maeve let everyone except Josie take the table apart and move the furniture back to where it should be. Then they all gathered around the TV to watch football. Aaron had never been much of a sports enthusiast, but he enjoyed listening to Herm and Boyd get all riled up over the ref's calls. After that, the women claimed the television and put on *It's a Wonderful Life*.

"A family tradition," Maeve explained. "Mom and I watch it together every year."

Of course it was and of course they did. Maeve was a female George Bailey.

He stole glances at her throughout the movie. When the bell rang at the end, he spotted her crying. She was trying to hide it, but he could tell. Then he noticed Josie and Maeve's mother were crying, too.

It was like being home with his mom and sisters. He felt uncomfortable. He didn't know where to look. What to say.

"What do you call a computer nerd with no sense of humor?" he blurted out.

"What?" Maeve asked.

"A memory stick-in-the-mud."

They all laughed, but it wasn't quite as real as the other night at the library. "Not one of my better ones?" he asked innocently.

"Awful, Aaron. It was awful." Maeve laughed. "Don't let your win the other night go to your head. Keep the day job."

"Got it. Stand-up is not in my future." But his bad joke had done its job. The women had stopped crying. After snacking on the leftovers, the guests began to leave.

As each one opened the back door, the tiny bell on it tinkled. Aaron might not have noticed the sound before, but after watching *It's a Wonderful Life,* it stood out.

He'd bet that Maeve had hung it on purpose with the movie in mind.

Aaron waited around on purpose, wanting to be the last one to leave, wanting to talk to Maeve alone about the idea that had been swirling around in his mind all afternoon.

"Well, thank you for coming," Maeve said once it was just the two of them. "I'm glad you joined us. You were a big help setting up."

She eyed the door and Aaron knew that had been a hint, but he wasn't ready to leave yet. "Let me help a little more. That's a mountain of dishes."

"The kitchen is too small for more than one person." The look on her face told him she knew that wasn't quite true.

"I'll stay way over to the side. You wash, pass them to me and I'll dry them and pile them on the table. You can put them away when we're done."

"Really—" she started.

"Really," he said, interrupting. "I want to help."

She sighed. "Fine."

"And I want to talk to you about something."

"Oh, what?"

He didn't want to jump right into things, so rather than reply he said, "I liked when you had everyone go around the table and say what they were thankful for."

She looked up from the glass she was washing. "I guess I'd add that I'm thankful you found some more work for Boyd."

"I know you won't believe me, but I do want to help." And as he said the words, he acknowledged that he did. "You're really planning to start some kind of charity that will help people find homes?"

"Yes. It was a dumb...spur-of-the-moment idea. I know it will require a lot more than a few days' consideration. Because I'm forced to wait now, I'll have time to really think things through. That's not my strong suit, you know. I tend to get excited about something and jump right in, without planning ahead. Like I did with the library."

"How did that idea come about?" He dried the last of the glasses and set it on the table.

"I was sitting in the kitchen, drinking a cup of coffee one morning and I looked out at the vacant library. It was a mess. The landscaping was totally overgrown. The town sent a maintenance crew over now and then to run a lawn mower, but nothing else. I remembered going in there when I was younger. Especially on rainy days. There was something so comforting in seeing the library all lit up and stepping into its warmth. The smell of the books. Mrs. Anderson behind the counter, smiling..."

She'd been lost in her memory, but snapped back as she handed him a plate. "Anyway, I was tired of waiting for the town to find the money to reopen it and decided to do it myself. One month later, it reopened a couple nights a week. Now, here it is, two years later and while it's still only open minimal hours, it is open most weekday afternoons and evenings, as well as Saturday mornings. There are new books on the shelves. People use it."

"You've actually made a case for your spur-of-the-moment ideas, rather than a case against them," he pointed out.

She handed him another plate. "I don't think remodeling a house over the course of a few weekends would have been that easy."

He almost laughed at her use of the word *easy*. He doubted opening the library had been easy by any stretch of the imagination.

"Anyway, it's a moot point. I'm sorry I was mad afterward. It's not your fault. Again, I probably owe you a huge thank-you for saving me from myself."

"What if I want to do it?" He set the plate on the growing stack on her table.

She passed him another one. "Do what?"

He took the dish and dried it. "The charity. The house charity."

"Not a charity. A foundation. People would ultimately be paying for their own homes."

"Fine. A foundation. What if I want to help with it?" he asked again.

"You'll be going back to your own life as soon as your uncle arrives in Valley Ridge. I'm sure you've got enough on your plate until then."

"I'm sort of between projects right now," he said. He'd been in between projects for two years. "And as for a lot on my plate, this is coming from the woman who has a full-time job, volunteers at a library in her free time, and is now going to take on a new—foundation? I think I can find the time."

"All right. I guess you could help research how other similar organizations are set up. Remember, rather than building new houses, we'll be rehabbing existing ones. I like the idea of the greenness of it. Rather than all new materials, we'd recycle and reuse what we can. I guess the silver lining is that I now have time to plan it properly. A friend of mine consulted a lawyer a while back. Maybe he can suggest someone to help us with the legal details."

Aaron set the plate down. "I have a very good attorney. If he can't help us with the legal mumbo jumbo, he'll know someone who can. But that's not exactly what I was talking about."

"Then what?" She started scrubbing another plate.

"I'll give you the house."

Maeve dropped the plate she'd been washing and let out a cry of regret when she picked up the pieces.

"I'm sorry. I shouldn't have spit it out like that."

"Not your fault," she assured him.

"Was it a special dish?"

She didn't answer. That was the most frustrating thing about Maeve Buchanan. He wanted to know everything, and she offered next to nothing.

"As for your offer, I'm not even sure that Boyd and Josie will accept the house."

"If they don't, then we'll carry on with your original idea and find another needy family."

He was fortunate that he was so well off. He'd bought the house on a whim. He thought he'd surprise his uncle. But to be honest, Valley Ridge Farm and House Supplies had enough space as it was. They didn't really need more.

"I can't pay you the same price you bought it for and still have money left over to fix it up," Maeve said. "You went over my budget. And realistically, I don't think any sane person can reasonably expect to start a foundation and renovate the first house in a matter of weeks."

"I think anything that's worthwhile happens because someone did what felt right. Because they had faith that they could make it work despite what naysayers might tell them."

Maeve stood holding the broken plate, staring out the window. She didn't say anything.

Since he sold his program, Aaron had made an important discovery...money talks. "Let me worry about the cost. I'll get in touch with the mayor and the attorney and we'll hammer all that out. Maybe this would be a crazy idea if you tried to do it on your own. But if you have help, it's not that crazy."

Aaron could see that was exactly what Maeve had been planning—to do this basically on her own.

"If you do this, then it has to be a community project," he said. "Something realistic. One house a year. Maybe a Valley Ridge Christmas tradition. The foundation buys back one property that's reverted to the town for taxes. They rehab it and let some deserving family move in and make payments on a sliding scale, according to their income. The payments go back into the foundation's savings. Something like that would be self-sustaining and self-perpetuating. Keep it on a small scale, not a lot of bureaucratic overhead." He shrugged. "I'm not really sure how it would work, but it definitely could work."

"And you don't want any money from me?" she asked slowly.

"No. I don't advertise it, but I'm pretty solid financially." That was an understatement. "I already bought the house, and I'm sure we can get the community to donate time and supplies."

She eyed him suspiciously. "There's a catch." He started to protest, but she held up a hand. "Don't deny it. I can see it in your eyes. You've got this devilish sparkle. So, what is it?"

"If we're both working on the house, I get to spend time with you. I don't understand you."

"Why do you want to spend time with me?"

He thought of the book in her room. "I don't want you to get the wrong idea. I'm not looking for romance."

"Phew." She wiped her brow with exaggeration. "I mean, nothing personal, Aaron, but you're not exactly the kind of man I'm looking for."

"What sort of man are you looking for?" he found himself asking.

She laughed. "I'm not sure, but I suspect I'll know him when I meet him. That's how it happened for my mother and father. And after Dad died, Mom thought she was done with romance, but then it happened again for her. Herm walked into the diner, ordered a chocolate milk shake, and to hear them tell it, it happened that fast."

"And is that how it happened with the string of weddings here in Valley Ridge?"

She nodded, her red hair swishing around her shoulders. She set down the plate and pushed her hair off her face. "Yes. You can tell just by looking at them that Sophie and Colton, Lily and Sebastian, and Mattie and Finn were meant to be together."

"Soul mates?" he asked. When she looked surprised, he said, "Hey, you don't have to read romance to know the term."

"Why do you need to understand me?" She finally set the cracked pieces of the plate down on the counter, and went back to washing the dishes.

She passed him another plate. As he dried it, he said, "I spent a month in detention when I was in eighth grade because I took apart a computer in the lab. When I come across a puzzle, I have to solve it."

She stopped, her hands still submerged in soap suds. "I'm not some computer that you can take apart and figure out."

"No. You're much more complex, and that makes you even more intriguing."

"Gee, Aaron, that sounds kind of stalkerish." She laughed, which told him she wasn't particularly worried.

"I'm..." He didn't know how to explain the way she made him feel. "You intrigue me. It's been a long time since I've been interested in someone.

It's as if you're too good to be true. People don't just go around buying houses for other people. They don't let strangers park their RVs in their driveway and invite them to Thanksgiving dinner. They don't open and run the town library for nothing in exchange. You're different than anyone I've ever met. I want to know what makes you tick.

"And I'll help. I'll help you set up the foundation, I'll help with the renovations, and I'll even help out at the library."

"But you don't want to spend time together in a romantic way?" she asked.

"I can't get involved with anyone, so, no. But I also can't get you out of my mind. I don't like anomalies. I don't like unanswered questions. And you are both those things." Aaron used to believe that people were basically good. That life was fair. That if you approached things honestly, everything would turn out all right.

He'd learned his lesson.

Maeve raked her fingers through her hair and they got snagged in a curl. That seemed to annoy her and she yanked her fingers free.

"I'll donate the house to the foundation and help get things off the ground. The store will donate materials and I'll pitch in my time."

Maeve snorted. "Most men, if they want to find out more about a woman, ask for a date. They don't give away houses."

"Most women don't want to spend their savings to buy a house for someone they hardly know." He shrugged. "So, maybe we should spend time together since we're obviously not *most people.*"

She stared at the sudsy water for a moment. "I'm not sure if I like you enough to spend the next month working with you as much as we'd have to work together. I wouldn't want to give you the wrong idea. You are not the kind of man I'd be interested in."

"Like I said, I'm not in a position to date anyone." He almost laughed at his choice of words. "I'm not interested in a romantic relationship. It's just that I don't understand your motivation. You said you were homeless once. It seems to me that would make you want to hold on to your savings rather than blow it on someone else."

She glanced at the wall behind him, and then she looked him in the eye, her hair wild and her hands immersed in a sink of dirty dishes. "If I say yes, you'll really help me get this off the ground, and get the house ready? If not for Josie and Boyd, then for some other family?"

"I will."

"And you're not in a position to date me—"

"Date anyone, not you specifically."

She nodded. "Anyone. But you're curious about me. You don't understand why I do what I do? I can tell you that even if you spend the next month working with me, you'll probably never understand. Because I don't have a clue why I do what I do. I see something and I think to myself *that might be a good idea.* And the next thing I know, I'm doing it."

"That may be, but you run a library that is a vital part of the community. You have an RV with people in your driveway. And now you have a run-down house. There might be something to your method of madness. I want to see for myself what that is. If you'll agree..." He held out his hand, and she dried hers on a towel before shaking his. "And the thing is you have free labor. I mean, if altruism is your goal, if you don't have some angle, then you should be jumping at this opportunity."

"Okay," she said. "I think you're wasting your time, but I'll agree."

Aaron felt something in him settle. He might not understand her, but he was pretty sure that Maeve Buchanan didn't go back on a deal.

"Great. So after we finish the dishes, we can sit down and map out a strategy."

"Oh, so you're one of those."

"One of what?"

"A strategy sort of guy."

"It's the programmer in me. Step A leads to Step B, leads to...well, pretty soon I've written a program. Or in this case, renovated a house."

"So, let's get a strategy." She washed the plate and handed it to him. "But you are crazy."

"You may be right," he admitted. "You definitely may be right."

CHAPTER SIX

AARON AND MAEVE finished the dishes. Afterward, they started their list for the house. Maeve seemed to feel it was only going to need some paint, a new porch and some other minor renovations.

He didn't want to tell her that he'd been inside and didn't think *renovation* was the right word. *Reconstruction* was more like it. She'd figure it out soon enough for herself.

It was almost eleven when he left Maeve's and strolled through Valley Ridge toward his uncle's. Farm and House Supplies. F&H Supplies. Valley Ridge Supplies. VR Supplies. They all had a nice ring. Much better than the current mouthful, Valley Ridge Farm and House Supplies. He thought about going up to the apartment, but he knew he was too keyed up to sleep, so he continued his walk through town.

It hadn't snowed in a few days and the sky was clear, but it was cold. The puddles had frozen into pockets of slush on their way to becoming ice. The boots he was wearing were a much better winter choice than sneakers.

Most of the shops and businesses had some sort of security lighting, but the light was blazing at MarVee's Quarters. He started toward it to investigate.

Back when he was a kid and visited his uncle during the summers, MarVee's had been called the Five and Dime. It closed down and was vacant for years until two women named Marilee and Vivienne had bought it. When they reopened the store, they changed the name from Five and Dime to Quarters...because of inflation.

He smiled as he reminisced. Valley Ridge, New York, was a small town. It had a great sense of community and a lot of heart in its hardworking citizens. And it definitely had its share of quirky residents. His uncle always said that they were part of the town's charm.

Aaron reached the big plate glass window at MarVee's and found the lights were on because old Mr. Mento was in the window setting up a train track. Not only a train track...an entire miniature town that was decorated for Christmas. There was a teenage boy helping him. They both looked up and waved.

Aaron waved back. He should have remembered that Mr. Mento's tradition was to set up the Christmas trains on Thanksgiving night. It was an elaborate display, so he knew the older man would be pulling an all-nighter. But finding the store window decorated was a Valley Ridge Black Friday tradition. His uncle had talked about it frequently. It was a sign that the Christmas holiday season had officially begun.

Aaron went on past the fire station to the town hall. The mayor's office was there. He'd bought the house there. The house he was using to bribe Maeve into spending time with him.

He'd told her he was curious about what made her tick. That was the truth.

He'd said he wasn't in a position to date anyone. That was absolutely the truth.

But it was more than that. He enjoyed being with her.

More local government offices marked the end of the town. The handful of blocks that made up the heart of Valley Ridge.

It had just started snowing again. Nothing like the blizzard that brought Boyd and Josie to town— merely a light dusting of flakes. He'd be surprised if there was more than an inch or two of snow come morning.

He turned around and walked back toward the apartment.

In some cities and towns a couple inches of snow would be enough to shut everything down, but here, along the southern shore of Lake Erie, two inches of snow was nothing. He'd always liked that about his uncle's town—they kept going no matter what.

He headed down the other side of the street, past the coffee shop. It was one of the new businesses that had opened since he'd last visited his uncle. He'd been there a few times for a good cup of coffee, something he didn't seem able to make on his own no matter what brand of coffee he used, or how he brewed it.

He walked past the pharmacy, the antique store and the dentist's office before he made it to his uncle's store. F&H Supply? In an age when acronyms and texting shortcuts ran rampant, the business's name was too long.

Maybe he'd talk to Uncle Jerry about switching to the shorter version.

Aaron was still too keyed up to sleep. And knew it wasn't the question of a new name for his uncle's store that was keeping him awake. It was Maeve.

He decided to copy old Mr. Mento and get a head start on his Christmas decorating.

He already had his employees coming in tomorrow an hour before they normally would to decorate the store.

He was pretty sure they wouldn't mind if he did some of it on his own.

He meant to string a few Christmas lights along the tops of the shelves and call it a night, but he got caught up in the moment. Soon black-and-red plaid bows hung from lights and his uncle's artificial tree stood in all nine feet of glory near the registers.

By the time his first employee arrived the next morning, Aaron had not only decorated, he'd set up a ten hour loop of Christmas music on the intercom system.

He looked at the clock. It was 8:00 a.m. on Black Friday. He knew his mom and sisters were decorating, too. Picturing his family made him feel lighter. He peered out the window, trying to decide whether the store should have some Christmas lights, when he noticed someone near the house he'd bought and given away.

He decided to throw on his coat and see what they were doing.

"Good morning," he called out. The person, bundled from head to toe, startled and turned to face him.

It was Maeve.

"I don't understand you, either," she said, her words muffled by her scarf.

"Good morning to you, too," he repeated cheerfully. "Want to go in?"

"Do you have the key?"

"There's no key. The city took over the house because of unpaid taxes, remember? It had been abandoned for years. I didn't have one made because I was going to bulldoze the place."

"So, how do we get in?" she asked.

"Lucky for you, your partner had tools and took care of that earlier. Let's go." He led the way and opened the door.

Aaron watched as Maeve took in the garbage-strewn living room. There were holes in the plaster. Raw wires hung from the ceiling where there had probably once been some sort of light fixture. Beneath the clothes and bags that littered the floor there was a carpet. A pumpkin-orange shag rug that had probably been all the rage in the seventies.

Maeve picked her way slowly across the floor and peeked into the kitchen. There were cupboards with no doors, dirty dishes in the sink and more garbage everywhere. The area that should have housed a table had torn boxes. The linoleum was a cool seventies gold and had huge gashes in it. He couldn't fathom why someone would have ripped up chunks of flooring like that, but he guessed it didn't matter. It would have needed to be replaced regardless.

He'd already decided to talk to his uncle about the supplies, which he'd pay for. It was the least he could do for this family.

"I'm a fool," she whispered. "I don't know what I was thinking."

She had been a little naive, but the situation wasn't as awful as she seemed to think. "It's not as bad as it looks. Nothing a Dumpster won't solve."

"I thought I'd come in a couple weekends, do some painting and sprucing up, maybe fix the front porch, and then we'd turn the keys over to Josie and Boyd. It wouldn't be the Taj Mahal, but it wouldn't be this—" she waved her hand, indicating the whole house "—either. In my mind, I imagined them seeing it for the first time on Christmas Eve. There'd be a tree in front of the window. It would be covered with lights and ornaments. There would be presents. Someone would be dressed up like Santa. They'd think we brought Carl to see Santa, but then he'd 'ho-ho' and hand them the door key. In my mind, I could see their look of surprise and then happiness as they understood what it all meant."

She tried to hide her disappointment from him, but Aaron could see how close to crying she was.

If asked he'd have said he found crying annoying, but that was before Maeve. All he wanted was to pull her into his arms and comfort her.

He shoved his hands into his pockets in order to resist the urge.

Maeve swiped at her eyes, stood up straight and faced him. "I have obviously spent too much time between the covers of books, reading fictional stories where there's always a happy ending. This was dumb. Thanks for the offer, Aaron, but do whatever you wanted to do with this house. Bulldoze it and make storage for your uncle's store. Bringing in a bulldozer is probably the kindest thing you can do for this house." She turned and started for the door.

"Maeve, wait."

She stopped and shook her head. "Really, it's okay. I'll see you at the library."

She left.

Aaron could see the room the way Maeve had. But he could also see the things she hadn't seen. The house had a solid foundation and a dry basement. What Maeve was looking at was cosmetic. Plaster that could be repaired or replaced. The ugly carpet that hid hardwood floors. All the place needed was time and effort.

Aaron headed back to the store. Black Friday sales would bring in the customers. He intended to lend a hand with the crowds. But first, he had some phone calls to make.

* * *

MAEVE HAD PASTED a smile on her face as she went over the winery's inventory.

Her boss, Gabriel, was over the moon with their Black Friday sales. No, they weren't a huge department store with their kind of numbers, but he'd sent everyone on the winery's mailing list a coupon and they'd had a steady stream of customers all day. Most were buying more than their regular bottle or two of wine, ostensibly stocking up for their holiday celebrations and purchasing gifts.

Her cheek muscles ached from maintaining the smile she didn't feel but wore as she went through the motions of holiday cheer. All she could think about was that wreck of a house and her silly dreams of making it a home by Christmas.

It was ridiculous, when she stopped to think about it. She'd been so mad at Aaron for outbidding her, but in reality he'd saved her. She'd worked so hard to save against some future disaster and she'd almost thrown her entire financial cushion away on that money pit.

Yes, she'd had the best of intentions, but good intentions weren't enough to keep a roof over anyone's head. She knew that better than anyone.

She bought a bottle of Gabriel's Perry Bicentennial wine. She'd take it to Aaron as a thank-you.

"Are you okay?" her boss asked.

"I'm fine, thanks. And you?"

"Better than fine after today's turnout. But you are definitely not fine. If you need something, you

154

know you just have to ask, right? I've got broad shoulders."

Gabriel was a nice man. When Tori had met him, she'd tried to set the two of them up, but Maeve had put the brakes on that immediately. Dating Gabriel would be like dating her big brother.

"Thanks, Gabriel," she said. "But I am fine. I almost made a fool of myself, but fate stepped in and saved me."

"And are you taking that wine to fate?"

She smiled what felt like her first genuine smile of the day. "Yes."

"Are you going to tell me fate's name, so I can check him out?"

"How do you know it's a 'him'?" she countered.

"Because that smile wasn't for a girlfriend," he said in a knowing way.

"You're nuts, but thanks." Gabriel's concern was enough to lift her spirits ever so slightly. Maybe it didn't matter so much that she failed to save the world. She had tried.

* * *

A SHORT TIME LATER, she parked her car in her driveway but didn't even bother going into the house. She did stop in at the RV to check on Josie on her way to the library. "How are you today?"

"Okay. Bored. I've read *Where the Wild Things Are* about thirty times." As if on cue, Carl growled. "That's his roar," Josie added.

"Why don't I take your *wild thing* with me to the library? The after-school crowd will be arriving soon."

"I didn't think there'd be school today because of Thanksgiving."

"There isn't. But a lot of parents still had to work and those who didn't had kids running off their pumpkin pie all day. I'm pretty sure I can think of one or two who would be happy to take a go at running Carl ragged for you."

"That doesn't sound like a very library-like activity."

"The beauty to operating the library is that I can do what I want. The second floor has a quiet room. I've got tables set up there and comfortable reading chairs. But the downstairs is pandemonium between three and five-thirty. Everyone in town knows if you want a quiet browse at the library, do it after dinner. Your *wild thing* will fit right in with the rest of the crew."

"Thank you, Maeve. You're a good friend. You've done so much for us—"

"Shh," Maeve said. She felt like a fraud. She hadn't done much of anything, but given them someplace to park their RV and fed them a Thanksgiving meal. "I wish I could do more."

She wrapped up Carl and carried him across the parking lot to the library. She dug through her bag for her keys and had just unlocked the door when a gaggle of kids came into view.

"Miss Maeve, guess what?" Mica Williams called as she sprinted toward her. Mica's big brother had become especially close to Sebastian and Lily. Through him they'd taken the whole family under their wing.

"This week was letter *M* week," Mica said, "and today I practiced even if I wasn't in school. I made letter *M* pictures with M&M's and monkeys, but I made two pictures of me, one for Daddy and one for you."

"You made me a picture?" Maeve asked. "Well, let's get inside so you can show me."

"Who's that?" Mica pointed at Carl.

"This is my friend Carl." The toddler growled at the sound of his name. "He's two and he's been reading *Where the Wild Things Are.* That's his *wild-thing* growl. He's come to help me at the library today."

Mica eyed the toddler. "I don't think he's gonna be much help. He drooled on you."

Maeve brushed at her damp shoulder. "It will dry."

She put Carl down, stripped off his coat and hung it on one of the hooks she'd installed on the interior wall. Then she took off her own. "Do you need help?" she asked Mica.

Mica shook her head and shrugged out of her coat, as the rest of the kids came in and did the same.

"Everyone, this is Carl. He'll be my assistant. Since there was no school, why don't you all get some toys, or color for a while, or look at a book. Then I have a treat. We're starting a new book for Christmas. One of my all-time favorites."

The kids all sat down at tables. Joe Williams, Mica's older brother, was there, along with their other sister, Allie. Carl found the bucket of blocks and set about happily stacking them as Maeve walked from child to child.

"Miss Maeve, here you go." Mica thrust a ragged-looking picture at her. There was a blonde stick figure and standing next to her was a taller stick figure with a mass of red squiggles.

"You put me in the picture?"

"Yeah, Mica starts with *M*, and Maeve starts with *M*, too. That's what my brother said."

Maeve smiled. "You're right, it does."

She leaned down and hugged the little girl.

"I wish you were my mommy," Mica said. "Or Miss Lily. You guys would never leave a little girl, like my mommy had to."

These were the kinds of situations Maeve hated. She never knew how to respond. Aaron walked in. He seemed pleased with himself and said, "Sorry. Am I late?"

"For what?" She disentangled herself from Mica and stood.

"To hang out here at the library, with you, rather than leave you to take care of everything on your own."

"I'm not on my own," she said, looking around at the room filled with kids.

Carl chose that instant to pick up a block and throw it right at a table of girls. The girls shrieked, which made the other kids laugh. Carl thought it was a great game and grabbed another block, but

Aaron sprinted over and stopped him midthrow. "Come on, Carl. Let's build with the blocks, not throw them."

Maeve returned her attention to the other kids, but she couldn't help sneaking glances at Aaron. Soon, he wasn't only entertaining Carl. The other kids gravitated toward him.

She never would have pegged Aaron Holder for a pied piper, but she had to admit it looked good on him.

Soon the kids started to chant, "Story! Story!"

Aaron joined in. "Story!"

"All right," Maeve conceded, picking up the book she'd hidden behind the counter. "Grab a carpet square."

The kids ran straight to the pile of squares that Aaron's uncle had donated. "Me, too?" Aaron asked.

"If you like." She took her seat and read out loud from *The Best Christmas Pageant Ever* by Barbara Robinson.

She was afraid that Aaron would inhibit her storytelling. But as she got going, she forgot he was there. She read the first two chapters, glanced at the clock and promised, "More on Monday. Cleanup time."

The kids groaned, but went about returning their carpet squares and putting away the toys. She might have relaxed the quiet rule, but she strictly enforced a no electronics rule. Sometimes she wished they had a couple of computers, especially for the kids who didn't have them at home, but it was all she could do to keep newish books on the shelves. She didn't bother worrying about what the library couldn't afford.

"So, I was right," Aaron said from behind her.

"Where's Carl?" she said, rather than ask him what he was right about.

"He's with a bunch of girls. They're playing house and he's the baby."

She scanned the room and spotted Carl sitting next to a pile of stuffed animals, which she guessed were the other babies.

"Aren't you going to ask me?" Aaron prompted.

She looked back at the disarming man who was suddenly everywhere she turned. "Ask you what?"

"What I was right about," he said.

"I'm sure you feel you were right about so many things that it's going to take some time for you to narrow it down to one thing." She smiled so he would know that she was teasing him.

"You are a natural storyteller. I could see bits of it at Riddlefest when you talked about *The Hobbit.* You set the scene so vividly."

She didn't know what to do with his praise. It made her uncomfortable, knowing he was watching her and paying attention to what she did. She shrugged.

"I was right about that, and you were right about the house, creating a foundation."

Maeve shook her head. "I meant it. It was a lovely dream, but there's no way I can realistically get it ready for Christmas. And odds are Josie and Boyd won't want it, anyway. Boyd's heart is set on going to North Dakota."

"Don't," he said sharply. "You're a dreamer. I don't know much about you and I certainly don't understand you, but don't ever change that."

"You're wrong. I'm many things, but at heart, I'm a realist."

"Let me put this in a way a librarian will appreciate and understand. You are Don Quixote. You see the world the way it could be. The way it should be. This library is a case in point. You saw the need and you dreamed the dream and here we stand. But you're right. You were a realist in that you didn't wait for it to magically reopen. You opened it. You did it all on your own and you continue to do it all on your own."

"No," she said. "I have help."

He scoffed. "I met your *help.* Tori, your personal matchmaker who doesn't even live in Valley Ridge, and a few other people who fill in for you on afternoons or the rare weekend you're busy with something else."

"It's not a big deal. If I weren't here, I'd be home. I read here. Otherwise, I'd be reading there. It's only a change of venue."

"I didn't see much reading going on today. I saw supervision and encouragement. I saw interest and the occasional hug. The only reading I saw was the book you read to the kids." He paused a moment and said, "Keep dreaming about the house. I'll follow your lead and help. I'm sure others will help, too, if you ask. If you let them."

She opened her mouth to protest, but he cut her off. "And if Boyd is determined to go elsewhere to look for work, I'm sure there's sombody who can be the foundation's first home owner. I was going to head over to Boyd's house—the RV, I mean—when I was done here. Boyd came in to the store today, you know. I've offered him full-time work, at least through the holidays."

Her eyes narrowed. "I thought you didn't need help." Boyd was proud. He wouldn't take a handout.

"It seems that I'm going to be busy setting up a foundation and renovating a house, so I won't be able to be as hands-on anymore at the store and one of my other guys is leaving soon. We can use more trained help."

How could she argue with that? This was a chance for Boyd to have a real job. A real chance.

"Do you really think we can get the house done in time for Christmas?" she asked.

Aaron smiled with all the confidence she'd lost the moment she'd seen how bad the house looked. "I do. And though I don't know you that well, I suspect asking for help isn't your forte. But this once, you're going to need it."

She didn't know how to respond to that.

Aaron said softly, "I suspect half of Valley Ridge would rally to your aid if you only asked."

He was right; asking people for help was so not her thing.

Out of the blue, he said, "How did you end up homeless?"

"My father died and we lost the farm." Maeve might have left her explanation at that, but there was a look in Aaron's eyes asking her to continue. The man was giving her a house, so how could she ignore him? "Mom tried to keep it going after Dad died. She didn't want me to have to leave the only home I'd ever known. But she couldn't keep up with the payments. We put most of our belongings in storage and lived in a short-term rental for a while, then in the car. Until—"

"Until?"

She decided that Aaron Holder posessed insatiable curiosity. If she kept talking, he'd keep asking questions and pressing her for more. Better to dole the stories out in smaller increments. "I told you something personal about me. More than I've ever told most people."

He didn't look satisfied.

"So, do you understand me any better?" she asked.

"No. But it's like writing a program. I've added another bit of data. Eventually, I'll have enough bits that I'll be able to put it all together. So when can you start work on the house?"

"You're really sure you want to do this? I mean, it sounded like a great idea to me, but then I saw the reality of it when we walked into the house. Christmas is only a month away."

"I looked beyond the mess and saw the potential. I'm sure."

Maeve nodded. "I open the library Saturday mornings for a couple hours, but that's it. And we're closed on Sundays. Weekdays are busy, but I can probably sneak a few hours in. Weekends will definitely be easiest for me."

"And probably for anyone else who volunteers. So, we'll work mainly on weekends. And now, I'm going to go see if Boyd's around. Tomorrow's Saturday, so why don't we meet at the house after you're done here?"

"I'll be there a bit after eleven."

She closed up the library after the last kids went home and picked up Carl and carried him through the parking lot. It was snowing again. A gentle dusting covered the ground. "Look, Carl." She held out her hand and the fat flakes fell lazily onto her glove.

Carl laughed and swiped at her hand.

She felt...almost giddy.

Maybe the house had been a ridiculous dream if she'd been left to her own devices. But with Aaron helping it could happen. And if Boyd had a job here, maybe they would stay.

"Let's go see how Mom's doing," she said to the toddler. She tapped on the door to the RV and then let herself in.

Josie called out, "I'm back here."

Maeve took off Carl's coat and mitts and carried him through the small living area of the RV into the bedroom. Josie was propped against pillows under the covers. "There's my guy. Mommy was so lonely without you."

Carl squirmed to be put down and when Maeve put him on the bed, he made a beeline to his mother. "Were you good?"

"Oh, he was good all right. I'm not sure if you realize what a flirt your son is. He's got all the girls wrapped around his little finger. He's got Aaron under his spell, as well."

At the sound of his name, Josie grinned. "Aaron came to get Boyd and offered him full-time work through the holidays. They just went over to the store for something."

Maeve didn't let on that she'd known Aaron was going to do that. "That's wonderful."

Josie flopped back against the pillows. "It was good to see Boyd smile. He's been so worried about me, about us."

"I have a feeling that this is going to be a magical Christmas for you all." Maybe she'd had her doubts, but in the face of Josie's optimism, she felt a renewed sense of possibility.

"You might be right," Josie agreed. She patted the side of the bed, and Maeve sat down gingerly, not wanting to jostle her pregnant friend.

"How're you feeling, really?"

"I'm feeling fine. Your friend Lily is coming over tomorrow to check me out, but I've only had a few more bouts of pain and every day brings me closer to the time when it's okay for the baby to be born."

"Can I get you two some dinner?"

"Boyd was going to celebrate the new job by picking up a pizza at the diner. I've been craving it. You're welcome to stay."

She knew that Josie meant it, but she'd be a fourth wheel. The family needed to celebrate on their own. "That sounds wonderful, but I haven't been home since first thing this morning. I really need to get some things done around the house. You call if you need anything before Boyd comes home, okay?"

Josie reached out and took her hand.

Maeve's first inclination was to pull her hand back. She wasn't a touchy-feely kind of person. She'd never been one. But looking at Josie, she held fast.

Josie gave her hand a squeeze. "You've been a true friend to us, Maeve. Like a kindred spirit."

Maeve thought about Mattie, Lily and Sophie—true friends and kindred spirits. They'd come together when Bridget had been sick. And the three of them had clicked. It was as if they'd always been a part of each other's lives. They were friendly with her, but she wasn't part of their inner circle. She'd never felt part of any inner circle until now. Until Josie.

"Who, me?" Maeve joked. Humor was an easy way to keep people at a distance. She knew Josie was right, though—it was how she felt, too. As if she'd found the friend she'd always been looking for, without knowing it. So she ditched the humor and said truthfully, "I feel the same way." She thought for a moment and added, "So, when I offer to help, you won't be able to say no because we're kindred spirits, right?"

Josie laughed. "Right. Are you sure you don't want to stay for pizza?"

"I'd love to, but I'm going to heat up some leftovers and head back to the library. An hour or so in the evening gives me time to clean up after the kids, and adults can come in and grab a book without the chaos."

"Well, thanks for giving Carl some playtime."

"I'll be at the library tomorrow morning for a bit, and then I'll be gone most of the weekend. You've got the key to my place, and I want you to feel free to go into the house for whatever you need. And please, think about eating some of those Thanksgiving leftovers tomorrow. I'll never finish them all myself." When Josie looked as if she might argue, Maeve pointed out, "We're kindred spirits and that means we're family, and that's what family does."

Josie laughed. "Yeah, that might have been a mistake admitting it to you."

* * *

MAEVE WOULDN'T HAVE admitted it to anyone, but she was a bit disappointed when Aaron didn't meet her at the library Friday evening or first thing in the morning. It was a quiet Saturday. With it still being holiday time, everyone's schedules were likely still in flux.

She was turning out the lights when Aaron showed up in the doorway.

"Are you done here?" he asked, smiling.

She switched off the last light. "Just about."

"Then put on your grubby clothes and let's go."

"You did mean it," she said.

He stood stock-still and nodded. "I guess we should start this off with me assuring you that I always mean what I say."

"I do, as well," she told him.

They stopped at her house. While Aaron waited downstairs, Maeve ran upstairs to put on a pair of old, holey jeans, a waffle-weave shirt and a sweatshirt that was miles too big and declared Perry Bicentennial Wine—Honoring Erie's History, One Glass at a Time. Back downstairs, she grabbed her old barn coat, a hat and her work boots from the closet and spotted the bottle of wine she'd picked up for him.

"Aaron, I got this for you to thank you for saving me from myself, but now it's a thank-you in advance for the help. My boss made this up special for the Battle of Lake Erie bicentennial. It was a big deal around here."

"Great." He eyed her as she put on her worn boots. "Your work clothes look as if they've seen actual work."

"I give mom and Herm a hand at the farm sometimes." She looked at him. His work clothes looked too new and not worn in enough, but she decided not to mention it. "So what's the plan?"

"You'll see."

"Cryptic..." she murmured.

Aaron didn't say much as they walked in the direction of the store. She knew he had something up his sleeve because he looked pretty happy with himself.

She didn't pressure him to tell her what was going on. To be honest, it was nice to have someone she could be quiet with.

Her mom and Herm had that kind of relationship.

She followed Aaron as he cut through the parking lot to the small picket fence that bordered the house. It had once been white, but all that was left of the paint were some grayish strips.

"This fence is on its last legs," he said, echoing her thoughts. "I thought we'd put up a nice wooden privacy fence. In the spring, we can plant some arborvitae. If we did it right, they'd never know there was a store past their backyard."

"That would be wonderful."

He climbed over the fence and she followed him as they walked along a trail that indicated he'd done this once or twice already today. He pointed with flourish.

"A Dumpster?" she asked. "How did you get it delivered so quickly?"

"I'd like to say I have connections, but actually Uncle Jerry does. They brought it right over."

The giant Dumpster occupied almost the entire driveway.

"If we clear out the house, then we can start taking down plaster and ripping out the kitchen."

"Aaron, I still don't know. This looks like too much work to get done—"

"When you opened the library, did you imagine it taking off like it has?"

"No. I thought I might open it one or two days a week. But the kids needed someplace to go after school, and people asked about book clubs and..."

"From what I can see, it's become an important part of the community. To be honest, I suspect it could be your full-time job."

"That would be my dream. Ray says that when he can find the funding in the town's budget, it will be. I don't have a library sciences degree, but he thinks my English major, and the fact I've been running it all this time is enough."

"But that's not why you reopened it, right?"

"No. I thought the community needed it and it happened gradually. First it was open on Saturdays, then a couple hours after school..."

"Then look at the house the same way. One step at a time. Sometimes when you look at a new project as a whole, it can be overwhelming. Instead, you just set an immediate goal. Today, it's garbage detail. We'll see where tomorrow takes us."

She studied this man who was inexplicably being very nice to her. He was tall, reed-thin. His brown hair looked as if it needed to be cut. To most, he wouldn't be considered a hot-looking guy. But as he stood there smiling at her, sharing his words of wisdom and pointing at the Dumpster, she knew that what was inside a person was what really mattered. "Fine. One step at a time."

"And I brought you a gift." He handed her a pair of thick work gloves. "I think you're going to need them."

* * *

ON AARON'S UMPTEENTH trip to the Dumpster, a man with glasses approached him and said, "Hi. Aaron, right? Jerry's nephew?"

He extended his hand. "Yeah."

"My wife's brother said you bought the Culpepper place." The man pushed his glasses up higher on his nose.

"Your wife's brother?"

"Sorry. I'm Finn. Finn Wallace. My wife, Mattie, runs Park Perks, the coffeehouse on Park Street. Her brother's the mayor. Ray. He said you bought the place out from under Maeve. That you're going to bulldoze it and turn it into more storage for the store."

"That was my plan, but it's changed." Aaron had forgotten how, in a small town, everyone seemed related to everyone else, or knew folks through one place or another. "Maeve's starting a foundation and this house is going to be the first one sold to a low income family."

"What kind of foundation?" Finn asked.

"You should talk to her. She's inside."

Before Finn could find her, Aaron stopped him. "Finn—"

The guy turned around.

"You said Maeve's a friend of your wife's, right?"

"Yeah."

"Listen, I don't think Maeve will ask for help. I don't think she's ever asked for help with the library, either, for that matter."

"No. People would have helped, but before most of the town knew what was going on, she had the place open. She did take some help from Tori this summer, but it actually started with her helping out my friends by giving Tori somewhere to serve her community service hours."

"That doesn't surprise me at all." It really didn't. He was beginning to suspect that Maeve Buchanan was exactly what she seemed to be. He couldn't find any ulterior motive behind anything she did. In fact, the only thing he could find was that wall hanging. *I can't save the world, but I can try.*

Well, maybe it was time someone tried to help Maeve. "Even though I still don't know her very well, the thing is, she's not going to ask for help with this, either, but she needs it. I'm planning on pitching in, but this is a big job. A huge job that needs to be done by Christmas Eve. If her friends offered—no, scratch that. If you all rolled up your sleeves and helped, well, she'd have to accept it."

Finn seemed skeptical. "But you don't know her well at all."

"No. Not yet."

He grinned. "Is another Valley Ridge romance brewing?"

"No. It's not like that. It can't be like that." Although, it wouldn't take much for it to be like that.

He dismissed the thought.

"Right. I'll go in and talk to her. Then I'll make some calls and send in the troops."

"Whatever you do, don't tell her I said anything. I made the mistake of facing her wrath when I called her Red. I don't ever want to be on her bad side again."

Finn laughed as he headed into the house.

Aaron tossed his garbage bags into the Dumpster, and then waited a few moments before he too went inside.

"Aaron," Maeve called. "We're in the living room. Finn was asking about the house. So, I explained the foundation to him, and about Josie and Boyd, and he wants to help."

Finn pushed his glasses up higher on the bridge of his nose and winked at Aaron. "She makes it sound as if she immediately jumped at my offer, but she's been finding all kinds of obstacles to my helping. Me, and everyone else. She thinks we're all too busy. We all have lives. Uh, Aaron, have you ever seen Maeve when she's not busy?"

He thought about that evening on her couch when they'd watched the movie together, but he didn't mention it. "She does seem to be in perpetual motion." His comment earned him a glare from Maeve.

In for a penny, in for a pound, his mother always said. "And we can use the help. There's a heck of a lot to do."

"Then, I'll rally everyone and we'll be here first thing tomorrow. What time, Maeve?"

"I..." She looked from Finn to him, then back again and sighed. "All right. I'll be here at seven, so anytime after that. And I suspect one of the people you'll be calling is Colton. Make sure he knows that Sophie is not invited, even though I know he wouldn't let her come help."

"What's wrong with Sophie?" Aaron asked.

"She's pregnant. I mean, even more pregnant than Josie. She's ready-to-have-the-baby-if-she-sneezes-hard sort of pregnant."

"Maybe she could stay with the kids?" Finn mused. "That would free me and Mattie up."

"That would work. And, Finn, please make sure everyone knows that this is a secret. I want to surprise Boyd and Josie. They might say no. But I want to give them the option."

Aaron knew instantly what she wanted. She wanted the house to be ready by Christmas Eve. A tree in the window, and the rest of the house decorated. Someone playing Santa.

He knew he'd do everything in his power to see that it worked out.

"I'm on it. Do you need any supplies?" he asked.

"You can ask Aaron. He's my technical expert."

He led Finn through the house and quietly explained that he was paying for anything they needed from his uncle's store and more. They'd have to hire an electrician, and probably a plumber. And the roof needed some new shingles, which would require an able-bodied person who wasn't afraid of heights to pitch in to get that done. "Listen, Finn, Maeve is nervous about how much there is to do, so I'm not overwhelming her with..."

"How much there is to do?" Finn said as he glanced around. "I'm a surgeon not a contractor, but even I can see how much there is to do."

"And it all needs to be done by Christmas Eve."

Finn looked around again. "Wow."

"Yeah. So, anyone who can give even a few hours will be welcome."

"We go to church in the morning. Let me put the word out there. And I'll tell Vivienne and Marilee—"

"MarVee's Quarters, right?" Aaron asked.

"Yes. If I tell them, everyone in town will know about it before the day's over."

"Remember to make sure they know not to say it's for Boyd and Josie. Maeve's got her heart set on surprising them with the offer on Christmas Eve."

"And I can see that what she wants matters to you," Finn said with a grin that made Aaron frown. "Don't worry. Everyone'll know it's a secret."

He spotted Maeve carrying two garbage bags out to the Dumpster. Finn looked out the window and watched her, too. "She's got a huge heart. She's always doing something for someone else."

"Yeah. I don't get it," Aaron said.

"You don't have to get it, but you better not break it. I know you said there's nothing like that between you two, but make sure she's aware of that."

"She is. We're..." He shrugged. "Friendly. Maybe becoming friends."

"As long as we're clear. Maeve is important to a lot of us. We'd take her being hurt personally." Finn nodded as if he felt he'd settled the matter. "As for the house, I'll pass the news along and we'll meet you here in the morning."

CHAPTER SEVEN

"AND YOU DON'T even bother to call your own mother?" Maeve's mom asked Sunday morning as half a dozen people showed up at the Culpepper house.

"Mom. What are you doing here?"

"Do you see my work clothes?" Renie Lorei was wearing faded jeans and an oversize flannel shirt over a black insulated one. She had on scuffed boots and a black knit hat that couldn't quite contain her mane of hair. Maeve had watched her mom's hair color fade over the years. She assumed hers would take the same route. That was okay with her because the gray had faded to straight-up white. It looked beautiful.

"Herm's in his, too," her mother said. "We're here to work, obviously. Honey, you could give lessons in discretion to a Carmelite nun."

Maeve didn't understand the reference and it must have shown, because her mother explained. "They take a vow of silence."

"Oh. I wasn't *not* saying anything for a reason. Everything at the house has happened so fast. I thought it was going to be a solo project and then Aaron came on board, and next thing I know, people are showing up." She still couldn't believe the crowd. "When I came up with this idea, I didn't realize how much work the house was going to take. Aaron said it has a solid structure. Well, that may be, but everything else is a mess. How did you find out?"

"Finn and Mattie mentioned it at church. I like the idea of working in shifts. Herm and I signed up from now until the cows need to be milked, so point me in a direction."

"They're tearing down drywall in the bedrooms."

"Tearing down is so much easier than putting up, so I'm there." Her mother stopped and kissed her cheek. "You're a very good person, Maeve. Your father would be so proud."

Her mom rarely mentioned her father and Maeve felt herself tear up.

"He was a good man," her mother continued, "but he was a proud man. He never asked anyone for anything. Not even me. He'd rather work outside all day in subzero weather, than let me help. Pride can be a good thing, Maeve, but there's nothing wrong with accepting help. There's also nothing wrong with asking for help. Next time, pick up the phone and call me and Herm."

"I will, Mom. I'm hoping I can get this set up so we can do one house a year. Then there will be plenty of opportunities to help."

Her mother kissed her cheek. "Well, I'm off to start."

Maeve watched as her mom joined everyone else in tearing down the drywall.

"You've got a lot of friends," Aaron said, startling Maeve.

"Valley Ridge is a special town. I love how everyone's pitching in to help Josie and Boyd. They're practically strangers here, and yet the whole town's taken them under its wing," she said.

Aaron shook his head. "That's part of it, but mainly, they're here for you."

Maeve kept silent and shrugged.

"What do you do for fun?" Aaron asked.

"I'm going to a wedding next weekend, so we'll have to work around that. Everyone in town will be there."

"Lily's, right?" Aaron asked.

"Right."

"I got an invitation. Well, Uncle Jerry did. But she asked me to come in his place."

"That doesn't surprise me. Lily's great."

"She seems very nice. The only problem is I don't know anyone in Valley Ridge, other than you."

Maeve shook her head. "Sure you do. You know Finn now, and there's Colton and Sebastian and..."

"I've met them, but I *know* you." Aaron liked the idea of seeing Maeve doing something fun. He'd seen her working at the library, working to put on a Thanksgiving meal, working here. Would she be different in a fun situation?

"No, you've seen me more than you've seen them, and you're trying to figure me out, but that doesn't mean you know me."

He ignored her comment and asked, "So will you go with me? I feel like a kid passing you a note back in grade school and asking you to check yes or no."

"Not as a date, right?" she asked.

"Right. We'll just be two friends who are going to the same place so decided to go together. You'd save me from feeling awkward." Maeve might not think he knew her, but he knew enough to realize that she'd find it hard to say no to helping him out.

"Fine. If you'd passed me a note, I'd check the yes box. The wedding's at two. Pick me up at one-thirty."

"Got it."

Aaron thought about hanging around her longer, but she was swept away by the bride-to-be and Mattie from the coffee shop. He went back to taking the drawers out of the kitchen cupboard. He unscrewed the backs of the handles and put them in a box. They'd decided to paint the cupboards—or rather, Maeve had. She might have trouble imagining what the house would look like when the mess was cleaned up, but she had definite opinions on what she wanted it to look like when—if—Josie and Boyd moved in.

The old white kitchen cupboards would have a fresh coat of paint on them. She'd declared the old farm sink was back in vogue and that old soapstone counters were, as well. All they needed was a good oiling.

It was nine o'clock that night before the last person cleared out. Maeve surveyed the kitchen and he could sense she was pleased.

"We might get this done after all," she said.

"I told you so," Aaron said, trying not to feel too smug.

"Vince is an electrician and he said he'd work after hours throughout the week, and TJ said the same about the plumbing. We can't work Saturday because of the wedding, but we can put up the drywall on Sunday. And I have the first coat of plaster on the holes and cracks out here..."

Aaron listened as she outlined her plans. She was back to her glowing optimism.

"I talked to my lawyer," he said. "He gave me the name of someone in Buffalo. I know you keep the library open most evenings, but is there any chance that you can take Wednesday night off? We can meet him at four, and then maybe go out to dinner or something afterward if you'd like."

At first, he thought she was going to say no to dinner, but she agreed. "If you'll let it be my treat."

"But—"

"No arguments," she scolded, teasingly shaking her finger at him. "You gave me a house. I get to buy you dinner."

"I didn't buy you a house, I donated it to..." He stopped and nodded. "Yes, you can buy me dinner."

"Great. It's a date."

"It's not a date," he agreed.

"I know, my dark, mysterious man. You're not in a position to date, though you're not overly forthcoming about why. For a man who wants to know all my secrets, you're not very good at sharing." She was smiling and he realized that she was teasing. "Thank you for everything, Aaron. You're a good man."

He shook his head. He was anything but that.

He insisted on walking her home, and afterward he went into his makeshift office in his uncle's apartment. He'd made a desk out of a small card table that he kept his printer on.

A stack of forwarded mail was piled in front of the keyboard.

He sat down and picked it up. He looked at the top envelope and knew what was in it, but he made no move to open it.

Before he'd met Maeve, he might have simply pushed the envelope to the back of his desk and forgotten about it. But since he'd met her, things had changed.

Maybe he was changing.

He wasn't sure how.

He wasn't sure why.

He put the envelope back down, unopened, but he left it where he could see it.

* * *

MAEVE GOT HOME from work on Wednesday, went into the house, took a shower and tried to decide what to wear.

It felt odd not to go to the library and open it up for the after-school kids.

She felt as if she were going on a date...only this wasn't that. This was meeting with a lawyer, then dinner. Dinner between friends, or, at least friendly allies.

She didn't have a clue how to dress.

182

She pulled out half a dozen tops, and then discarded them in a pile on her bed.

She wanted something that said, *competent businesswoman.*

She looked at the pile and finally pulled out a plain white blouse, a black cardigan and a pair of black pants.

She dressed and looked in a mirror.

She looked as if she was on her way to a funeral.

She glanced at the clock and realized Aaron would be there any minute, so she ripped off the cardigan and pulled out a kelly-green one. She took her mountain of hair and wrapped it into a loose bun.

Good enough for a meeting and dinner—a dinner that wasn't a date.

She was zipping up her black leather boots when Aaron pulled up in a SUV.

She grabbed a coat and hurried outside.

Josie stuck her head out of the RV. "Don't forget your curfew," she called, teasing.

"Don't forget you're supposed to be a bed-bound, or at least couch-bound mother-to-be."

Josie was still laughing as she shut the door.

"She seemed happy," Aaron said as Maeve got into the SUV.

"I couldn't tell her about the attorney, so I just said we were going out for dinner. I assured her it wasn't a date, but Josie lives in a world where losing your home might be a good thing. She believes in fate and angels. She probably believes in Santa Claus. Nothing I said could convince here this was anything but a date." She shrugged. "I don't want you to think I made it out to be more than it was."

"It's okay, Maeve. I wouldn't think that. Half the time I'm still not sure you even like me."

"Half the time, neither am I," she assured him, half joking, half serious.

He took the comment for a joke and laughed. She learned something she'd suspected since Riddlefest—he had a sense of humor and a contagious laugh. She couldn't not join in.

Aaron's laughter broke the sense of awkwardness she'd felt when she got in the car.

They talked about the house, the foundation and the holidays.

And when they got to the attorney's office, they talked about the same things again with him.

When they left his office an hour later, Maeve admitted, "I don't think I'll remember half of what he said tomorrow. I don't think I have a head for business."

"That's okay, I do, and he does. He's done this kind of thing before. He'll make sure our *i*'s are dotted and our *t*'s are crossed."

"So, this is really going to happen." It was a statement. Not a question any longer. Her dream was going to become reality. And if the crowd over the weekend was any indication, they'd have no problem getting the house done in time for Christmas.

All that was left was finding out if Josie and Boyd would stay.

She sank back against the heated, leather seat and sighed. Maybe this would actually work out.

* * *

Aaron glanced over at Maeve, as he drove to the restaurant.

He wondered what she was thinking.

She seemed excited about the charity. The Valley Ridge Home for Christmas Foundation had a nice ring. But she just stared silently out the window. He was at a loss for what to say.

He pulled into a parking space. "We're here."

She nodded and got out.

"Is every thing okay?" he asked when he got out of the car. "You seem upset."

"I'm not upset. I'm thrilled. Happy."

"It's hard to tell what you're feeling at any given time. Well, except when I've annoyed you. That I can tell."

"I tend to be private."

A maître d' showed them to a table. They placed their orders. Maeve was still quiet.

When the waitress left, she said, "You know, I've never told anyone else my mom and I were homeless for a time."

"No one?"

"No. My principal must have guessed. She called me to her office every day on some pretense or another, well, at least at first. She always had packed too much for her lunch and shared it with me. She finally came out and asked."

"Did you tell her?"

Maeve shook her head. "Not at first. I didn't want to, but she...insisted. After that, she'd come in early in the mornings, and Mom and I would take showers in the gym. She brought me lunches. She..."

"What happened?"

"She talked to Hank. I was so mad. I can't even tell you how mad I was. But Hank has an apartment behind his house. Lily's mom lives there now. He let us stay there and gave Mom a job at the diner."

Aaron knew what happened next. "And that's where she met Herm."

"He fell in love with her chocolate milk shakes." Maeve twirled her straw in her glass, swirling the ice and lemon wedge around.

"And no one at school ever knew?"

"I got a reputation for being a bad girl." She looked up as the lemon lazily made another loop around the glass.

He laughed. "I can't believe anyone bought that."

"You don't think I have the makings of a bad girl?" She sat a little taller.

He studied her a long moment, then shook his head. "I see more of a bookworm than bad girl."

She sighed. "Yeah, that's what I was afraid of. But since no one ever knew what I did, they were a bit hesitant to mock me for my bookworming ways."

"Now, that's a bonus."

She got quiet again.

"Is there a problem?"

"I don't know how to do this." She waved her hand between them. "I know it's not a date, but even then, small talk escapes me."

"You were doing fine. I'm not known for my small talk abilities, either. I'm a computer nerd. I'm more at home with my laptop than I am socializing."

"So, what you're saying is we're both hopeless?" She smiled and looked more comfortable.

"Yes."

"That does make it easier."

"So, let's enjoy the dinner."

And they did. Maeve told Aaron stories about Valley Ridge and its inhabitants. No gossip, which he liked, but interesting tidbits.

"Most of the socializing takes place either at the schools or at the church. We don't even have a bowling alley in town. But the beautiful thing about Valley Ridge is we're between North East, Pennsylvania, and Ripley, New York. And just beyond those two smaller towns, there's Erie and Buffalo. And then there's the lake. Erie's got Presque Isle, North East has Freeport Beach, and there's *the beach* here in Valley Ridge. For as long as I can remember, there's been talk about giving it an actual name, but it's not developed, so it's just 'the beach.' It's one of the few accessible beaches around here, but it's owned by one of the farmers. Ray's been working with town council to actually buy that small stretch for the town."

Aaron listened to Maeve and realized how deeply her roots were sunk in this town.

"You love it here," he murmured more to himself than to her.

"I do," she said. "A lot of kids move away. It's a small town and farming's our biggest industry, but the town proper has experienced a rebirth. There's talk that people are looking at buying up empty storefronts. Ray's been working to bring tourists into town. The current theory is that with the recession, people long for roots. That's what we offer. A place to plant roots."

He realized that the gift she wanted to give Josie and Boyd was more than a house; it was those roots. "Is that why you came back after college?"

"It's home. I missed being near my mom and I missed the town. I missed knowing almost everyone. I know I'm not very outgoing, but people seem to accept me regardless. I guess that's what I like. The acceptance. The looking out for each other."

She paused, and then added, "Hank has dementia. Some days you can hardly tell, and others, you can't miss it. But the whole town knows and keeps an eye on him. If he starts to leave the diner, invariably someone asks if they can go with him to keep him company. He's cared for. That's the best example I can think of."

"And he's one of the ones who helped you and your mother."

She nodded. "More people would have, but my mom is a proud woman and didn't want to be a burden to anyone. Hank insisted. He's stubborn."

"It seems to me that you got a fair dose of pride and stubbornness, too."

"And you don't have either of those?" She grinned at him in a way that said she wouldn't buy it if he said no.

It was a fair question. One he'd never asked himself before. He thought about the envelope on his desk. Maybe it wasn't his heart, but rather his pride that was stinging. Maybe his resistance to signing the papers he knew were inside was more about stubbornness at this point.

That question stayed with him long after they'd finished dinner and returned to Valley Ridge.

Heart or pride?

CHAPTER EIGHT

IT HAD BEEN a long week. Aaron went to bed exhausted every night, and had a heck of a time waking up every morning. But somehow he'd made it through until Saturday.

What surprised him was that Maeve seemed to do twice as much as he did, but she didn't seem fazed by it. She was like that bunny on television. It played its drum and kept going and going....

He'd seen no evidence of her slowing down.

Since the meeting with the lawyer, he'd started the paperwork. That meant that, as he sat at the computer each day, he had some legitimate work to do. It might not be his work, but it was something. And maybe it was like priming a pump, because he'd actually started to work on his own stuff, as well. Certainly not at the frantic, all-encompassing pace he used to work, but he'd worked.

That was something.

When he saw Maeve, he tried to steer their conversations toward her. He wanted to talk about her.

She wanted to talk about the house.

They talked about the house.

He hoped that today would be different. There would be no working on the Culpepper place. It was Lily and Sebastian's wedding, and he'd convinced her to take the whole day off, despite the fact that Maeve seemed hell-bent to get the place done.

He couldn't get over all the stuff she did. Work full-time. Take care of the library. Help with Carl. And now, she was coming over at the end of each day to work on the house, as well.

Well, today, there was no library. No house. It was a day to relax.

Normally, going to a wedding would be at the low end of things he wanted to do, but today, he couldn't wait because he was going with Maeve.

Not going with her in a way that implied a date, but rather they were two friends going together.

He thought about the damned envelope. Broken heart or injured pride? The question kept popping up. He still didn't have an answer and he still hadn't opened it.

Aaron crawled out of bed and looked out the window. It was snowing again. Not enough that he needed to go out and plow, at least not yet.

Something caught his eye. Movement at the Culpepper place.

She wouldn't.

He threw on some clothes and hurried out.

Maeve Buchanan was in the kitchen cleaning out a paintbrush. She had huge curlers in her hair. The last time he'd seen a woman with curlers in her hair, it had been his grandmother.

She looked up as he entered the room and he could see the flash of guilt on her face. "Good morning, Aaron."

"Maeve, I though we agreed you'd take a day off."

"I'm finishing up. I woke up early and couldn't sleep. The wedding's not until this afternoon, so I thought I'd come put another coat of paint on the cupboards. They look awesome, don't they?"

He looked at the white cabinets and had to admit they did. They'd found the missing doors in the basement and now old wooden cabinets looked like new.

But that wasn't the point. "The point is you need a day off."

"The point is, I had time and I decided to spend it here. I'm finishing up and heading home to change."

"Maeve, I've seen your schedule. You can't keep going like this." As he said the words, he remembered Tracey saying the same thing to him. Telling him to slow down. To take a break. To get out of the house and away from his computer. To spend time with her, or with his family. He hadn't listened to her any more than Maeve was listening to him.

Heart or pride?

"Aaron, while I appreciate everything you're doing, that doesn't mean you get a say in how I live my life." Despite the fact she had curlers in her hair, and old painting clothes on, Maeve managed to make the sentence sound haughty.

"When's the last time you went out with friends?" he asked.

"I went out with you last week when we met with that lawyer."

"That wasn't fun—that was dinner after a business meeting."

She looked hurt. "Well, I had fun."

Damn, that's not what he intended. "We talked about this house."

"I'm having fun with this house. And I told you, I don't know how to make small talk. If that's what you wanted, you should have taken another friend with you."

"But you need to do something other than work. What's the last thing you did that was strictly for your own enjoyment?"

"I took a bubble bath the other night. I lit some candles, read my book and refilled the tub at least three times. That was fun."

He could see that Maeve meant the statement innocently, but her words had anything but an innocent effect on him. He could picture her in the tub, surrounded by bubbles that slowly disappeared as she added more water...

He took a deep, steadying breath. "Maeve, I think you know what I mean."

She shook her head and her curlers rattled. "Aaron, I never know what you mean."

"Pardon?"

"You say we can't date, yet you're with me all the time. You say you don't understand me, but that's only fair because I don't understand you. You try to tell me what to do, what to enjoy, how to spend my personal time, not seeming to realize you don't have the right. And, let me point out that you've dug around, trying to find out things about me. And

I've let you. I've told you things I've never told anyone else. And yet you remain closemouthed about yourself. You say you can't date anyone, but you don't say why."

She was right. He tried to think of a retort, but before he could, she said, "Now, if you'll excuse me, I need to get home and get ready for the wedding."

She stormed out of the house, curlers bouncing, without a backward look.

Once again, Aaron had managed to anger her.

At one-thirty, he pulled into her driveway and she came out the door before he could even open the car door.

She was bundled in a long black wool coat but she didn't have on boots. She had on some strappy shoes that didn't look nearly warm enough, despite the slight increase in temperature. He thought about suggesting she go back and grab some boots, but thought better of it.

You try to tell me what to do, what to enjoy, how to spend my personal time, not seeming to realize you don't have the right. She was right, he had, and he didn't, so he didn't mention her inappropriate footwear.

"Told you I'd be ready," she said as she climbed inside the car.

"You smell like oranges."

"It's my body butter."

Aaron didn't have a clue what body butter was, but the words sent his mind spiraling down paths it shouldn't go. He tried to block the images on the short drive to the church.

Dylan was directing traffic. "That's nice of him," he said.

"It's penance," Maeve murmured.

She must have read the question in his expression because she added, "Dylan RSVP'd late, and when dealing with Lily, that was not wise."

She waved at Dylan as they drove by. "Word of warning—don't annoy Lily."

"I think I've annoyed my share of women for the day." He shot her a look and she was grinning. Feeling as if he'd earned a reprieve, he promised, "I'll be on my best behavior."

"Were you really mad that I went over and worked this morning?" she asked.

"I thought you were mad at me." He pulled into a parking spot, but left the car running.

"I'll confess. I don't like people telling me what to do."

"I'll try not to let it happen again. But we've become..." He looked for a word to describe what they'd become. "Friends, I guess. I worry about you. You don't seem to ever stop moving. You're a whirling dervish of energy. I'm afraid you're going to crash."

"I don't know how to not do something. I didn't go to the library today, and it seemed like a long time to sit around doing nothing for the sake of doing nothing, so I went over to the house. I'm sorry if it annoyed you."

"That's not it. Although, as someone who has spent a lot of time with you, let me say that you could probably use some downtime."

Her back stiffened. "Thank you for your opinion." Her voice was so tight it practically crackled.

He sighed. "I didn't mean to annoy you again."

"You never mean to, but you do seem to manage it on a regular basis." She paused and added, "Sometimes I have a short fuse. Sorry. Let's start over. I am really looking forward to today. Thanks for asking me to go with you. It's always awkward going to a wedding alone. So, let's go in."

Aaron turned off the engine and walked ahead of Maeve. He purposefully shortened his stride leaving footprints for her to step in.

They walked into the large white church together. He heard Maeve's sharp intake of breath as they caught a glimpse of the church's interior. It sounded like a swoon. When he'd seen that romance book on her nightstand on Thanksgiving, he'd suspected it, but now he knew with utter certainty: Maeve Buchanan was a romantic.

* * *

MAEVE STOOD AND took in the decorated church. White bows festooned the end of each pew, a sprig of holly the only color. The altar was flanked with a myriad of poinsettias. The decorations were simple but beautiful.

She sighed again. Lily had done beautiful work.

There was a long coatrack along the side of the entryway. She unbuttoned her coat and took it off. Aaron drew in a long breath. "Wow," was all he said.

Maeve smiled. "That was a very nice compliment. Thank you."

She'd found the deep green vintage dress on eBay. She'd looked at local department stores and couldn't find anything she liked. This was perfect, and reasonably priced.

She'd felt good when she put it on, and she felt better knowing Aaron had noticed it. Not that she wanted or needed him to notice.

She glanced at her escort. His black suit was fitted. He wore a muted red shirt, and a trendy black tie. "We look like a Christmas decoration," she said.

He stood next to her looking at the back of the church and said, "Guess we'll fit in here, then."

Maeve smiled, seeing Lily's hand on everything as Aaron escorted her into the church. She reached out and touched one of the sprigs of holly. "It's so lovely."

Aaron didn't say anything. He merely gave her a knowing smile.

"What?" she asked.

"You're all dewy eyed. You're a romantic. I know you said that Mattie, Lily and Sophie wanted to start the romance book club, but I think you must have been secretly thrilled. I bet you were over the moon that someone else suggested it. You so wanted a romance book club because you, Maeve Buchanan, are a romantic."

Maeve shook her head. "Am not."

"Are, too." Aaron grinned in a totally annoying way.

She wondered why it was that Aaron always seemed to get under her skin. He always seemed to evoke some strong emotion.

Frequently, he annoyed her.

Sometimes he touched her, like when he gave the foundation the house.

And on occasion he amazed her, because as much as he complained she worked all the time, she'd seen him at the house—he was no slacker himself.

"I'm not going to bother arguing with you. Let's find a seat." She walked midway up the aisle and slid into a pew. "I'm not admitting to being a romantic, but I have gone to an awful lot of weddings in the past few months."

"Really?"

"Well, there was Colton and Sophie's wedding in June, only that was, uh, interrupted and didn't happen. Then there was Mattie and Finn's wedding in August, which turned into Sophie and Colton's wedding, too. Now this." She gestured at the beautiful church. "Lily and Sebastian's is the third wedding."

"Fourth if you count that one in June that didn't take," he pointed out.

"But they made it eventually. I think when people are meant to be together, they will figure it out, no matter what their obstacles."

He didn't say anything, but she knew what he was thinking. He was thinking it so loudly there was no way to ignore it.

"I'm not a romantic," she whispered.

"Ha," was his response.

"Oh, shut up."

"Red," he whispered so softly she almost didn't hear it.

That should have set her teeth on edge. She wanted to be annoyed. But it was so obvious he was teasing and he shot her a grin that almost challenged her to get annoyed at him.

"You are not an only child are you?" she asked, knowing he wasn't. She could see the signs. Aaron had definitely grown up picking on siblings.

"Three younger sisters," he admitted slowly.

"Yeah, it shows." She felt smug at his look of confusion. "Now, sit back and behave and enjoy the ceremony."

Feeling as if she'd finally had the last word, Maeve was content to let her banter with Aaron take a backseat. She wanted to savor the moment, because—while she'd never admit it to Aaron—there was a chance that she was a bit of a romantic.

Even if she wasn't, it would be hard not to feel like one today because Lily and Sebastian were so utterly meant for each other. She resisted the urge to sigh over the romance of it all. Instead, she watched the guests funnel in. Maeve smiled and waved at half the town. Her mom and Herm joined them in their pew. "You look beautiful," she said to her mother.

"Thank you," Herm said, laughing.

"You look beautiful, too," she assured her stepfather.

She knew that some people had rocky relationships with stepparents, but she'd always liked Herm. And even if she hadn't, she would always be thankful that he'd made her mother happy.

Soon, Miss Helen started playing the organ. The older woman had taught music for the school district for years. Even though she was retired and her health wasn't the best, she still played the organ every Sunday and occasionally at a wedding.

Soon, Sebastian was at the altar, Colton and Finn at his side.

Mattie walked down the aisle. Her bridesmaid's dress was gorgeous—strapless with an empire waist. The top section was off-white while the bottom of the dress was a muted red.

Sophie was next. She wore the same dress as Mattie but with more material on the bottom. The empire cut allowed the lower fabric to drape over her giant baby bump.

Miss Helen began to play the traditional wedding march. Everyone stood as Lily came down the aisle with Hank on one arm and her mother on the other. Vera Paul was new to town. When she'd arrived this summer, she seemed quiet, almost mousy. But now, walking Lily down the aisle, she practically glowed.

There was no "practically" about Lily; she was glowing.

Maeve watched Lily's expression as Sebastian came into view.

She fought to hold back tears. The love between them was palpable.

Maeve didn't want to cry. Aaron was standing next to her, giving her those you're-such-a-romantic looks of his. She knew if she cried she'd only be giving him more ammunition. But she felt the tears start to well in her eyes, and then her nose started to run.

She wished she was a pretty crier, but the fact was, she was a nose-running, bloodshot-eyed, ugly crier. She tried to hold the tears back, but when her mother reached across Aaron and passed her a tissue, she gave up the fight.

"Romantic," he whispered in her ear.

She discreetly stepped on his toe. Not hard, but enough to make him chuckle.

"Shh," she whispered as they sat down.

She was thankful that her mom had passed her the tissue as she listened to the couple's vows.

"...I promise to love you, to honor you and to challenge you to one-handed basketball whenever you need it," Lily promised, then added, "I don't promise to obey, though."

The congregation laughed. Lily had literally played a one-on-one game with Sebastian last summer with one hand tied behind her back. That basketball game had become a town legend.

Maeve totally lost it as Sebatian's scarred hand came up and caressed Lily's face. When he'd come to town, he'd hidden his injuries, but now, he didn't seem to care who saw the scars. Lily turned his hand to her and kissed his palm.

Maeve's mom passed her another tissue.

Maeve never brought her own because she was always convinced she wouldn't cry.

And she always did.

As the minister pronounced them husband and wife, Sebastian and Lily kissed, then walked toward the back of the church. As Mattie and Finn, and Sophie and Colton joined arms and walked down the aisle after them, she couldn't have stopped crying if she wanted to. All three couples were so perfect for each other.

She waited until it was their row's turn to exit and then joined the crowd waiting to congratulate the new couple.

She realized her mom and Aaron were talking.

"...she was always like that. A tenderhearted little girl. I got a note from her teacher her second week of kindergarten asking me to please send in crayons for her."

Maeve knew what story her mother was going to tell and she groaned. "Oh, come on, Mom, Aaron doesn't want to hear this."

Aaron shot her mother his most ingratiating smile. "Please, Mrs. Lorei, finish."

"Maeve gave her crayons to one of the boys whose parents couldn't afford them. She gave him her pencils, too. Although she kept her pencil box. Go on and ask her why she kept that one item when she gave away all the others," her mother instructed.

Aaron looked at Maeve expectantly, as she felt her cheeks heat up.

"It was pink," she admitted. "I offered it to him, but he didn't want it."

Her mom laughed, and then turned to talk to Mrs. Esterly.

"Before you say anything," Maeve warned Aaron, "I want to state for the record that I only gave him the stuff because he was the tiniest boy in kindergarten. He was already a target. Even at five I knew that being smaller and different made you a target. I didn't want his blood on my hands."

"It was kindergarten, Maeve, I don't think he was going to be targeted by the mob because he didn't have crayons." Aaron had a puzzled expression as he studied her.

Maeve suddenly understood how animals in a zoo felt as visitors studied them. "You don't understand me, I know. Well, join the club because I don't understand me most of the time, either."

She was thankful that they'd reached Lily and Sebastian and he couldn't respond. "Everything was beautiful, Lily. And I love everyone's dresses."

"Tell that to Mattie. By the way she kibitzed, you'd have thought I asked her to wear sackcloth." Maeve glanced over at Mattie, who was tugging at her dress.

Maeve kissed Sebastian's cheek. "You're a very lucky man."

The ex-marine and newest town council member smiled and assured her, "I know."

She moved down to Mattie. "I'm supposed to tell you—"

Mattie waved her comments aside. "I know. A dress isn't going to kill me. That's what Lily says. Personally, I'm not sure."

Maeve laughed. "You're worse than the kids."

As if on cue, six-year-old Abbey Langley launched herself at Maeve, trusting that she'd catch her. "Did you see my dress, Miss Maeve? Aunt Mattie wasn't sure it was okay for a wedding, but Aunt Lily said I looked beautiful and she's the bride, so she got the say-so and now here I am."

Abbey had on a red-and-white striped shirt with a green jumper over it. A jumper with a giant candy cane on it. It looked more appropriate for school than for a wedding, but looking at Abbey's pleasure, Maeve knew she'd have had the same response as Lily. "You look absolutely beautiful. It's a very festive dress."

"Yeah, I know." The little redhead nodded so hard she whacked her head on Maeve's cheek. "Sorry," she said. "But I told Aunt Mattie it was a good wedding dress."

Maeve rubbed her cheek as she laughed. "I'm sure you did."

"And who is this beautiful lady?" Aaron asked.

Abbey turned her attention to Aaron. "I'm Abbey Langley. And I got a new dress for the wedding."

"I can see that," Aaron said. "You look stunning."

Abbey's eyes narrowed. "Is that a good thing or not?" she asked Maeve.

"A very good thing. It means you look princess beautiful."

Abbey threw herself from Maeve's arms toward Aaron.

Maeve couldn't help but wonder if it meant something about Aaron that even though Abbey didn't know him, she trusted him to catch her. He stepped out of the receiving line, still holding the little girl as she imparted a long story. Aaron gave her his complete and utter attention.

"Sophie, you look beautiful," Maeve said.

"I look like a house, but thank you for lying," Sophie said.

Her husband kissed her cheek. "I like houses."

Maeve laughed. "That was the wrong response, Colton. You're supposed to tell her she's beautiful and not the least bit houselike."

"She is beautiful," he said.

Maeve stepped out of the reception line. Tori, Sophie's daughter, was at the back of the church. "You came with a date," she said. "I'll have to call off the troops."

"What troops?" When Tori didn't respond, Maeve sighed. "I thought we had a discussion about fixing me up. Don't. I'm totally happy with my life. I don't need a man messing it up."

"Yeah, men do make life messier, but when you see those three guys—" Tori pointed to Colton, Finn and Sebastian "—with their wives, you've got to admit, sometimes messy is worth it. I'm the daughter of two wonderful parents who are still in love. Even my grandparents are still crazy about each other. You could say they've all corrupted me."

Maeve looked at the three couples Tori was pointing to. "They do look happy," Maeve admitted. "But I'm happy, too."

Tori pointed at Aaron, apparently engrossed in whatever Abbey was saying. "He seems very nice."

"He..." She hesitated. If she'd been asked the first day she met him, she'd have assured Tori that he wasn't nice, that he was annoying as all get-out. But looking at him today, she didn't feel even mildly annoyed, despite the fact that he'd called her Red again and accused her of being a romantic. "He's okay. He's been helping me with something big."

"Oh, the house for those people in your driveway. Yeah, I heard. Mom and Dad said we can stay late tomorrow so we can help. You lost a whole day of work today because of the wedding."

That wasn't quite the truth. Maeve had gotten those few hours of painting in. But after Aaron's reaction, she thought it was better not to mention that. She was silent and let Tori continue.

"We figured you could use the help. And Dad, he can do anything. He said we'd come up the next weekend, too, and bring Papa."

"How did you hear already?" Maeve asked.

Tori laughed. "Maeve, you know this is Valley Ridge, right? We stopped at the bed-and-breakfast, and JoAnn told us all about it before we unpacked. We were going to stay at Sophie's, but we figured she'd be busy with wedding stuff, and with my new brother on the way, we didn't want to wear her out."

"Oh." Of course. The Valley Ridge grapevine was stronger than the grapevines in the vineyards that surrounded the town.

Tori waved at her parents. "I'll see you at the reception. Dad's motioning for me to hurry up." She flew out the door.

Aaron came back over, sans child attached to his hip. "I got thrown over for a younger man." He pointed to Abbey who was standing with Joe and his sisters.

"Women are fickle creatures," Maeve teased.

"Are you ready to head over to the reception?" he asked.

"Yes."

After they'd retrieved their coats, Aaron wrapped her arm through his.

It felt nice.

They walked across the church's parking lot to the reception hall. It was the largest gathering place in Valley Ridge. Not quite as big as Colton's barn, but more than ample enough for a reception.

The hall was beautifully decorated, too. Lily had strung garland, woven with small twinkly lights, across the ceiling. At each point that the garland swagged up to the ceiling, there was mistletoe. Poinsettias were placed on the serving table and gift tables.

The dining tables were covered with red table clothes. Candles in hurricane lamps were surrounded with evergreen branches.

"Beautiful." She hadn't realized she'd spoken aloud until she caught Aaron grinning at her. "I'm not a romantic," she said, even though he hadn't said a word. He still smirked. "Oh, let's go drop off our gift and find our seats."

"We got a gift?" he asked.

"We came as a couple, so yes, *we* did."

"What did we buy them?" he asked. She handed him the package and he hefted it.

"A book?"

"Not just any book. We got them a beautifully bound album called, *Our First Year.* There's room for pictures and for notes on things they did. There's a section for them to write in their history as a couple. The wedding. The honeymoon. Their first holidays."

"That sounds very...romantic," he teased.

"And we got them a weekend at a winery in the Finger Lakes," she continued.

"Wow," he said. "We are generous. I wrote them a check. You gave their gifts a lot of thought."

"I've given the book at every wedding I've gone to. As for the weekend, I know the owner and he gave me a deal," she said, trying to downplay the gift.

"Still, that's a lovely gift because you obviously gave it a lot of thought."

She felt uncomfortable with Aaron's praise. "I wanted to do something special for them."

"Maeve, from what I can see, you spend a lot of time doing special things for other people. When do you do anything for yourself, or better yet, let someone else do something for you?"

He studied her as if she was a lab experiment gone wonky, but at least this time he didn't mutter anything about not understanding her. She didn't want this to turn into some serious conversation where he tried to discover everything there was to know about her while telling her nothing about himself, so she teased, "There was that bubble bath, and I'm letting you and half of Valley Ridge help with the house."

"The bubble bath was fine, but I think you know that's not what I meant. And the house isn't for you so I don't think it counts."

"I don't know what your problem is today. Suffice it to say I do exactly what I want when I want. I'm happy with my life. Now, let's find where we're sitting for dinner."

* * *

Aaron wasn't sure what was up with him, either. He'd officially annoyed Maeve twice today by worrying she was doing too much.

Maybe that was fair, because her innocent comment about a bubble bath had conjured up images that would be haunting his dreams tonight.

He took a long breath and watched her as she listened to Finn give a toast to the bride and groom. "...Sebastian told me that his grandfather once compared Mattie, Sophie and Lily to wines. Sophie was champagne, all bubbly and effervescent. Mattie was red wine, earthy and comfortable with herself. And Sebastian's Lily was

Riesling, slightly sweet, with a bit of a bite. I have to say, as someone who managed to marry one of these three ladies, I count myself lucky. And Colton and Sebastian feel the same way."

Someone in the audience made a mocking sound.

Finn glared in the direction of the noise, then went on, "Yes, these three women mean everything to me and to my friends. Our lives have changed up fundamentally. Sebastian is a better man because of Lily.

"I wish them both nothing but happiness. To Lily and Sebastian."

Maeve had tears in her eyes as she raised her glass and tapped it against Aaron's. "To Lily and Sebastian."

Aaron looked at Maeve, her red hair cascading down the back of her green dress. She smiled up at him.

"They'll be happy together," she said. "They just fit. All three couples. Watching them fall in love over the past year has been a lesson in what love should be."

She got very quiet and watched as the bride and groom danced together. After the first song, other couples joined them on the dance floor.

"Look, that's Lily's mom dancing with Hank, Sebastian's grandfather. They both look so happy. Did you hear the bells as Lily walked up the aisle? She put them in her bouquet for Hank. Bells and chimes remind him of his wedding. They seem to have become a Valley Ridge tradition."

Aaron had noticed the bells tinkling as Lily walked up the aisle. "I thought it was just something to do with the season."

"That, too. I love the sound they make—it's so hopeful. When your doorbell rings, or the phone, you never know who it's going to be. There's a sense that anything is possible."

"Sometimes it's bad news," he pointed out, thinking of the envelope he'd signed for last week. The unopened envelope that still sat on his desk.

"Sometimes, I guess. But I'd rather hope that it's something good."

"So, when you get married, you'll have bells, too?"

"Maybe." She looked up at him and grinned. "You know, most men get nervous bringing a woman to a wedding, much less mentioning that woman's future wedding."

"I'm not most men," he assured her.

She tilted her head to one side, as if she'd see him more clearly from a different angle. She studied him for a moment longer than was comfortable, then finally agreed. "No, you're not."

He couldn't decide if she meant it as a compliment or not.

As if she could read his mind, she laughed and said, "So now you're trying to figure out how I meant that, because you're a man who needs to understand things. So, this once, I'm going to help you along and say it was a compliment."

"Thank you."

"You're welcome. So, now that I've been so very complimentary, you have to ask me to dance."

"I'm an awful dancer. I mean, really bad."

She took his hand and pulled him to his feet. "I'm feeling brave and fearless. I'm going to take my life into my hands and dance with you."

A few years ago, he'd walked into his parents' living room and found them dancing, although there had been no music playing. He'd stood in the doorway and watched them. His mother pressed up close against his father's chest, holding on as they turned circles. Instantly, he'd known that was what he wanted.

Hell, that's what he thought he had.

He didn't mention the memory to Maeve. After all his teasing about her being a helpless romantic, it didn't seem wise. But the song was perfect, he admitted to himself as he took Maeve in his arms for the first time. She fit. She fit perfectly. And he could almost imagine holding her like this beyond this one dance.

For the past two years, he'd been so angry. Hurt, too. Confused. But those feelings felt like a distant memory as he danced with Maeve in his arms.

The rest of the world melted away.

They were surrounded by other couples, dancing to the same song, but all he could focus on was Maeve Buchanan. As the song ended she took his hand as if to move off the dance floor. But Aaron didn't want to go back. He didn't want the moment to end.

As he had that thought, Maeve reached up and gave him a chaste kiss on his cheek. "Thank you."

And suddenly, Aaron wanted more than a friendly peck on his cheek.

Without thinking about it, or weighing his action, he leaned down and kissed her on the lips. A kiss that told her without words that he thought she was anything but most women. A kiss he hoped told her how much he was growing to care about her. A kiss that said...

He suddenly remembered that envelope at home on his desk and realized what he was doing. He pulled back. "Maeve, I'm so sorry. I shouldn't have—"

She laughed and started toward the table. "Relax, Aaron. Believe it or not, I've been kissed before, and I didn't mistake it for anything more than it was. Even though we're at a wedding, and you mentioned my potential future wedding, I promise, I won't be picking out a china pattern tomorrow. Someday, I plan to fall deeply in love, but I'm not in a rush."

Aaron thought about the big envelope sitting on his desk at home. He realized that he was cheating. He pulled back and stopped short of the table. "That should never have happened."

Maeve's smile faded. "Aaron?"

"I want to, but I can't."

"Why not?" she asked. "You're free. I'm free. I know you're only here until Jerry comes back. I know that if we start something, it will hurt when you go, but I'm not asking for forever. I told you I wasn't ready to pick out china patterns."

He didn't respond because he didn't know what to say.

Maeve started to look concerned. "You're not a priest, are you?"

He shook his head.

Her eyes locked onto his as she slowly asked, "You're not seeing someone back home are you?"

He shook his head again.

"And you're not married...?" She must have seen the truth in his eyes because she let her open-ended question hang there.

There was no way to ignore it. No way to misunderstand it. "I'm not *precisely* married."

Her teasing expression disappeared in the blink of an eye. "I know that I'm from a small town, but I do know there are some issues that are black-and-white with absolutely no shades of gray. You can't be *not precisely pregnant.* You can't be *not precisely married.*"

Aaron had heard all the generalities about redheads' tempers. He'd seen Maeve annoyed, but not truly upset until now. Her fury was palpable. "I want to explain."

"Are you married to someone?" she asked.

"Legally, yes, but—"

She nodded. "Legally is what counts. At least as far as I'm concerned. I don't think we should see each other again."

He felt a sense of desperation at her declaration. He couldn't imagine never seeing Maeve again. He still didn't understand her. And he didn't want to let her go.

"What about the house?" he asked. "You're going to throw that away because of this? If you'd let me explain—"

She stopped in her tracks and turned around. "If the house was for me, I'd tell you exactly where to shove it. But it's not, so I'll be there in the morning, like we planned. I know you said you didn't understand me, and you've told me that you need to understand things, so here you go, in order to help you understand me...

"I. Do. Not. Date. Married. Men. Ever. I respect myself too much to do something like that, and I..." She hesitated and added softly, "And I don't respect you at all for putting me in this situation."

"Maeve, I forgot..." He wanted to explain that he'd forgotten he was married until after he'd kissed her. That when he was with her, all he could seem to think about was her. Not his ex. Not the anger and the humiliation of their breakup. But anything he could tell her sounded lame and like an excuse. He was legally married until he signed those papers in that envelope on his desk.

Some men might think that a two-year separation was enough, but he wasn't some men. He hadn't dated, or looked at, another woman until Maeve.

He told himself he wanted to understand her. He wanted to figure out what made her tick. But if he was honest with himself, he simply wanted to be with her.

He'd been so angry and hurt the past two years.

Well, maybe not so much the past year. He'd simply fallen into the habit of thinking he was still angry and hurt. Because right now, he could hardly remember his ex's name. He couldn't even picture her. All he could see or think about was Maeve Buchanan.

And he'd done her a terrible disservice. "Never mind. I'll see you in the morning, and don't worry, that will never happen again."

"You can be sure of that." She turned and walked away from him.

* * *

How the heck did you forget you were married?

For half a moment, as he kissed her, Maeve had thought...

Well, never mind what she'd thought. She glanced at the wedding party dancing in the center of the floor.

She looked over at the table where her mom was sitting nestled close to Herm.

She saw Tori and her parents. Yeah, they had it, too.

That's what she wanted.

And that would never be with Aaron I-forgot-I'm-married Holder. He might be generous and funny, too.

He might even be cute.

But that wasn't enough.

She was surrounded by loving couples. She knew what love should look like. She'd even seen what lost love looked like. When her mom lost her dad it was there. When Hank talked about his wife, it was there.

She wasn't sure she could describe what *it* was, but Maeve knew that she wanted *it.*

She'd sensed a possibility of *it* with Aaron. But that was gone, as surely as if it had never been.

He was married.

Maybe that was okay with some women, but she wasn't one of them. She'd meant what she said—she respected herself far too much to put herself in that situation.

"Maeve, is everything okay?"

She turned and spotted Sophie's daughter standing behind her. The summer they met, Tori's hair had been a vivid blue, but today, there was only a streak of color in it. Tori must have noticed Maeve looking because she said, "People have told me that it was lucky I had blue in my hair for Sophie's wedding, and Mattie's, so I added it for Lily's. It'll wash out."

"I like it on you," she assured her young, sometimes assistant. "It was a beautiful wedding, wasn't it?" Maeve said, ignoring Tori's question.

The girl grinned. "Yeah, Lily and Sebastian look so happy."

Maeve put her arm around Tori and they both watched the newlyweds twirl around the dance floor. "They do, don't they?"

"And you and Aaron looked happy up until he kissed you."

Maeve swung back to Tori. "You saw that?"

"Everyone saw that," Tori assured her.

Maeve groaned. In a town like Valley Ridge, that meant even people not at the wedding would hear about it soon enough.

"And," Tori said slowly, "they saw you stop kissing and you get mad."

"Oh, wonderful. Becoming Valley Ridge gossip fodder was high on my to-do list." She knew that the talk wouldn't be malicious. People in town cared for each other. That was one of the beautiful things about Valley Ridge. But sometimes living in a fishbowl could be hard.

Tori nodded. "I get that. But look at it this way, if people want to know what's going on, they might show up at the house to help you renovate. I've been talking to a bunch of people about it. You might have a few extra helpers tomorrow."

"Really?" she asked.

"Maeve, I know I'm only a kid. I know that sometimes grown-ups think they know so much more than we do. But despite the fact that I'm only fifteen, we're friends, right? That means, I get to worry about you."

When she'd first met Tori, the girl had been angry. There wasn't a trace of it left. This sweet, caring girl was all she saw. "We did become friends but, sweetie, you don't need to worry about me. I'm a big girl and I can take care of myself."

"That's the problem," Tori said with a heartfelt sigh.

"What is?" Maeve asked.

"You think you can take care of yourself. But as your friend, I'm telling you that you don't have to do it all yourself. My dad grew up on a commune and he's always spouting off about community and taking a village to...well, he says raise a child, and then tells me with a child like me he needs more than a village's help. But you get what I'm saying."

"I need a village?" Maeve asked.

Tori held up a hand, as if to ward off an argument. "Listen, I won't press my luck. You're always the first one in line to help someone, but you're the last person to let people help you back. And, Maeve, you need to let people help you. Not only at the house, but at the library and maybe with Aaron."

"Maybe you're right." Maeve knew there was no maybe about it. Her parents, her boss, her friends...they'd all said as much, though not as directly as Tori was saying. "Okay, so there's no *maybe* about it. You're right. And there's so much to do at the house, of course, I'll take any help that's out there. But there's nothing between me and Aaron to help with."

"That kiss?" Tori asked, toying with the strand of blue in her hair. "Everyone saw that kiss and it wasn't 'nothing.'"

"It was an anomaly." She didn't kiss married men. Not ever.

"You're sure?" Tori asked.

"I'm absolutely positive there's nothing now, nor will there ever be anything between me and Aaron Holder."

Tori digested Maeve's declaration and nodded. "Okay. Well, then, let's go make the rounds and see if we can find you someone else to dance with."

"Listen, I'm not—" Maeve protested.

Tori interrupted her. "I'm not saying you have to suck face with him like you did Aaron, but you're not leaving here without hitting the dance floor with someone."

Which was why ten minutes later, Maeve found herself dancing with Dylan Long, who was wearing his police uniform. "You didn't want to buy a suit?" she teased. Dancing with Dylan was safe because they'd both become friends. Not friends who were looking for anything more with each other.

"I'd planned to change, but I left my suit on my couch. And we don't expect any trouble, but Lily's still nervous about her father showing up and harassing her mother. Vera served him the divorce papers last week. I didn't want to chance going back for my suit, so—"

"I was teasing, Dylan." He was a nice man. Valley Ridge had a three-man police department, and Dylan was the youngest and newest member of the small force, but he'd taken his role of protecting the town to heart.

He was a very nice man.

A man who should be easy to fall in love with.

And yet, she'd never felt the slightest urge to kiss him.

Not like she had with Aaron.

Dylan interrupted her thoughts by asking, "So, is Tori trying to fix you up, or me up?"

"Me," she said.

"Phew." He looked relieved.

"She's only a kid," Maeve assured him. "I don't think a big cop like you needs to be nervous about her."

"Yeah, she's only a kid. A kid who decided we should dance, and here we are on the dance floor dancing."

"You've got a point." She spotted Tori dancing with Joe on the other side of the small dance floor. "She does have a way of accomplishing what she sets out to do."

"I could bow to the inevitable and ask you out for dinner," Dylan offered.

"Dylan, you are so sweet, but..." She didn't know what else to say. She didn't know how to tell someone that she didn't feel any spark of chemistry with them. And she wanted that. She wanted more than someone nice, someone comfortable.

"Yeah, I saw you kiss Aaron, but then he left and I thought maybe..."

"It's not Aaron. Him and me, we're not going to happen," she said with certainty.

There were some things that were undisputable. The sun would rise tomorrow. The tides would come in and go out. And she wouldn't be kissing Aaron Holder again.

"Aaron and I aren't going to happen, but I'm pretty sure neither are we. I think if either of us had really been interested in the other, we wouldn't have needed a fifteen-year-old to fix us up. We're friends. And I treasure our friendship too much to throw it away by trying to chase after something that's not there. Someday soon you'll meet the right person."

"So, you're a romantic. You believe in soul mates and happily-ever-afters."

"Well, I don't know that I'd put it like that," she said slowly. She pushed thoughts of Aaron Holder teasing her about being a romantic away and concentrated on Dylan. "No, I wouldn't put it like that, but yes, I guess you're right. I think when I meet the right man, I'll know. Deep down, I'll know. I care about you too much to try to force something that isn't there, and ultimately ruin our friendship."

He nodded. "Well, as your friend, can I offer to come over and help at the house tomorrow?"

"Yes. I've been told by another certain bossy friend—" she nodded her head in Tori's direction "—that I need to let my friends help me. So yes, please come."

"Tori said that?"

She laughed and nodded. "She's like an eighty-year-old woman trapped in a fifteen-year-old's body."

"She's a force to be reckoned with," he agreed. "So what do you need for the house?"

"Everything. I originally thought it would only need a few gallons of paint and a good cleaning. I pictured doing it myself over a couple of weekends. I was very naive, and maybe overconfident in my abilities."

"What abilities?" he asked.

"Exactly—what abilities? I had delusions of ability from having watched *This Old House* for years."

Dylan smiled and said, "Did I ever tell you about my uncle's barn?"

There was a wicked gleam in his eye. "No, you haven't mentioned your uncle's barn."

"You've seen that television show on hoarders? His barn should be an episode. There has to be at least fifty years of stuff in it. He saves everything. And he was a contractor, so he saved things from all sorts of jobs."

Maeve kissed Dylan's cheek and squealed. "So, if I put together a list, do you think he'd let us go shopping?"

"It's not up to him. My aunt would practically pay you to come shopping."

Maeve squealed again, and then stopped abruptly when she spotted Sophie walking toward the restrooms. There was something in the way she was walking that gave Maeve pause. "Can I call you later? I have to go see a friend. But, thanks. I'll happily come shopping with you at your uncle's if he won't mind."

"He might, but my aunt will love you for it," Dylan assured her.

Before he could say anything else, Maeve hurried across the reception hall to the restrooms. She found Sophie coming out of a stall in the restroom. She looked pale.

Maeve's heart gave a little lurch. "Sophie, are you okay?"

For a long moment, Maeve wasn't sure Sophie was going to answer, but finally she said, "No. Not really. I've been having contractions since the ceremony started. I was hoping I could wait until after the reception, but I'm pretty sure my water broke."

"Since the ceremony? Oh, Sophie. You should have spoken up. Lily's going to be so mad that you didn't say anything." She was babbling. She didn't have a clue what to do when a woman was having a baby.

"Deep breath, Maeve. Babies take time. It was like that with Tori," Sophie said. "There's nothing else to do. I could go home, but I'd rather enjoy my friends. Though now I don't think this baby is going to wait until after the reception."

How on earth could Sophie be so calm? "Do you want me to get Colton? Lily and Mattie—"

"No, not Lily and Mattie. I don't want to take anything away from the wedding. I'm going to go out into the foyer. If you'd find Colton and point him that way..."

Maeve wasn't someone prone to hugging people, but this once she couldn't help herself. She hugged Sophie. "You're going to have a baby soon."

"Yes." Sophie laughed, then grimaced and took a deep breath. "Go get Colton."

"Right, I'm going." She sprinted toward the bathroom door.

"Maeve, slow down. Look relaxed. Look like you don't have a care in the world."

Maeve pasted a smile on her face and started a circuit around the packed hall. Once she'd gone a full circle, she found herself face-to-face with Aaron and sighed. "Have you seen Colton?" she asked.

"Why, so you can kiss him, too?" he asked angrily.

"What?"

"I saw you and the cop," he accused.

"That wasn't—" She stopped short. She had kissed Dylan, but it was just a peck. A friendly peck on the cheek. "Listen, I don't owe you an explanation. I'm unmarried and unattached, and as such can kiss whomever I want. It's only people who are married—even those who aren't *precisely* married—who shouldn't be kissing anyone. So, thank you anyway, I'll find Colton myself."

He sighed. "I saw him head into the kitchen with Finn."

"Thank you." She turned, wanting nothing more than to escape Aaron Holder.

"Is something wrong?" Aaron asked.

She turned and faced him. "Other than you're married and you kissed me, nothing at all." She started toward the kitchen.

"I'd like to explain," he called after her.

"I don't have time. But frankly, it doesn't matter what your explanation is, it won't change anything." She waved her hand over her back at him.

She found Colton and Finn in the kitchen like Aaron had said. She whispered in Colton's ear, "It's time. Sophie's waiting for you out in the foyer. She wants to keep it quiet so as not to interrupt the wedding."

"What's wrong?" Finn asked.

"It's time?" Colton repeated it like it was a question. "It's time," he said again, this time with more conviction.

"Time for what?" Finn asked, and then said, "Oh."

"Sophie wants to keep it quiet," she told the two men. "She doesn't want to distract from Lily and Sebastian's night."

"Yeah, like that's going to happen," Finn said. "This is Valley Ridge, a town where there's no such thing as a secret."

"I've gotta go," Colton said.

"Walk, don't run," Maeve warned. "And try to look casual."

What Colton did was as closely related to walking as jogging was related to sprinting. It was a walk, but a power walk. Certainly not a walk designed not to call attention to himself.

"Will someone call me when the baby gets here?" she asked Finn, sure that he was right, this wouldn't be kept quiet for long.

"Absolutely," he said.

She wished she could leave the reception, but she felt she should stay until closer to the end of things, especially now that Sophie and Colton had left.

"Did you hear about Sophie?" Tori asked. "Mom and Dad are going to take me to the hospital, but we'll be at the house tomorrow. I wanted to say good-night. I saw you dancing with Dylan." Tori looked as if she might pass out or burst from excitement.

"Breathe, Tori. And yes. Sophie sent me to find Colton for her, so I heard."

"And Dylan?" Tori pressed.

"He's a good guy, but he's not the one for me." Which was a shame. She genuinely liked Dylan. He was kind and funny, not to mention easy on the eyes, with those surfer good looks. But they just didn't click as a couple.

Tori nodded. "That's what I thought when I saw you two dancing. Maybe—"

Anxious to head off more matchmaking, Maeve interrupted. "Go. You'd better head to the hospital and wait for your baby brother. Will you text me when he arrives?"

"You'll be the first one." Tori hugged her, and then sprinted toward the door.

Maeve found a table in the corner and counted down the minutes until she could head for home. Watching Lily and Sebastian dancing, so obviously in love, she felt a pang of jealousy. Not that she begrudged them their happiness, but she longed to find someone who would love her like Sebastian obviously loved Lily.

Sometimes she wondered if she'd ever find that kind of love for herself.

CHAPTER NINE

MAEVE WANTED TO get a head start on the day. She went through her morning routine and was out the door before seven. There was a light on in the RV. She shut her door quietly, but Josie must have heard her. She'd barely gone two steps before her friend opened the door and waved her inside.

"Where are you going so early?" Josie asked as she took a seat on the small couch. She motioned for Maeve to join her.

Maeve hadn't prepared an excuse, and lying wasn't her forte. She struggled for a moment, and then said, "I'm going to help Gabriel with some inventory."

"You were walking. You can't walk all the way to Ripley."

"Uh, no. No, I can't. Of course I can't. I'm meeting him at the diner first. Gabriel's treating me to breakfast as a thank-you, and then he'll drive me to the winery."

"Oh. Do you have a few minutes to fill me in on the wedding? Boyd worked all day yesterday and I spent the day fantasizing about it."

"I'm so sorry the doctor nixed your going. Lily would have welcomed you."

"She did call and invite me, but although she's been lovely to me, this was a day for her close friends and family. Even if I could have gone, I wouldn't have. But that doesn't mean I don't want to hear about it."

Maeve allowed herself a few minutes and sat down next to Josie on the couch. She described Lily's dress, and Sophie's and Mattie's. She described the church and the reception. "Poinsettias will always remind me of Lily's wedding," she said. "It was perfect. And when she danced with Sebastian? The whole world seemed to stand still."

Josie's eyes narrowed. "I heard there was some excitement."

Maeve smiled. "*Excitement* is the exact word for it. Sophie went into labor at the reception. Tori texted me at two this morning. I should have said so immediately. It's a boy. Benjamin Sturgis. Both mother and baby are fine."

"Lucky lady." Josie's hands rested on her huge stomach. "I feel like I'm never going to give birth. I dreamed last night I was in a nursing home, still carrying this baby."

Maeve laughed. "I promise it won't be that long."

"You can promise. So can Boyd, but I'm not sure I'm buying it. We were so worried when I was pregnant with Carl. The whole pregnancy was fraught with problems. But this pregnancy has gone so well, until these past few weeks. And the doctor said the baby would probably be fine if he or she was born now, but it would be better if they waited the month."

"Sometime after Christmas you'll have this baby. And you'll forget all the waiting and worrying." She almost said *And a month will go by fast* but from Josie's expression, time was crawling by, so she said, "You've only got a few more weeks."

A few weeks sounded much better than *a month.*

Josie sighed. "A few weeks isn't so bad, plus Dr. Marshall promises that I can get back to a normal routine soon. I remember when I was young, time seemed to slow to a standstill at Christmas. Turns out, the same time distortion happens when you're pregnant."

"Can I do anything to help?" Maeve asked. Josie seemed down today, and though they hadn't been friends for long, that wasn't the norm. "I mean it, tell me what would make it easier on you."

"Don't look so worried. I'm fine. It's just one of my feeling-as-big-as-a-house days. You've distracted me. I'm going to imagine the wedding, and finish my present for Benjamin." She held up a crocheted blanket. "I want to finish the hat. It looks like an owl when it's all done. And there're booties, but those go very quick. When they're done, would you take them to Sophie?"

Maeve looked forward to having an excuse to go see the baby. "I would be happy to." She stood. "I've got to get going or I'll be late."

"One more thing before you go?"

Maeve nodded. "Yes?"

"You told me everything about the wedding...everything except the fact that you kissed two men."

Maeve sank back down on the couch and looked at Josie whose expression seemed innocent, although a sparkle danced in her eyes. She was new to town. How could she be part of the Valley Ridge grapevine already? "Seriously, you heard about that? How?"

"Well, JoAnn and I hit it off at the library and she stopped by after the wedding to check on me, and she might have mentioned it."

Maeve sighed. "Really. It's ridiculous how things get blown out of proportion around here. I did kiss two men. A peck on the cheek for both Aaron, who'd asked me to dance, and one for Dylan who is doing me a favor."

Both statements were true. Not mentioning that Aaron had kissed her afterward wasn't a lie, it was an omission.

Josie was silent, waiting, her focus on Maeve.

Maeve threw in the towel and admitted defeat. "You are going to be such a great mother when Carl and this new baby get bigger. You can holler with just your eyes."

Josie still didn't say anything.

"Fine." She wasn't used to someone taking such an interest in her goings-on, much less insisting she talk about them. "So, Aaron kissed me after I kissed his cheek. Then we got in a fight."

"Did you fight because you didn't want him to kiss you?"

"Yes. No. Well, maybe, but it turns out, Aaron's married."

Josie didn't say anything, but her mom-look gave way to a murderous look that didn't bode well for Aaron Holder.

"It's fine," Maeve added hastily. She had no clue why she was protecting him. "He said he wasn't 'precisely' married. I'm not sure what that means. It struck me as one of those black or white issues. You are or you aren't. Anyway, I let him know in no uncertain terms that I don't date, much less kiss, married men."

She'd tried to think of any and all excuses for Aaron as she tossed and turned last night. Maybe he'd married someone to get them a green card. Maybe he'd married someone who went into witness protection and now he couldn't get a hold of them to get the divorce papers signed. Maybe he'd married someone after a drunken night in Vegas and didn't know who they were in order to divorce them. Maybe...

She wanted a logical explanation, but nothing felt plausible.

"Did you ask him to explain?" Josie asked.

"No. Sophie went into labor, and then..." Maeve shrugged. "There was really nothing left to say after that."

Josie took Maeve's hand and gave it a squeeze. "I'm sorry."

"Don't be. Someday I'll find my someone. I know what love should look like, and Aaron wasn't it."

"You're sure? I've seen you two together and I thought there was potential there."

"I'm positive." If she was honest, she had thought that maybe they had something special, but that was squelched the second he'd told her he was

233

married. "I've got to run. But if you need anything today, you text me. I can be here quickly."

"Thank you." Before Maeve got up, Josie hugged her. Josie's huge stomach pressed against Maeve's and she felt the baby kick.

Josie pulled back from the hug. "He's going to be a gymnast, I swear. Do you want to feel?"

She'd never actually felt a pregnant woman's stomach. It always felt like a cheeky request. Maeve nodded, and let Josie guide her hand to a spot. She felt a series of kicks or moves. "Wow."

"I know. When they first start moving, it's amazing. But at this point in the pregnancy, I want him or her to settle down. I'm pretty sure he's bruised a rib."

"That's awesome. Not that he bruised a rib, but the whole baby thing." Someday, she'd like kids, but maybe it wasn't in the cards. Maybe she'd stay in Valley Ridge and express her maternal urges toward the kids who came to the library.

She looked at the clock on the other wall of the RV. "I really have to go. But I'll stop back in and see you tonight. And, Josie, thanks for being on my side."

"We're friends. Even after Boyd and I leave, you and I will be friends. I'll always be on your side. And Aaron Holder better watch out."

Maeve felt warm in the glow of Josie's friendship.

If Josie got her hands on Aaron, he was in real trouble. That shouldn't make her feel better, but strangely enough, it did.

* * *

Aaron was in real trouble. He'd brought five dozen doughnuts to the Culpepper house thinking it would be plenty, but as he looked around at the number of people who'd come to help Maeve, he didn't think it would be enough. The house was alive with the sound of hammers, a circular saw that Finn had brought in and the hum of conversation.

This house that had sat vacant for so long was suddenly alive. He wanted to find Maeve, stand by her side and savor the feeling.

And Maeve was at the house. But standing by her side wasn't in the cards because she was anywhere but where he was.

Everyone was buzzing about Sophie and Colton's new son. He knew without asking that the boy was named Benjamin Sturgis—two family names. He knew the baby was twenty-one and a half inches long, and weighed eight pounds and ten ounces.

He also knew that was a huge baby for someone as petite as Sophie to deliver.

Aaron knew all this without asking because every other person working in the house wanted to know if he'd heard about the baby, then, even after he assured them that he had, they would give him all the details again.

The fact that seemed to delight everyone the most was that the baby was born at 11:59 p.m., which meant that he was born on the same day Lily and Sebastian got married.

235

Aaron heard from more than one person how special that was because Sophie and Colton shared an anniversary with Mattie and Finn, and now their baby shared a birthday with Lily and Finn's anniversary.

He started taking down the dining room chandelier, which would have looked totally at home in some '70s disco.

"Those three couples seemed destined to be tied together," Stan, the former mayor, told him. "They all fell in love at Sophie and Colton's first almost-wedding. It was destiny."

It was on the tip of Aaron's tongue to call the retired mayor a romantic, like he'd called Maeve, but before he could, Stan said, "Yeah, I know how I sound. I blame Maeve. I joined the girls' romance book club at the library. Oh, hell, don't tell them I called them girls. Women. I meant women. Anyway, they've got me hooked on HEAs."

"HEAs?" He unscrewed the bulbs and handed them down to Stan.

Stan nodded. "HEA, short for happily-ever-after. It's a must in a romance. There's something nice about reading a book and knowing you'll be happy at the end."

"You read romance?" Aaron couldn't imagine admitting that he read romance in public. He'd like to think he was secure in his masculinity but there were limits.

He eyed the metal cover that hid the chandelier's wire and began to unscrew it.

The older man laughed. "Yes. And while you might scoff, I've learned a lot about how women think. And what they think about it. My first wife, bless her soul, would have loved the fact that I read them. Romance is a genre most men run scared from, so the meetings are all women. All women and me. I either learned enough from reading, or improved my odds enough that I'm dating again. Well, *dating* is a strong word. We're neither one in a place for that. *Keeping company* is a better description."

Aaron had heard that Stan had gone out with Vera, Lily's mother, once or twice. "Congratulations."

"I only mention it because maybe you could learn a thing or two about women if you read a romance or two. After that kiss, then the fight with Maeve, you could use some help. That girl has a bit of a temper, and more than that, she has a streak of pride that's a mile wide."

"How did you—"

The retired mayor shook his head. "Well, last night, most everyone at the reception saw you kiss Maeve. And most noticed the fight after. Right now, you're in the calm before the storm because they're all focused on the new baby. But you can bet that they'll come back around to you and Maeve in a day or two."

Aaron handed the rest of the fixture down to Stan. The power was still off to the living room and dining room, but to be on the safe side, he used the voltage meter to test before he began to disconnect

237

the wires. "I live in Orlando and it's nothing like this."

"Florida is full of transient residents. Snowbirds, vacationers. This is Valley Ridge and the people who are here are here for the long haul. We were born here. We went to school here. We work and farm here. We're lifers. And Maeve's one of our own. We care about her and we're watching you."

What had started like a friendly conversation was ending like a mafia movie. Aaron realized that he was being warned. "I'll keep that in mind, sir."

"You do that, boy." Then the romance-reading former mayor smacked Aaron's back and went off to spackle the drywall in the master bedroom.

Someone else smacked his back as he stared after Stan. Aaron turned and found Finn Wallace grinning at him. "So, the mayor gave you the I've-got-my-eyes-on-you line?"

"It was more like he warned me that the entire town has their eyes on me." Aaron suddenly felt very vulnerable here at the house, where people wandered in to work then left. Most checked in with him, but now he felt they were checking him out, as well.

"We'll he's not wrong," Finn said slowly. "We all saw the kiss and then the fight."

Aaron felt as if he needed to explain. "I—"

Finn held up a hand. "No, don't tell me. Really, I might have been born here, but I spent a lot of years in Buffalo. I had a condo there. I could recognize my nearest neighbors to wave at them, but I didn't know any of their names, and I

238

certainly didn't know, or care, about who they kissed or fought with. But I'm not in Buffalo and neither are you—"

"Florida," Aaron corrected. "I'm not in Florida." Florida—the sunshine state. Where his lanai sat unused. It was snowing again today in Valley Ridge. He was pretty sure it wasn't snowing in Florida.

"Florida. And here in Valley Ridge, people do care. It's the blessing and the curse of a small town. And everyone in town cares about Maeve."

Before Aaron could think of anything to say to that, Finn added, "Make it right. Say you're sorry or whatever you need to say, but make it right. I know that not every woman's as simple to understand as Mattie is...well, Mattie didn't always seem simple."

"But she is now?" Aaron asked. He grew up in a house full of women, and he'd never found any of them to be simple.

Finn got a weird smile. "Yes. Take Christmas for instance. Some men worry about buying jewelry or other stuff. You know what one of my presents is for Mattie? I guarantee, no matter what else I give her, it will be her favorite."

"What?" Aaron still had his family to shop for and he'd take any hints for gifts he could get.

"The Sunday paper," Finn said. "I can't promise every Sunday, because some days I'm on call, but when I'm home, I am giving her a year of Sundays hiding out in the bedroom with a carafe of coffee and the paper before church. I will feed the rabble and get them dressed for church. And unless you've ever tried to herd cats, you can't imagine what that entails."

"And that'll be her favorite present?" Aaron wasn't sure any of the women in his family would think that was the best present ever.

Finn didn't look the least bit worried. "I guarantee it. But what I'm trying to say is, talk to Maeve, listen to what she says, and maybe even more importantly, listen to what she doesn't say. Pay attention. Women like that."

With that sage advice, Finn pushed his glasses up on his nose and walked away humming *Waltzing Mathilda,* if Aaron wasn't mistaken.

He'd barely recovered from Finn's conversation and was eyeing the chandelier wires when Maeve's mother came up to him and shoved a finger in his chest. "You."

"Me?" He tried to sound as if he had no idea why Renie was *you*-ing, but he knew.

She shook her head. "I know everyone else in town is caught up in the baby news, but I'm not everyone. I am Maeve's mother." Renie took a deep breath as if to calm herself. "Now, I know Maeve is an adult and she wouldn't welcome my interfering, so I'm not going to interfere, and if she asks you, I'd appreciate you telling her that I didn't interfere. But I'm going to say this. If you hurt her..." She didn't say any more. She just gave him a fierce look.

Well, he knew it was supposed to be fierce. But as much as Maeve had the temper of a stereotypical redhead, her mother didn't. He didn't think Renie Lorei had a fierce bone in her body. But he knew that was the look she intended, and so he tried to look sufficiently cowed and nodded.

Then, as if to emphasize how un-fierce she was, she kissed his cheek. "I'm sorry I had to get tough with you. Now, I'm going to go wallpaper the bathroom."

I know everyone's talking about the baby, but...

If Aaron heard that phrase, or a variation of that phrase, once, he heard it a hundred times during the course of the day. According to everyone, they'd all witnessed the kiss and the fight. The fight that had grown to epic proportions by some people's accounts.

Aaron had been offered motherly advice.

Aaron had been offered friendly advice.

Aaron had been offered guy advice.

Aaron had been offered a woman's perspective.

And more than once, Aaron had received Godfather-esque warnings.

What it came down to was that Maeve Buchanan was part of this town. Probably more a part of it than she realized. And the townspeople took a real interest in her well-being.

He wished he could talk to her and try to explain, but not only was she avoiding him, there was no way he was opening himself up to even more gossip by having that discussion in public.

He ordered in pizzas from North East Pizza for lunch, but couldn't bring himself to eat with everyone.

Instead, he carried garbage bags from the back porch to the Dumpster.

On his second trip, he felt something whack his shin. "What the—" He cut off the expletive and turned to see who was there to read him the riot act this time.

Tori, wearing jeans and a T-shirt that announced CSA: America's Farming Future, glared at him.

He knew why she was there, but in the hopes of staving off yet another lecture, he tried, "Isn't it too cold to be out here in only a T-shirt? I know I'm from Florida and you all think I have thin blood, but seriously, I don't think it's even hit thirty today. You're going to catch a cold."

"Colds are caused by viruses, not by being out in a T-shirt in cold weather. Plus, it's a long-sleeved T-shirt."

"What's CSA stand for?" he asked, feeling encouraged. She hadn't started her lecture yet, maybe she'd forget.

"Community Supported Agriculture, though I've heard it called Community Sustained, too." She didn't miss a beat as she said, "I might be a kid, but I know what you're doing and I'm not falling for it. What did you do to Maeve?"

"If you know what I'm doing, why would you ask? Because if I'm avoiding your third degree, like you think I am, there's no way I'm going to answer. I'll try to deflect your rather impertinent question. You're a child. I'm an adult. Maeve's an adult. We've got it handled."

She stamped her foot, acting her age for the first time since he'd met her. "Aaron, you and I both know there's no deflecting me. Ask my parents what happened when they tried to keep me from finding out about my birth mother. So, I'll ask again, what did you do?"

"I threw some garbage into the Dumpster," he said, playing obtuse.

She took a deep breath and seemed to be counting. Then she slowly said, "No, last night at the wedding. I saw the kiss and then..." She didn't go into detail, but she kicked him again. "What did you do?"

"Listen, I appreciate the fact that you care about Maeve—that the whole town cares about Maeve. But I'm not explaining myself to you." He'd have liked to believe he was saying that because he didn't owe Tori any details, but the truth of it was, he just didn't like those details.

Tori gave him a look that was far fiercer than Renie could ever have managed.

He didn't respond.

Her eyes darted from him to some point beyond him.

"Tori?"

He turned and saw what she was looking at. Who she was looking at.

Maeve.

"What is going on? Why did you kick Aaron?" Maeve seemed annoyed and she was far more intimidating than Tori.

"I don't know what he did to you last night, but he'd better fix it, or else."

Maeve took the girl by her shoulders and said, "Tori, you know that I love our friendship, but, honey, I'm a grown-up and I can fight my own battles. When there is a battle. And I'm not saying there is a battle."

"But he..." Tori must have seen something in Maeve's look, because she sighed. "Fine."

"No more kicking. I'd think I'd have to warn Abbey or Mica that kicking isn't a good option, not you."

Tori looked at some indistinct point on the floor. "Fine."

"Your mom and dad are looking for you."

"They probably want to go see Sophie and Ben before we leave for Ohio." She threw her arms around Maeve.

He saw Maeve hesitate a moment, then hug the girl back.

"We're coming back down next week." Tori shot him a look over Maeve's shoulder and he knew that her comment had been meant for him. A reminder that she'd be back and she expected him to fix things with Maeve before then.

"Great. I'll see you then." Tori ran back inside and Maeve remained standing next to the Dumpster. She didn't have a coat on, either. What was it with Northern women? He'd put a coat on before braving the walk from the house to the Dumpster. He thought about mentioning it, but after Tori's reaction, he decided not to.

"So, rough morning?" she asked. She didn't seem annoyed, but rather, concerned.

"A lot of people turned out to help," he said, avoiding her question.

She tilted her head slightly and narrowed her eyes. "And most of them have had words for you?"

"I wasn't sure you even noticed I was here."

She sighed. "I did. How could I not? But I'd hoped to avoid more gossip by avoiding you."

"Yeah, that's not working so well," he admitted.

"I can see that."

"You've got a lot of friends in town."

She shrugged, and he wasn't sure she really understood how important she was to the community. "Half the town came to tell me to fix things with you, the other half warned me that if I hurt you, they'd take care of me."

"No one's going to hurt you," Maeve said. "But no matter how much you want, you can't fix the fact that you're married and you kissed me."

He wasn't sure how to explain himself to her, mainly because even after two years, he didn't understand what had happened to his marriage. Why it had fallen apart. "It's not like that. I'm one signature away from being divorced."

"And how soon will that signature come?" she asked.

"I don't know. It's..."

"Complicated, I'm sure. Divorcing someone normally is, not that I've had personal experience, but how could it not be? That being said, I don't kiss married men. Even if they're only one signature away."

"I know. I don't, either. Not kiss married men, but get involved with someone else while I'm technically still married. I don't... I've never..."

"Listen, Aaron, you obviously have things you need to work out. Let's just say we're friends. We'll work together on this house, and on starting the foundation. Spring will arrive, your uncle will come back and you'll leave." She shot him a look of sympathy.

He'd have preferred her anger. "You'd like that, right?"

"What?"

"If that's how it went down. If I agreed to be friendly with you until I leave. You know, you didn't even ask me about the married part. About the circumstances. Don't you want know?"

She shook her head. "No, I don't need to know the circumstances because they don't matter. You're married. Period."

"The details do matter. They really do. I agree with you, you know—married is married. But I've been separated from my wife for two years. I have our final divorce papers sitting on the desk right now. She's already signed them. So I meant what I said, I am one signature away from being divorced."

"But the fact is, you haven't signed them and you're still married."

"Black-and-white," he said. "That's how you're going to see this."

"There are no grays with marriage," she said primly. "You're either married, or you're not."

"Maeve, I made this so easy on you. You can push me away and not even try to find some excuse to hide behind."

"Excuse me?" she asked.

"You are the loneliest person I've ever met."

"Are you kidding? I'm surrounded by people all day. At the winery. The library. Now here." She pointed back at the very full house. "How can I be lonely?"

"Because while you might be surrounded by people, you don't let any of them in. How many people in town know you were homeless?"

She shrugged. "A few."

"How many?"

"My mom, Herm, Hank, you..." She paused, looking as if she was struggling to come up with another name. "My principal. Mrs. Anderson knew."

Aaron shook his head. "You hold yourself apart. You don't share, and because you don't, other people who like you very much, stay half a step back. Sharing is a two way street."

"Wow, for a man who's been on the verge of divorcing for two years, you have a lot of wise observations. If you have those papers on your desk, why haven't you signed them? Maybe you're saying I keep myself apart because so do you. Like recognizes like. There's an old saying about a man seeing a pebble in another's eye and never noticing the boulder in his own. I'm not pointing fingers, but, Aaron, don't blink too hard."

"I think it was a log, not a pebble. Maybe a plank?" Picking on her word choice was easier than acknowledging she was right.

She shrugged. "Fine. Log. Boulder. Whatever. You've got issues, too, Aaron."

"And what will you do if I deal with those issues? If I sign the papers and I'm officially divorced. What will you do then?"

"There's more to it than just signing the papers, isn't there? And I don't know that you can move forward until you look backward and figure out what went wrong. I think my plan is a wise one. Let's be friends."

She was the most infuriating woman he'd ever met. The loneliest woman he'd ever met. And every part of him wanted to pull her into his arms and kiss her again. But he wouldn't because she was right; he wasn't free to do so. So, he'd help her renovate the house because it mattered to her. And the fact that it mattered to her made it matter to him.

He wanted to please her.

Maybe that's what had been missing in his marriage. He'd cared about his work more than he'd cared about his wife and what mattered to her. And for the first time in two years, he didn't feel as angry when he thought about his failed marriage, he felt guilty.

Aaron realized he had a lot of thinking to do. He looked at Maeve and smiled. "Then as your friend, I'll heed your advice and try and deal with my baggage. Maybe you should consider doing the same."

"But—"

He turned and walked away from her because if he didn't, good intentions or not, he was going to kiss her again.

* * *

I<small>T WAS AFTER</small> nine before the last person left the Culpepper house. Maeve wasn't sure she could face going into her quiet house. The light was on again at Josie's. She didn't know she'd made a decision until she was at the door knocking softly.

A moment later, Josie opened the door.

"I'm sorry. It's late. I saw the light, but obviously...I shouldn't be here." She started to turn around and head home.

"Don't be silly. Come in," Josie said. "Boyd and Carl are both down for the count. I was sitting out here, definitely not sleeping. I could use the distraction. I think the baby has more than bruised my ribs. I think they've actually cracked."

Josie patted the couch for a second time that day and asked, "So, what's wrong?"

Maeve wasn't sure why she was there. She wasn't the type to complain to a friend. She felt awkward and uncomfortable. "Really, I shouldn't have come. You've got enough on your plate without me whining—"

"Maeve, you are the least whiny person I've ever met, and I never have so much on my plate that I can't listen to a friend," Josie said. "What is it?"

Maeve thought about what Aaron had said, and before she could second-guess herself, she said, "I was homeless, too. When I was in school. My father died, we lost the farm and Mom and I lived in the car for weeks. Then Hank found out and gave us the apartment behind his house. The one Lily lived in, and her mom lives in now. Hank gave Mom a job at the diner. That's where she met Herm. But we lost everything, and then Hank helped us and we bounced back." Maeve didn't know what to say after her confession. She settled on, "I wanted you to know I get what you're going through, and that's why I helped you."

"Okay, but I'd bet that even if you'd never been homeless, you'd still have helped us. That's not what's been eating at you. Tell me. What's going on?"

"Aaron says I'm the loneliest person he's ever met." She wished she were Tori's age and he was there because she'd kick him in the shins, as well. The mental image was enough to make her relax a little. "I laughed and said I'm surrounded by people all day, but he told me that didn't matter."

"Maeve, we're friends, right?" Josie asked. "I mean, I know we haven't known each other a long time, but we're friends. When I leave, we'll talk on the phone, and visit. Because we're friends. That's why you're here, right?"

Maeve nodded.

"Then I'm going to speak to you like a friend. Like I'd talk to a sister if I had one. Aaron's right. I know that's not what you want to hear, but there it is. I haven't been here long, but I've got nothing to do all day but watch and observe. You are surrounded every day by people. People who care about you. People you care about. People you hold at arm's length. And if you hold them at arm's length, they can't really get to know you...and you can't really get to know them, either."

"I'm here talking to you," Maeve said.

Josie nodded. "I think that's because I'm safe. Boyd and I will be leaving. You and I, we can make a connection, but you know there's an expiration date. We'll keep in touch, but I won't get too close. I won't make you uncomfortable."

Maeve flopped back on the couch. "So, what you're saying is I'm hopeless."

"No, what I'm saying is, now that you're aware of the problem, change. Let other people in. And I'm not just talking about letting them help you with the library and stuff. I mean, really let them in."

"I tried to avoid Aaron today, but he caught up with me. He tried to explain the kiss and his being married."

Josie went from looking friendly and considerate to looking downright dangerous. "It better be good," she muttered.

"It's been two years, he said. He said the divorce papers are on his desk and he only has to sign his name, and then he won't be married anymore. But he hasn't done it. They're on his desk, but he hasn't signed them."

Josie looked considerably happier. She gave a little sigh. "We'll that's not quite as bad as I was thinking. I liked him, and I didn't like thinking that he was less of a man than I'd thought. But I wouldn't kiss him again until he's signed the papers."

"I'm not kissing him again, period," Maeve stated with utter certainty.

She waited, expecting another lecture from Josie, but instead of a lecture, Josie asked, "Did I ever tell you about the first time Boyd and I kissed?" She wore a small smile that said the memory was a sweet one.

"No, you didn't."

"It was when we were in kindergarten. He came up to me one day and said I smelled like oranges, then kissed me on the cheek. I slugged him and we both got sent to time-out. He steered clear of me for a long time after that, and I had to wait until high school until he kissed me again. Well, frankly, I kissed him."

"Your point is?" Maeve asked.

"I don't think it's going to be nearly that long until Aaron kisses you again." Josie was grinning.

Before Maeve could come up with some sort of retort, the door at the back of the RV opened and Boyd came out wearing flannel pajama bottoms and a football T-shirt. He looked so much younger, sleep tousled and worried. "I heard voices. Is everything okay, honey? Is it the baby?"

"The baby's fine. Everything is fine, honey. Maeve's keeping me company. You can go back to sleep."

"Thanks, Maeve. 'Night." He waved and stumbled back into the bedroom, shutting the door behind him.

Josie stared at the door, and then turned back to Maeve. "Normally, you could drive a semi next to the bed and Boyd wouldn't wake up. He must be sleeping lighter because of the baby. He's still worried about me. I tell him that each day brings us a day closer. Dr. Marshall said everything is looking good."

"It'll be soon."

Josie rubbed her stomach. "I'd say not soon enough, but I'm really hoping the baby waits a bit longer. Boyd's got work tomorrow at Aaron's. That's thanks to you."

"No, that's thanks to Aaron." There were so many things about Aaron she liked. The fact that he'd found work for Boyd was one of them. The time he was spending working on the house, and the fact that he'd donated it to her foundation—she liked that, too.

But he was married, she reminded herself. Until he signed those papers, he was married.

As if she was reading Maeve's mind, Josie said, "You came here because we're friends and you want my honest advice, right?"

Maeve wasn't sure she wanted anyone's advice, but she found herself saying, "Yes."

"As soon as Aaron's signed those papers, kiss him again. Kiss him and don't stop kissing him." She paused and added, "And I suspect he'll be signing them soon."

"I don't know."

"My mom used to say, in for a penny, in for a pound, so I've got one more piece of advice," Josie said. "Let other people in, Maeve. When Boyd and I leave, let someone else get close to you. You're surrounded by people who care—people who are just waiting for you to take a step in their direction. Just take that step, Maeve."

She thought about Gabriel's comment the other day, about her not saying much about her personal life. Then Aaron. Now Josie. There had to be some truth in what they were saying. "I'll try."

"So, I finished that romance novel for the book club tomorrow," Josie said. "Maybe that's what you need?"

"I already finished the book. It was a good one."

"No, I didn't mean the book, at least not specifically. And yes it was good. What I'm talking about is the romance aspect of it. You need a good romance."

Maeve groaned. "You and Tori."

"Tori and I are right. When Aaron's signed the papers, kiss him." Josie went on, talking about the book, about the baby, about Boyd's job. And Maeve made a conscious effort to share. To not hold back.

And she realized that as she sat talking with Josie into the wee hours of the night, she didn't feel the least bit lonely.

CHAPTER TEN

MAEVE SURVEYED THE library on Monday night. The romance book club had drawn another good crowd. Winters were long and cold on the shores of Lake Erie, so all of the winter book clubs were usually well attended. People were looking for places to go and things to do.

Lily wasn't there because she was on her honeymoon, and Sophie was at home with baby Ben. But Josie had come again—under strict orders from Boyd not to move from the couch. He'd assured them all that he and Carl had important boy things to do.

Josie smiled indulgently. "And by boy things, he means they're going to watch the train in the Quarter's window for a while, and then they're going home to watch football. Boyd is trying to teach Carl to like watching sports because he's created a majority-rules rule for the television. He's hoping this new baby is a boy so that I'll be even more outnumbered, but he assures me even if it is a girl, he's going to brainwash her, too." Josie heaved an exaggerated sigh, but Maeve could tell she was okay with the idea of being outnumbered.

Mattie was there, plus about fifteen other people. They had all read *The Secret Santa Club,* which combined the holiday and a handful of short romances.

"I liked the idea of turning the term *Secret Santa* into a verb. *Secret-Santaing* people," Josie said when the meeting got rolling. "And I liked that all the short stories were different. Sometimes the lead characters were the recipients, sometimes the giver."

"Oh, I hadn't thought of it, but I liked that *Secret-Santaing* became a verb, too," Maeve put in.

Josie was on a roll. "I liked that the recipient wasn't always in financial need. I mean, that's a big thing. But sometimes the people most in need don't need money, or things. They need love. They need to feel as if people care. Sometimes they have to learn to open themselves up to what's all around them and let people in." She eyed Maeve.

Maeve got her point and rolled her eyes at Josie, who grinned. She'd been thinking about what her friends had said and had come to the conclusion that they were right. She'd tried to figure out why she cut herself off. It had started after she'd lost both her father and her home. She'd been so afraid that people would pity her that she'd kept her homelessness a secret. She'd stayed a bit removed from others. After a while, it became her standard.

"I agree," a voice said from behind her. "Some people need to open themselves up and see who's around them, waiting to be let in."

Maeve didn't need to turn around to know who it was. Aaron pulled a chair over beside Mayor Tuznik and announced, "Us guys need to stick together."

Maeve lost track of the discussion after that, which thankfully took on a life of its own.

What was he doing here?

Aaron kept giving her odd looks throughout the course of the discussion and she studiously tried to avoid looking at him.

She busied herself after the meeting, trying to avoid Aaron. It wasn't all that hard, since everyone was mingling over the cookies and punch she had put out.

Mattie waved her over, which was fine since Aaron was across the room sitting with Josie.

"Hey, what's up?" Maeve asked. "Did you see Sophie today?"

"I did. She's doing well, and so is the baby. I know I might be biased, but Ben is one of the most beautiful babies I've ever seen."

"I don't think boys are supposed to be beautiful," Maeve teased.

"Don't tell Colton, but this one definitely is." She laughed and then turned serious. "Are you okay? You don't seem like yourself."

"I'm fine," Maeve said and realized her response was exactly what Josie was talking about. Her first instinct was to leave it at that, but she forced herself to add, "Sorry. That's not quite accurate. I'm okay, but I'm not sure how to act around Aaron." There. She'd made a personal remark and was still standing.

"Yeah, the kiss and the subsequent fight have been making the rounds." Mattie grinned. "It's not

257

every day *you* are the focus of the Valley Ridge gossip mill."

Maeve groaned. "It's worse than Twitter."

"Do you want to talk about what happened, what he did to upset you?" Mattie asked. It was a genuine offer based on concern, not some need to gossip.

Maeve actually kind of did want to talk, but she still hesitated. "Thanks, not right now."

"Well, if you don't want to talk about it, would you like me to take care of him for you? I grew up with Ray and Rich, and the kids have been giving me a refresher course in wrestling. Aaron might be big, but I could take him out if you wanted."

Maeve smiled, which she knew had been Mattie's intent. "No, it's fine. I feel awkward. I don't tend to go around kissing men, and I don't know what the protocol is after."

"There's no right or wrong, Maeve." Mattie paused, and then said, "But it's not easy feeling as if everyone's watching you. I think the entire town was placing bets on when I'd pack up and leave."

"I never thought you would." Maeve grew up watching Mattie and her best friend Bridget. They took friendship to a level closer to sisterhood. When Bridget got sick, Maeve had known with utter certainty that Mattie would come back. And when Bridget passed away, she hadn't been surprised that Mattie stayed to take care of her kids.

Mattie took her hand and gave it a squeeze. "You were one of the few. But you've got to ignore the gossip and everyone's advice. You need to follow your gut. If you really don't think things with Aaron will work, don't let anyone try to talk you into fixing them."

Maeve thought Mattie was done, but she added, "There's a saying. *A friend knows where the body's buried. A good friend helps you dig the hole.* You're a good friend, Maeve. If he gives you problems, remember, you have friends who will help dig the hole if you need us to."

Maeve laughed. "I doubt it will come to that, but thank you."

If she'd told Mattie she was okay, Mattie would have let it go at that. But because she'd opened up Mattie had offered to help bury someone. Maeve was definitely feeling a warm glow at the offer.

"Not to change the subject," Mattie said, "but Josie and Boyd don't know what's going on with the house still?"

"I don't think they have a clue. I'm not sure that they'll stay or that they'll even want the place, but if it's not for them, then someone else will take it. Aaron's helping me with the paperwork so we can turn this into an official foundation. Something we can do every year. I like the idea of it being a Valley Ridge Christmas tradition."

"Finn and I will be at the Culpepper place on Saturday, but if you don't mind, I'd like to do some outdoor work. I know the porch was fixed, and they put new shingles on the roof. But all those trees need pruning."

"You can work wherever you want."

"Are you going to ask why?" Mattie asked.

"Do you want me to?"

Mattie nodded.

"Why do you want to prune trees, Mattie?"

"I'm pregnant."

Maeve started to hug her, but Mattie whispered, "Be cool. We're not telling anyone about Jack for a few more weeks, but if I didn't tell someone, I'd explode. And I didn't want you to think I was slacking, but there are all those paint fumes inside, and I don't want to take a chance."

"Jack?" Maeve asked.

"That's what Finn and I are calling the baby. It works for a boy or a girl. Jackson. Jacqueline. Either way, it's going to be Jack. We like how androgynous it is."

"Of course you do." Maeve grinned. "Congratulations. I'm so happy for you and Finn. We've all known from the moment Finn started spending so much time in town that you're such a perfect couple—"

Mattie snorted. "Definitely not perfect. He was spending time in town because he was suing me for custody."

Maeve liked to complain about how quickly news spread in Valley Ridge, but this particular piece of news had never reached her. "Pardon?"

"Don't say anything, please. But he was. And we spent time together for the kids' sake, and gradually, so gradually I hardly noticed it was happening, I fell in love with him."

Maeve didn't know what to say to that.

"Listen, love isn't always like tonight's stories. Sometimes it's messy. Sometimes it's unexpected. Sometimes it's easy. No matter how it comes about, it's worth fighting for. Thanks for letting me tell you about the baby."

"Thanks for trusting me. I won't tell anyone about Jack until you do."

Mattie nodded. "Now, why don't you send me a list of things you still need at the house. I'll remind folks at the coffee shop."

"I can't tell you how much I appreciate that, Mattie."

"Maeve, you've done so much for the community. We were all talking about it the other night. You've got such a vision for the town. Sebastian was saying that he wants to get your advice on what other things need to be done. But before you get any more involved, you should let others help more. Lead the way, and we'll follow. You don't have to thank me, or any of us for that. You're the one we should all thank."

Maeve felt heat rising in her cheeks. One of the big problems with being a redhead with a fair complexion was that she blushed easily.

Mattie laughed. "You're awesome. We all think so."

"I—"

Mattie interrupted, "My mother always says, when someone offers you a compliment, just say thank-you."

Maeve laughed. "Thank you. But you're—"

"Stop at the thank-you, Maeve."

Aaron came up and joined them. "Can we talk a moment?"

He looked tired, but she refused to worry about him. "After the book club," she said. Mattie glared at Aaron.

"Don't forget my offer, Maeve," she said, before she stalked off.

"Her offer?" he asked.

Maeve wasn't about to tell him about the body. "Mattie asked me to make a list of what we need for the Culpepper place. She'll keep it at the coffee shop. She's coming with Finn this weekend to help."

She turned and went back to the group and concentrated on giving Aaron a wide berth. As the meeting wound down, ex-Mayor Tuznik was one of the last to leave. He came up and whispered, "Go easy on the boy. I'm not asking what happened, but he's obviously on the losing end of things. He was snubbed all night."

"I didn't ask... I don't want..."

He gave her a hug. "I know. But that's how things go in Valley Ridge. You're ours. He's an outsider. You win, no questions asked."

She thought about Mattie's mom's advice and said, "Well, thank you. But could you spread the word that he didn't do anything that warrants a snubbing?"

The former mayor nodded and winked.

Maeve looked around the room and realized that she and Aaron were the only people left. He was already stacking chairs. "Thanks, but you don't have to do that."

"Listen, I won't keep you. I know you've had a long day... I just wanted to say, I signed the papers."

"How long had you had them?" She concentrated on adding another chair to her stack rather than look at Aaron.

"Awhile," he admitted. "I don't want you to think it was a rebound kiss. My wife...my ex and I have been separated for two years."

"That you've been separated that long should make me feel better, but it doesn't. There must still be something there between the two of you if you've had the divorce papers for *a while.*"

He paused a moment, then nodded. "Anger, mostly."

She looked up from the chairs. He did look tired. Exhausted, even. "Listen, Aaron, you were right. I have been holding back. But I talked to Josie last night. Really opened up. And tonight, when Mattie asked about our fight, rather than give her a short answer designed to stop the conversation, I talked to her." And Mattie had told her about Jack in return. "So, I owe you a thank-you for that insight. I don't think I'll ever be someone who wears their heart on their sleeve, but I'm going to try to change."

"I'm glad. You may even be surprised, you know. There are a lot of people who really care for you."

She thought of the former mayor's comments. "You're right about that, too. But, Aaron, even if you've signed the papers, even if it's been two

years since you've separated, you're not ready to...
I was going to say date, but that's not really what
we were doing. So, whatever you call what was
growing between us, you're not ready for it. You
can't move on until you let go of the past. And I
value myself too much to be with someone like
that."

He seemed to consider that. "You might be right.
I've been mad at Tracey for a long time. I probably
do need to figure out a way to let that go. But I
don't think I'm the only one holding on to old
baggage. In your case, you have to get out of the car
you and your mom lived in and start letting other
people in."

Maeve nodded. "I think it would be best if we
went back to being friends. We'll work on the
Culpepper place together and that's it. It was one
kiss, Aaron. No more, no less."

"Maybe it was only a kiss, but I think there's a
chance it could be more. I care about you, too,
Maeve. You live with the motto, *I can't save the
world, but I can try.* Well, you've changed me. Likely
in ways I haven't even realized yet, but I know I'm
different because I met you."

"We barely know each other." She shook her
head. "You don't understand me, remember?"

"I'm beginning to. And whether I understand you
or not, you have affected me. You know, I had
never read a romance until the book club. Some of
those characters had huge obstacles in their way. I
think the thing standing between us is letting go of
the past."

"I guess it doesn't sound as big as some problems, but maybe it's bigger." She thought about the three new Valley Ridge couples. They'd all had obstacles to overcome, but they overcame them. Heck, Mattie said Finn had sued her for custody. That was major. Yet they'd gotten past it.

But she wasn't sure that would hold true for her and Aaron. "Our past makes us. It forms us. I don't know how to let mine go without changing myself. I don't think you do, either."

"Like I said, you've already changed me."

She frowned. "Seriously, you should stick to the general fiction book club because that sounded really schmaltzy."

He looked rueful. "Maybe. But I know that I'll never read a book again and not think about you and your leather-bound copy of *The Hobbit.* I'll never hear a bell ring and not think of angels getting their wings. You're a part of me now. I know that you might not have intended it, but no matter what, I'll be taking a piece of you with me when I move back to Florida."

* * *

As the words came out of his mouth, Aaron realized that he hadn't say *when I move back home.*

When he moved back to Florida.

Since he'd come to Valley Ridge, he'd been fantasizing about his lanai. About working outside in the warm Florida sun. He had the perfect lounge chair. It faced north, so the sun was never in his eyes. He looked out at the pool and the trees that lined the back of his lot. He'd lean back and prop his laptop on his thighs. He had a small table on his left where he could set a drink.

"I'll think about what you've said," he told Maeve. He realized he'd made at least one decision, so he added, "I might be out of touch for a few days. But I'll see you Saturday at the house, if not before."

"It would probably be best if we didn't see each other until then. I've got work and the library. You've got your work. You can't let things slide at Valley Ridge Farm and House Supplies." She paused. "You know, that is the most cumbersome name for a business, ever."

"I've said as much myself. I keep telling my uncle that he needs to come up with something shorter. Catchier."

"Something like VR Supplies," she suggested.

It had been an option he'd thought of. "Yeah, something like. I'll see you this weekend."

"Right. See you then."

He started to walk away, but turned around and said, "Maeve, this discussion's not over."

"Unfortunately, it is, Aaron."

He left the library and headed for his uncle's. A steady snow was falling.

He watched the flakes under the streetlights. And as he looked up, he saw a full moon shining through a bank of fluffy clouds.

It was beautiful.

Cold, to be sure. Different from Florida. But beautiful.

Maeve was right. Signing the divorce papers wasn't enough.

He'd heard people talk about closure. He'd never had that. One day, Tracey had simply been gone.

He should take her the signed papers and talk to her. They hadn't done much talking. Their lawyers had talked a lot.

Maybe that's what hurt the most. She hadn't talked to him. Instead, she'd sent her lawyer in to talk to his lawyer.

He'd sold his patent for the technology he'd created and all that money had barely hit their account before she was gone and asking for half.

He'd been so mad. Only fights, recriminations and accusations followed. But no discussion. No closure.

He needed to be in Valley Ridge on Saturday to work on the house, but there was no reason he couldn't go see Tracey before then.

Maybe if he figured out what went wrong between them, he'd be able to move on.

* * *

IT SEEMED AS if one minute Aaron was in snowy Valley Ridge, thinking about finally having a conversation with Tracey, and the next he was in sunny Florida, sitting in a cab.

The temperature was in the upper sixties, and the driver spent the entire ride complaining about the cold.

Aaron almost laughed in his face. This wasn't cold. This was balmy. This was shorts and flip-flop weather.

But he didn't say that. He sat in silence as the cabbie groused and took him to Tracey's.

He got out of the cab, suitcase in one hand and clutching the envelope with the divorce papers in the other.

He studied the white stucco house that backed up to a dock on one of the myriad of channels that led to the ocean.

He remembered the first time he'd seen Tracey. They were in high school. He was a nerd. He didn't wear glasses, and he had younger sisters who made sure he dressed well, but at heart, he was a nerd. He was way more comfortable playing computer games in the basement than talking to girls.

Not that he didn't notice girls.

He did.

But despite his sisters' best efforts, they hadn't noticed him.

Until a Monday morning, midway through his sophomore year when the teacher introduced a new student. Tracey and her family had just moved into the district.

His first bit of luck was that she was new to school and hadn't grown up knowing he was a nerd.

His second bit of luck was that she was assigned a seat by him in three classes, one of which was math. He'd been asked to see to it she was caught up.

His third bit of luck was that his last name was Holder and her last name was Holt. They were frequently thrown together when the teacher assigned seats or partners alphabetically.

They became friends.

And by the end of his sophomore year, they were a couple.

"I see you out there," Tracey called from the front door of the house. "You might as well come in."

He wheeled his suitcase behind him and walked up the brick walkway to her front door. "It's good to see you, Aaron." Tracey looked like a Viking. She was tall, pale and very blonde. And unlike the last time he'd seen her, she was smiling at him. He realized it had been a long time since he'd seen her smile.

"It's good to see you, too." He said the words by rote, but the second they were out of his mouth, he realized that he meant them. It was good to see her.

Tracey Holder—no, she'd gone back to her maiden name—Tracey Holt, didn't look a day older than that Monday his sophomore year when she'd walked into his classroom.

"You haven't changed," he said. Her blond hair was still in an untidy ponytail, as if she couldn't be bothered to do anything else with it. Her jeans had holes in them and she wore a bulky sweatshirt. But it was her eyes that had always drawn him. They were bright blue and honest as she assessed him.

"You have," she said. "You need to get out from behind the computer and into the sun now and then, Aaron."

"I do. I mean, I get out from behind the computer, but there's not much in the way of sunshine in Valley Ridge, New York, in December. It's gray and overcast more often than not."

"That sounds depressing." She beckoned for him to follow her.

He left his suitcase in the foyer, clutching the divorce papers as he walked into her sunny living room. "You'd think it would be, but there's so much snow that its brightness sort of counters the gray skies. I hardly notice the lack of sunshine, and when there is a sunny day, the entire town talks of nothing else."

"How is your uncle?" She motioned to an overstuffed chair.

The room definitely had Tracey's style. It was haphazardly thrown together and comfortable. Tracey had always been comfortable with herself.

"He's in Arizona for the winter. His arthritis has been bothering him a lot. That's the family line, at least. I think it was an excuse to guilt me into overseeing the store for him."

"And yet, you're not in Valley Ridge, you're here."

"I brought you these." He held out the envelope. It looked a bit worse for wear as he handed it over. "I signed them."

Tracey took the dog-eared envelope and looked up at him. "Why now? You've had them for months."

"It was time."

She looked at the envelope again, then back at him. "You could have mailed them, Aaron."

"Listen, Tracey. I didn't understand then, and I still don't. What happened between us?" If he could understand that, maybe he'd have a chance with Maeve.

And as he had the thought, he realized that was what he wanted...a chance with Maeve.

"We grew up, Aaron. We grew apart. I know it sounds trite. It sounds like a cop-out, but that's what happened." She lowered her voice. "You accused me of leaving the minute you signed the papers and sold that damned program of yours. But I left you a long time before that. You were so preoccupied with your work, you didn't notice. I stayed with you out of habit, because you were so wrapped up in your work that I felt I had to take care of you. Do you know how long it took you to even realize I'd gone back to school?"

He shook his head.

"I was midway through my second term. I'd been studying for a term and a half—studying big text books at the kitchen table, and you never noticed. For all you knew I could've been reading romance."

Her comment made him think of Maeve. "Speaking of which, I've read my first romance."

271

He'd known Tracey his whole adult life, and he'd never seen her look so surprised. "Excuse me? I must have misheard."

"I read a romance. An anthology of holiday romance novellas, to be exact. It was pretty good. And I read *The Hobbit* for the first time, as well." Since he'd already flabbergasted her, he decided to go all in. "What do you call a computer geek who's swearing?"

Tracey looked totally bemused as she said, "I don't know."

"A cursor." He laughed again. Maybe he wasn't ready for stand-up, but he still thought it was a pretty funny joke.

"Just what is in the water in Valley Ridge?" she asked. Then she paused and studied him in a way that only she could. "So, you've met her."

"Her?" he repeated.

She nodded. "*Her.* I knew *she* was out there. And I knew *she* wasn't *me.*"

"Why wasn't she you?" He'd married Tracey fully intending to spend the rest of his life with her. He still didn't understand why that life had derailed.

"Aaron, I waited patiently while I watched your work consumed you. I went about my life. I worked. I went back to school. You didn't even notice I was gone. But I waited. I thought that if I stuck it out while you finished the program, I'd get my shot. But you finished the program, sold it for enough money that you could do anything you wanted to do. Anything. We could have lived more than comfortably for the rest of our lives on what you'd been paid. We could have traveled the world, or built a dream house. We could have bought the boat you'd always talked about owning. I waited and I thought, *here it is. It's my time. He's going to notice me and we're going to do all the things we've dreamed about.* And do you know what you did?"

He didn't answer.

Finally Tracey said, "You started a new project. And that day when I walked in and saw you back in your chair on the lanai, bent over your laptop, I knew. I knew with absolute certainty that I wasn't *her.* I was never going to be *her.* I could wait around for the rest of my life, and I'd still never be *her.* Right after that, I realized that we'd never dreamed together. I'd dreamed for both of us. I'd planned a life with you, but you weren't interested in what I wanted. You found me comfortable and familiar. Like an old college sweatshirt. Something that had been your go-to outfit for years. I wanted to be more than that. And I wanted you to have more than that. So I left."

Her voice was soft as she added, "I've missed you, Aaron. To be brutally honest, I didn't miss you in a husband sort of way, but in a friend way. You will always be my friend."

If they'd had this discussion last month, even last year, he wouldn't have understood what she was saying, but he thought he did now. "I'll always be a friend, but I'm not *him?*"

"No," she said gently. "You're not *him.*"

"Have you found him?" He waited to feel some pang of jealousy as he thought about Tracey with someone else, but it never came.

He remembered seeing Maeve and Dylan on the dance floor and felt that same wave of jealousy all over again.

"No, I haven't found *him,* but I'm patient. I didn't want to start looking until you and I had resolved things."

"What if we never did?" he asked. "What if I'd dragged the divorce out even longer?"

"Eventually, you'd figure it out. I had faith in you. You're a very smart man," Tracey said with grin. "If you didn't figure it out for yourself, I knew your sisters would eventually beat it into your thick skull. And to be honest, I was busy at school. I got my Ph.D. last spring, you know."

"Really? Congratulations."

Aaron sat back and talked to Tracey. Probably the first real conversation they'd had in a very long time.

She had two job offers and was currently weighing her options. She sounded happy. Happier than she'd been with him.

"Thank you," he said a couple of hours later. "Thank you for knowing me better than I knew myself."

"You were my first love, Aaron." Tracey kissed his cheek.

"You were my first love, too." And because he finally understood what she'd been trying to say all along, he added, "But you weren't her."

"And you're not him," she replied.

"There might be a romance novel here," he said with a laugh.

"Really, this woman got you to read something that wasn't some tech magazine or Manga? I'm shocked. And I hope I get to meet her sometime, if that isn't too weird."

"I don't think it's weird," he said. "I don't think she will, either. But if you do meet her, don't tell her what a geek I am. I don't think she's figured it out yet."

"Oh, she will," Tracey assured him. "And she'll like you all the more for it."

"Let me know where you decide to go."

"I will. I still talk to your sisters," Tracey said a bit hesitantly, as if she was afraid she'd disrupt their new truce. "They're my friends, too. I know it may seem strange, but they are. I spent more holidays with them than with you."

He remembered all the times he'd sent her to his family functions while he holed up with his work, and nodded in understanding. "Well, you're a braver person than I am. They still scare me, frankly. Speaking of my family, I'm going to go see them and spend the night. Then I'm heading home tomorrow."

Valley Ridge was home. He knew that now, as surely as he knew that Tracey had never been *the one for him.*

"Good luck with her, Aaron."

"I'll need it. She's angry that I kissed her before I signed the divorce papers." He hurried to add, "It was just one kiss, that's all."

Tracey smiled. "Buy her some jewelry and apologize."

"Yeah, I don't see that helping. I bought her a house...well, not for her. I bought a house she wanted to give away, so I gave it to her so she could. I'd buy her another house if I thought that would do the trick, but she's already working herself half to death on the first one. I could buy her a book."

Tracey studied him. "Love looks good on you, Aaron. She sounds like an interesting woman."

"You know that curse, May you live in interesting times? Well, I think there's a second one, May you love an interesting woman."

Tracey shook her head. "Aaron Holder turned comedian. I never thought I'd see it, but like I said, it looks good on you. Good luck. And maybe I'll come visit you in Valley Ridge sometime."

He nodded. "Do. I think Maeve would like to meet you, too."

The cab he'd called pulled up in front of her house, and he kissed Tracey's cheek. "Merry Christmas, Tracey."

"Merry Christmas, Aaron."

He walked toward the cab and the bell at the church down the street start to ring out the hour.

Angels' wings.

His lanai.

His family.

276

His ex.

Maeve.

Thoughts rolled over in his mind.

He'd said goodbye to his past. To his anger.

Tomorrow, he'd go back to Valley Ridge—he'd go back home—and see if he could find a future.

CHAPTER ELEVEN

"So, where's Aaron?" Josie asked on Friday as Maeve sat with her in the RV, watching Carl play with some blocks.

"No one knows." Maeve had hoped that Josie would know where he was

"Well," Josie said, "according to Boyd, he's called and checked in at the store every day, but no one's seen him since Monday at the book club meeting."

Well, that was a bust. Josie didn't know anything more than Maeve had already known.

She should be happy. She'd told him that she wanted some space and he'd obviously taken her at her word. Maeve changed the subject. "How are you feeling?"

"Great. I went to see Dr. Marshall again and he said everything looks fine. If I promise to continue to take it easy, I can start getting out more. I want that so bad that even grocery shopping sounds like a treat. I'm going to head over after dinner and pick up a few things."

"I'll be at the library." Maeve fished in her pocket and pulled out her keys. "Take my car."

"I'd like to argue, but odds are you'd win, anyway."

It was good to see her friend looking so happy. "Because I'm such a good friend, why don't you drop Carl off at the library and go all by yourself."

Josie hugged her. "I love my husband and son, but I'm so ready for ten minutes to myself. I've got a pile of coupons and Boyd's paycheck. I'm ready to party."

Maeve laughed to see Josie so jubilant. "It doesn't take much to please you, does it?"

"The secret to a happy life—" Josie leaned closer and stage-whispered "—is to find joy in the small things."

"You may be right," Maeve admitted.

"Do you want some dinner?" Josie asked. "I made a lasagna."

She'd smelled the tomato sauce when she walked into the RV. "No, but thanks. I had dinner already."

Josie frowned. "A peanut butter sandwich?"

"No, Miss Smarty-Pants. I had a tomato and bean sprout sandwich today."

Josie shook her head. "That's not a dinner. I'm not sure what it is, but it's not dinner."

"It'll do. I'll see Carl in a bit."

"I'll drop him off in a little while."

By seven o'clock that evening, Maeve realized that Carl had saved her sanity. She'd been so busy chasing after him that she didn't have time to wonder where Aaron was. Or at least, she didn't have as much time.

Only three people wandered into the library to check out a book. Vera, Lily's mother, brought Hank in and they were the only ones left as Maeve started tidying up the mess so she could close up for the night.

Vera picked up her books and tucked three dollars into the small container on the counter, like she did every time she visited.

Tori had put the container out a few months ago to collect money for new books, but Maeve felt guilty taking Vera's money. Maeve knew that Vera's job at the diner didn't leave her a lot of extra cash and it touched her that she was so willing to share what little she had with something that benefitted the community.

"Thank you, Mrs. Paul." Carl reached for the donation can. Maeve handed him a stress ball instead. "You really don't have to donate every time."

Lily's mom laughed. "It's my pleasure. But I wanted to ask you if I could do more. My evenings are pretty quiet. Maybe I could come work an evening in your place? Maybe Fridays? A young girl like you shouldn't be working every Friday night."

"You're right about that," Hank said. "All the eligible men are getting snapped up, Maeve. You'd better get out there."

Hank held out his hand to Carl and said, "We're going to leave you two girls to work this out. Come on, kid." He took Carl over to the kids' corner and picked out a book.

"So, how about it, Maeve?" Vera pressed. "Friday nights off? I know you don't have any book clubs that night. I can read here as easily as I can in my apartment."

Maeve glanced at Hank and Carl cuddling in the rocking chair, studying a book. Her first instinct was to assure Lily's mom that she had it covered, but she was trying to really think about how she always responded automatically. Having Friday nights off might be nice. "If you really don't mind, Mrs. P—"

"Call me Vera, dear. I've watched you here for weeks now and I'm sure I can manage if you walk me through the computer checkout system."

"I can show you right now," Maeve said and motioned for her to come around the counter so she could show her the very basic system she'd set up.

"I know you're working on the house tomorrow," Vera said. "What if I come over and help out here in the morning? My shift at the diner doesn't start until one."

"Mrs. Paul—Vera—that would be great. There's so much still to do at the Culpepper place."

"I think what you're doing is wonderful. I'm so glad I moved to Valley Ridge with Lily. This town...well, it's special."

"It is." Maeve promised to come over and unlock the library the next morning and get Vera set up before heading over to the house.

After Hank and Vera left, Maeve gathered up Carl and got ready to leave. She'd finished putting on his coat when the doorbell rang and Aaron came in. "I'm not too late. I thought you might have closed."

"Carl and I were just about to go. It turns out bundling a toddler up in the winter takes a while, so you have time to find your book if you move quickly."

"I'm not here for a book." Aaron hefted the bag in his hand. "I came with a St. Nicholas gift for you and Carl. I was going to stop in at the RV next with his, but since he's here with you, you saved me a stop."

"St. Nicholas?" she asked. She added as primly as she could manage, "I don't accept presents from married men."

He ignored her last comment and answered the first. "St. Nicholas Day is a German tradition that my family observes with our own twist. On St. Nicholas Eve, you leave out your shoes. If you're behaving, you get a treat. A small toy or some candy. And always an orange. I don't know why, but that's what we always got. If you haven't been very good, then you get a lump of coal. It's an early indicator of how you're doing before Santa comes."

"Did you ever get a lump of coal?" she asked in spite of herself.

"Just once. I got one in my shoe yesterday. I was told to pull my head out of my a... Well, let's just say my mother read me the riot act and told me that I'd better be home for Easter since I'm not going back for Christmas. Then she called my sisters, who still live nearby and they pretty much told me the same thing, only not as politely as my mom."

"What about your dad?"

"He didn't say a word. When Mom and the girls get going, that tends to be the best thing to do." He thrust a package at her. "Here. St. Nick left it at my house for you." He handed a bag to Carl. "And he left this for you, champ."

Carl dug into the bag and pulled out an orange, a pack of Cranraisins and a Nerf ball. He seemed delighted and threw the ball.

"Open yours," Aaron said.

"Aaron, I meant what I said about us being friends, but really, I can't accept anything from you."

"I'm not married now. I'm happily divorced."

"I'm glad that you signed the papers, Aaron, but it's not only that. There's a whole host of reasons why—"

"I bought it used, Maeve. Or rather, St. Nicholas did. We can't return it." When she still didn't move, he said, "Open it, please."

Aaron looked so excited about the gift that Maeve couldn't not open it. She gently peeled back the tape and unfolded the ends of the package. She pulled off the paper and took out an old, leather-bound copy of *A Christmas Carol.* She couldn't resist opening the book. The spine gave the slightest groan, as if it hadn't been opened for years and it was enjoying the experience.

She looked at the inside of the front cover, and there was an inscription. She read out loud, "June, May you treasure the memories of our Christmases past. May you relish each moment of our Christmas present. And may we have many, many Christmases future to explore. All my love, Leon."

Leon's words to June touched her. She put her finger on them and traced the curly signature. It looked as if it had been signed with a fountain pen. "It's beautiful."

Aaron grinned. "I thought you'd like it. There was a slightly nicer copy at the used bookstore, but when I read that inscription, I knew this was the copy that was meant for you. And I think you and your romance book club have done something to me, because I keep wondering if—and hoping that—Leon and June had a lot of holidays together."

Maeve hesitated. "I know I said I shouldn't accept this, but there's no way I'm giving it back. Thank you."

"Good. I wouldn't have taken it back, anyway."

She waited for him to tell her what happened, why he'd finally signed the papers, but all he said was, "Happy St. Nicholas Day. I'll see you at the house tomorrow."

"I'll be there first thing. Lily's mom will open the library. She's taking over Friday evenings for me from now on, too."

"Great." He left without a backward glance.

"Well, what do you think of that, Carl?"

"Balls." He held his Nerf ball out for her to inspect.

"Yeah, I agree."

She got Carl into his coat, mittens and hat, and with her book in one hand, and the toddler's hand in her other, they left for the night. She'd planned on continuing her holiday movie-fest later, but was pretty sure she was going to spend the night with her nose buried in a book instead.

* * *

Aaron spent Saturday and most of Sunday outside. The small garage had been filled to the rafters with junk. He'd emptied most of it into the Dumpster, but he'd found a couple boxes of holiday decorations that must have belonged to the Culpeppers.

Maeve would love them.

Wooing some women might mean expensive dinners and jewels, but he was pretty sure those things wouldn't work on Maeve. He'd given her a house and a book. Next, he was going to give her a box of antique ornaments.

He knew she'd come in before she said a word. He felt her presence.

"Aaron? Are you going to avoid me forever?"

He turned and smiled because avoiding her was the last thing he wanted. "I'm not avoiding you. I've got most of the garage cleared out. Except these." He pointed to the half dozen or so boxes. "I thought you'd like them." He reached inside a box and held up an ornament, a weirdly shaped, silver-and-red one with sparkles.

She took it in her hand and exclaimed, "Oh, it's perfect."

"Once we put up the tree, you can decorate it with these. I remember what you said about having a tree and Santa giving the house keys to Boyd and Josie."

She seemed surprised. "You remember that?"

"I remember, Maeve." He wanted to tell her how much he remembered. How much everything she said meant to him. How much she meant to him.

But he was trying to take it slowly. Although, last night, when she'd seemed so pleased with the book, he'd wanted nothing more than to kiss her.

And more.

Much more.

Looking at her now, kneeling by the box of ornaments in a pair of torn jeans and an old jacket, a black knit hat pulled low on her head, he wanted to kiss her even more.

She carefully removed the top layer of ornaments, examining each one individually. "They're lovely."

He also wanted her to understand him. "Are you going to ask me about my divorce?"

She looked up. "Probably not. Do you want to talk about it?"

"Do you want me to?" he countered.

"Not yet," she said simply.

It irked him that she wasn't curious. "But I'd like to spend time with you."

"As friends," she clarified.

He nodded. "Friends." Silently he added, *for now.*

"I stayed up way too late last night rereading *A Christmas Carol.* The book is beautiful. And I'm almost positive that June and Leon had many happy Christmases together. I'm back to watching Christmas movies tonight."

"Which one?" he asked, though he knew it didn't matter. He'd watch whatever Maeve wanted if he could finagle an invitation.

"Nestor, the Long-Eared Christmas Donkey."

Aaron chuckled. He'd had a friend, Chris, from Philly who always told some joke about a donkey in a manger. The joke used to make him crazy. He hadn't thought of the joke, or thought of Chris, for years.

Here he'd accused Maeve of cutting herself off from people, when he'd done the same thing. He couldn't remember the last time he'd gone out with friends. He couldn't remember the last time he'd taken Tracey out before she left him. He'd been consumed by his work to the extent that he'd pushed everything and everyone else away.

Maybe that's what was different here in Valley Ridge. He was finding balance. "I don't think I've ever heard of Nester," he said.

"Give me a half hour to shower and meet me at my house. Bring some tissues. You'll need them."

She cried over donkey movies? He'd like to say he was surprised, but nothing about Maeve surprised him anymore. "What if I bring pizza?"

She got up and gently lifted the box of ornaments. "Only if you get extra cheese and mushrooms."

"Done."

Two hours later, the pizza had been eaten, the movie had ended and Maeve had fallen asleep on the couch. She was wearing a pair of old sweats and a maroon-and-yellow sweatshirt. Her damp hair was gathered in a messy bun and she didn't have a lick of makeup on. He'd been watching her for the past half hour, thinking about waking her up, but loath to disturb her.

He was pretty sure her outfit was meant to scare him off. He didn't want to tell her it had the opposite effect. He loved her freckles, and in her sleep, she looked younger than she did when she was awake.

She was wary around him. He could sense the difference tonight as they sat and watched her movie. She'd cried every time Nester's mother reminded him about his ears. She'd tried to hide it, but he'd noticed.

He'd wanted to put his arm around her and pull her tight, but he'd resisted. He was going to give her the time and space to decide if she'd forgiven him.

He'd really made a mess of things.

She was disappointed in him and he didn't blame her.

"You're thinking very hard," Maeve said as she sat up and stretched. "You were thinking so hard you woke me up, which was only fair, since it's rude for a host to fall asleep on their guests. I apologize. I was more tired than I thought."

"Given your schedule, I think it's allowable."

"My schedule's not all that bad. Vera took over at the library Saturday, so I actually worked less than usual this weekend." She raked her fingers through her sleep-mussed hair, and more strands escaped her sloppy bun.

"Wrong, you didn't work less. Vera was at the library, so you came over to the Culpepper place early and worked straight through the weekend."

"Well, I will be taking it easier. Vera wants to work Friday nights and Saturday mornings for me. Once the house is done, I'll have less to do." She sat up straighter and glared at him. "A lot less."

"I'm sure there will be paperwork for the foundation, and meetings, and setting up a board, and finding a house to be next year's project, and the library and..." He was exhausting himself. "I don't think you'll slow down."

"We've been here before. This is where you mutter to yourself that you don't understand me, then you look at me like I'm some bug under a microscope and try to figure me out."

"I think I have figured you out." And as he said the words, he knew that he had. He'd figured out Maeve Buchanan as much as he ever would, as much as he needed to.

She shot him a look that said she didn't believe a word of it. "How's that?"

"You're pretty perfect." And that was that. She was pretty perfect. Perfect for him.

She snorted. "Wow, you're deluded."

"No, I mean it. You've got a caring and generous heart."

"If you've been studying me like a lab animal and that's the best you've come up with, you're sadly lacking in observational abilities."

He smiled at her.

"I have all kinds of flaws. Jealousy is one of the biggest ones."

"Who are you jealous of?"

She pushed a piece of hair back and seemed to consider his question. "I don't know if we have time to list everyone I've ever been jealous of. When I was in school, I was jealous of the kids who were athletic, the kids whose grades came easily to them. I have two left feet and worked hard to get my grades. When Mom and I lost the house, I was jealous of people who had a home. When I went to college, I was jealous of my friends who had parents who could foot the bill. I worked almost full-time in order to pay for my education. And..."

"And?" he pressed, fascinated by what Maeve thought was her greatest weakness.

"And I'm jealous of all my friends who have seemingly found their soul mates so easily. Not to mention my mom's found her perfect guy twice."

"May I point out a couple things?"

She nodded.

"I don't think there's anyone alive who hasn't envied someone else who seems as if they've had an easier time of it. Whether it's school, or love or life in general."

"But I—"

"But nothing. I've been around Valley Ridge long enough that I've heard most of the stories. Finn sued Mattie for custody of their kids."

"They worked that out."

"That's my point. They worked it out and look at them now. And I was at Lily and Sebastian's wedding. I saw how in love they were, but according to the town grapevine that's not how it was when Sebastian first came home. They didn't get along at all. Something about a huge fight and Lily playing basketball with one hand literally tied behind her back."

"But—"

He interrupted her again. "Then there's Sophie and Colton who canceled their first wedding—when they were standing at the altar."

"I know, but see how they are today."

"Yes, today they're great. Exactly. And none of them are perfect. None of them had an easy time of it. I've read a few more romances since book club and I've noticed that most of them are fairly honest about how love takes time. Even if two people have an instant attraction, they need to put the effort in to turn that into a lasting commitment. So there are bumps. I guess what determines who makes it and who doesn't depends on how people handle those hurdles."

"You're probably right."

He'd wanted to wait until she asked, but changed his mind. "And let me leave you with this thought. I was wrong to kiss you, but I haven't been with my wife for almost two years. The divorce papers have been languishing on my desk for months. I was mad. Furious that she left me. I thought she waited for the right moment. I thought she waited until I sold my program for lots of money and then she took the cash and left. But I was wrong. Completely wrong. She was waiting for me to pay attention to her.... I'd become accustomed to the idea of loving her. And that's very different than actually loving someone. We'd been together so long. Maybe love shouldn't be that comfortable. Maybe it should require work, be an investment, if only so you don't ever get complacent.

"So, I'll agree, I shouldn't have kissed you until I was completely free and clear. But I'm completely free and clear now. Legally and emotionally, which means it's okay to do this..."

He leaned in and kissed her.

For a moment, she froze, and he started to pull away, but Maeve wrapped her arms around him and deepened the kiss.

It was everything their kiss at the wedding should have been. Could have been. He knew he could stay like this forever, but Maeve shifted slightly and pulled back.

"Aaron, I—"

"In the two years that Tracey and I were separated, I never looked at another woman. But, Maeve, from the second I saw you I couldn't look anywhere else. I said that it was because you were an anomaly and I wanted to figure you out. I tried to tell myself that. But it's become so much more."

She moved farther back to the corner of the couch. "I don't know what to say."

"There's nothing to say. I signed the papers and I made my peace with Tracey. I made my peace with my past. I know I screwed things up by not telling you sooner. I'm sorry. I'm glad you've decided we can be friends. I won't kiss you again."

She started to speak, but stopped.

"I won't kiss you, but I would very much like it if you kissed me." Feeling as if he'd said what needed to be said, Aaron got up, grabbed his coat and made a quick exit before he broke his promise and kissed her again regardless.

* * *

Seeing to the house became part of the rhythm of Maeve's busy life, but that next week was especially frantic.

She fell into bed exhausted each night. And she slept so heavily that her internal alarm clock gave up. She had to rely on the actual clock by her bedside.

And she dreamed each night, too.

Of Aaron. Of Josie, Boyd and Carl. About the Culpepper place.

The dreams of Aaron were the most disturbing.

He wasn't going to kiss her again, but seemed to be waiting for her to kiss him. She kept circling back to that thought as she tried to convince herself that it was best to just be friends with him. She might have convinced herself if it wasn't for the dreams. One, in particular. In it, she was dancing with Aaron, but they weren't at Lily's wedding. Instead they were dancing on the snowy Culpepper lawn, though Maeve wasn't the least bit cold. There were colored lights glowing. They came from a Christmas tree in the window.

As she and Aaron danced, he whispered, "There's something I need to tell you."

She held her breath, anxious to hear his words. "Maeve, I..."

That's where she woke up, every time.

Which was why she was feeling tired and out of sorts the following Saturday.

She gave the nut on the screw that held the toilet to the floor an extra hard thump, and then tried unscrewing it again. It didn't budge.

She took the can of industrial lubricant and doused the screw, thumped the nut again and got her pliers to try to turn it. The nut still didn't move.

She found her hammer and whacked at the nut as hard as she could.

Harder.

"I think it's dead."

She turned and saw Aaron standing in the bathroom doorway, grinning.

"I told the plumber I'd do the demo in here, and the stupid toilet is stuck. I don't know what else to do."

"We're replacing it, right?"

"Yes. We're replacing both with dual flush toilets."

"Dual flush?"

"They're very water efficient. You use one button for little jobs and one for big..." She could feel her cheeks heating up. "Needless to say, they're a green alternative. Tori's dad suggested them. He said as long as we were doing all this work, we might as well make the house as green and energy efficient as possible."

Aaron sank down next to her and examined the bolts, then turned so that his face was inches away from hers. "You are the first woman I've ever met who can get excited about a dual flush toilet."

Maeve shrugged. "That's me. Save the earth...one flush at a time. But only if I could get this nut off the bolt."

"Let's try it together."

She shook her head. Aaron was already too close for comfort. "No, that's okay. I'll get it."

"Nervous?" he challenged.

She played ignorant. "About what?"

Aaron tsked at her. "I don't know what you could be nervous about. You tell me."

"Fine." She gripped the pliers and Aaron fitted his hands over hers. "Pull."

They both strained against the pressure, and the nut became loose enough to twist.

Maeve pulled her hands out from beneath Aaron's. "Okay, thanks. I've got it from here."

His face, still too close for comfort, moved even closer. "Well, I'll let you get back to it, then."

He got up and left the small powder room.

Maeve shook her head. She couldn't believe she'd just raved about toilets to the man she...

She wasn't sure what she felt for Aaron.

She was so mixed up.

He was divorced now, but he'd been good to his word and hadn't made a move to kiss her again.

She wanted to do as he'd said and kiss him.

And more.

He'd told her that she'd climbed into the car when she and her mom had been homeless and that she'd never gotten out.

It was time to get out of the car. It was time to live her life and take some risks. She'd been willing to sink her savings into this house. She hadn't needed to, but she'd been willing. She'd turned over some of her library hours to someone else.

She'd started opening up to people. To Josie, and even Mattie.

Maybe it was time she took a risk with Aaron. He'd said he wouldn't kiss her, but she could kiss him. Maybe it was time to try it.

* * *

As HAD BECOME his habit, Aaron waited for everyone else to leave, and then offered to walk Maeve home.

He stuffed his hands into his pocket, not only because it was cold, but because he was trying to keep his hands to himself. It was getting harder and harder to do. Some men might be impressed by a woman who was dressed to the nines and made-up, but he'd never seen anyone as attractive as Maeve had looked, sitting on the bathroom floor, swearing at a toilet bolt. He'd wanted to kiss her with every ounce of his being. But he'd managed to keep his promise. He would wait for her.

Even if it killed him.

They walked in silence through his uncle's parking lot. Rather than turning toward her house, Maeve turned and went in the other direction.

"Where are you going?"

"I'm too antsy to go home yet. I thought I'd watch the train at MarVee's. I like watching it at night."

"You've got to be exhausted," he said.

"Maybe."

"Listen, if you're that tired, why aren't you heading home to bed?"

She didn't answer him. Instead, she asked, "When is your uncle coming home?"

"He's been very vague about that."

She stopped in front of the well-lit window at MarVee's. The railroad track wound through an elaborate village. She pointed. "Mr. Mento has been adding a new building every year. Look at that one. It's Mattie's Park Perks."

He bent a little closer and saw that it actually said Park Perks on the window of the miniature version. "I hadn't noticed it."

"There's the township offices, and if you look very closely that's MarVee's Quarters. There's even a tiny train in the window. Mr. Mento wanted to make a whole train set, but his eyes wouldn't cooperate, so he settled for the engine."

"I've walked by this so many times, and I've noticed the trains, but I never took the time to look closely."

Maeve watched the train, but he was no longer looking at old Mr. Mento's masterpiece. He was looking at her. "Why did you ask about my uncle?"

"I just wondered how much longer you'd be in town."

"Uncle Jerry hasn't said specifically, but I'm here for a few more months at least."

She nodded. "Even if you're here through March, that's only three months."

He did the math in his head and nodded. "Yes, something like that."

"That's not very long."

"No."

"And you've signed the papers. You're officially divorced." It wasn't a question, but rather a statement that seemed to beg for confirmation.

"Yes."

She continued to stare at the train, though Aaron wondered what the internal monologue in her head sounded like. He sensed that something fragile hung in the balance, but he wasn't sure what.

"You asked why I'm not heading home to bed if I'm so tired." She paused.

"Yes," he prompted.

"I am exhausted, but in a good way. The reason I haven't hurried home to bed every night is that every night, I dream. Most of those dreams seem to feature you. And I couldn't help but wonder what would happen if you were in the bed next to me. Maybe I'd manage to sleep and really get some rest."

"If I were in the bed next to you, I don't think you'd be getting much rest at all."

She turned from the train and looked at him. The lights from the window cast a beautiful glow on her face. "Maybe we should give it a try."

He released the breath he hadn't known he was holding. "Don't make the offer if you're not sure."

"You're only here a few more months and you've recently ended a long, obviously painful relationship. I'll make the perfect rebound relationship. Something that, by its nature, must be short-lived."

She took his hand. It was the first time she'd touched him since that kiss on the dance floor.

No, he took that back. She'd let him hold her hand when they'd unscrewed that bolt on the new dual flush toilet. He smiled as he remembered her enthusiasm.

He'd follow her willingly, but he didn't respond to her rebound comment. He might be a total mess, but he was certain of one thing—Maeve Buchanan was so much more than a rebound.

He looked at the woman holding his hand as they stood in the soft light from the window display. She leaned forward with such agonizing slowness. He wanted to move toward her, but he forced himself to wait, to let her take the lead. Her lips finally touched his and she kissed him.

As they explored one another, he held her at the waist, pulling her close. He knew exactly what Tracey had been talking about.

He knew with absolute certainty *who* Tracey had been talking about.

When the kiss ended, Maeve said, "Let's go home."

And he recognized, without a doubt, where home was. And it wasn't Florida. It wasn't the apartment over his uncle's store.

It wasn't even the house where Maeve lived.

Home was wherever Maeve was.

She talked about what they were starting tonight as if it were a short-term affair. Something she was willing to begin because she thought he'd be going in the spring.

He had another idea entirely, but he kept it to himself.

For now, the only thing on his mind was giving Maeve Buchanan a night she'd never forget.

* * *

MAEVE WOKE UP at 5:00 a.m.

Despite her late night, she wasn't tired.

She rolled over and checked out the man sleeping next to her.

He was a blanket hog. He'd pulled at the covers, and then somehow practically cocooned himself in them.

She'd eventually given up any hope of wrestling the covers back from him. She tiptoed to the chest and found a spare quilt.

He looked so peaceful. It took all her willpower not to reach over and run her finger along his unshaven cheek.

"What on earth could you be thinking this hard about at—" He pulled an arm out of the cocoon and peered at the clock. "Five after five in the morning?"

"I was thinking that I can't believe we waited so long to have sex."

"Make love," he corrected.

She ignored his comment and slid closer. "I learned something last night."

"What?"

"You hog the covers."

"Really, after last night, all you have to say is, I hog the covers?" He grinned. "I was expecting something more like, *Aaron your rocked my world,* or—"

"And you snore," she blatantly lied. She giggled as she made a loud, snoring noise. "I mean you sounded worse than Sebastian's reciprocating saw." She snored again.

"Liar," he said. "Come on, I know I hog the covers, but I don't snore."

"Worse than the jackhammer you used to take up that front walk." She giggled even harder.

"Maeve, you tell fibs."

"And you snore."

He moved quickly, despite his purloined blanket cocoon. He pinned her to the bed and said, "Take it back."

"What will you do to me if I don't?" she challenged him with a grin.

"Oh, I can think of something."

She reached up, put her arms around him and very softly said, "You snore."

And it turned out he did have some very inventive ways to make her pay for her lies.

* * *

MAEVE MANAGED TO shoo Aaron out of the house before the town began to wake up. She got ready for work and went to the RV to check on Josie. She raised her hand to tap softly on the door, as had become her routine, but the door flew open before she was able to. "So, how was he?"

"Huh?"

Josie hustled her into the RV. "I saw Aaron taking his walk of shame. Although, if you ask me, the only shame is that you two waited so long."

Maeve felt a rush of heat sweep over her face. She didn't need a mirror to know she was blushing. That was one of the curses that came with her red hair.

Josie laughed. "I swear, I won't tell. You're a private soul. I get that."

"I'm trying to be more open," she said. "But I don't ever think I'll be *that* open. Maybe I'm a prude?" She thought about her night with Aaron. "Never mind, I'm definitely not a prude. I'm just private."

Josie cracked up. "Wow, Maeve. Joking about Aaron Holder? Things have changed."

"Well, he did sign those divorce papers," she said. It was important to her that Josie knew that.

"That's a good start. Last night was an even better start. What comes next?"

Maeve didn't say anything, not because she was private, or because she was a prude, but because she didn't have a clue.

The Culpepper place was almost done. And in a few months, Aaron's uncle would come home and Aaron would go back to Florida.

That didn't leave a lot of options.

Suddenly her bright day didn't seem quite as bright anymore.

* * *

THE SUNDAY BEFORE Christmas Eve, Maeve stood in the center of the refurbished living room of the house she would soon be presenting to Boyd, Josie and Carl. She was admiring the view when her mother entered the room.

"That's it. Herm and Aaron have the crib set up. Aaron said you had sheets somewhere?"

"They're on the table. I'll get them." She glanced around her. "I can't believe we did it."

"Really? Because I think everyone who knows you knew it would be finished in time."

"Well, it's not officially finished until we put up the tree. Aaron offered to let me use the store's truck. I'll stop by tomorrow to get the tree."

"Herm could have brought you one."

"I really want to pick it out myself." She'd started this project with Aaron, and it only felt right that she finish it with him. Putting up the tree was the final step. After that, it was up to Josie and Boyd.

Her mom took her hand. "Does it help?"

"What?"

"I know that losing the farm all those years ago hurt you. I saw you change. You'd been such an

303

outgoing little girl. But after that, you became so closed off. You didn't want people to know about our circumstances, and even after they improved, you couldn't go back to that girl you'd been. Does giving someone else a fresh start help heal the hurt?"

"Maybe not how you think. Yes, losing our home hurt, but I have learned something. Home isn't so much a place—it's the people in your life. Josie taught me that. Right now, her home is the RV because that's where Boyd and Carl are. As long as I had you, I had a home. Whether it was in the car, or at Hank's apartment or later with Herm. I never really lost my home, because I never lost you."

Her mother teared up. "That is probably the loveliest thing you've ever said to me."

She hugged her mother. "Then that's something else I've been doing wrong. I love you, Mom."

"And I love you, too, Maeve."

"We'd better turn around and turn around quick," Herm said from the doorway. "When women are crying and hugging, it's best not to be present."

"Oh, Herm." Her mother went to her husband and hugged him. "Thank you."

"For what?"

"For being my home," her mother managed mid-hiccup.

Aaron came up to Maeve's side and whispered, "What's happening?"

"Don't worry about it. Let's get the sheets for the crib."

"After we put them on, we're done. It's time to go home."

Aaron had spent every night with her since the first time they'd made love. She enjoyed every second she spent with him, but after her talk with her mom, his word choice at that moment meant something more to her.

"Home," she murmured, thinking about her parents, her friends. It wasn't so much a place as a person.

She glanced over at Aaron and wondered if she'd found her home.

CHAPTER TWELVE

CHRISTMAS EVE HAD arrived. Maeve hung the last of the antique ornaments on the tree and stood back to admire her effort.

That tree was so much more than just a Christmas tree to her. In it, she saw future Christmases. Josie, Boyd and a house full of children.

"It's beautiful," she whispered.

She could hardly contain her excitement. She hoped Josie and Boyd would accept the house, but she remembered how she'd had to fight Boyd to get him to park the RV at her house and she worried.

"It certainly is beautiful," Aaron, aka Santa Claus, said. Instead of staring at the tree, Santa was looking at her as he said the words.

"I'm not sure if I've said thank-you enough. We'll know soon if they want to take the house, or not. But even if they don't," she said to remind herself, "this is a positive thing. Families will now have homes because of what we've done."

"Because of everything you've done," he corrected. "The real Santa might have a workroom full of elves building his toys, but they don't hold a candle to you when it comes to getting things accomplished."

She hugged Santa, hoping to distract him. "Let's not start this again."

He managed to return her hug despite his well-padded stomach getting in the way. "I'll never stop it, Maeve. You have this ability to see things the way they could be—should be—and then make them happen. That is a rare gift."

She stepped back. She never knew what to say to compliments like that, so she put her new response into practice, "Thank you." She couldn't help but add, "I'm not sure I agree, but thank you, anyway."

"Before everyone arrives, I want to show you something." He walked over and dug through his giant Santa sack and pulled out a handful of papers. He handed them to her.

"What's all this?" She thumbed through the pages. She thought it might be foundation or house stuff, but it wasn't either. She saw the address for the store.

Aaron tapped the header at the top of the page. "That's a sale agreement between my uncle and me."

"What are you selling?" she asked.

"I'm not selling, I'm buying. The store. My uncle has decided to stay in Arizona, and I'm going to own the store. VR Supplies will be its new name."

She remembered suggesting that as an option. She eyed the stack of papers, then handed them back. "Oh."

"So, I'm staying here," he said slowly as if she might not have understood him.

She'd thought that what they had was temporary. Aaron would leave in the spring. But if he was still going to be in Valley Ridge? That changed everything. "What about your home in Orlando?"

"That wasn't my home. It was never my home. It was a house I lived in for a while. I've discovered that my true home is here."

"Oh."

"That's all you want to say?" He seemed annoyed.

Maeve wasn't sure what he wanted from her. She hadn't asked him to stay. As a matter of fact, he'd never mentioned it or asked her opinion. "Um. Congratulations? Finding out where you belong is a gift."

He sighed. "And I want you to know that I offered Boyd a full-time job at VR Supplies. With Boyd's past experience managing the plastics plant, he's by far the best candidate for the position. Having someone to handle the day-to-day operations will allow me to work on my next project. I'm going to use my uncle's old apartment as my office."

Maeve's heart felt full. "If Boyd has a job, then they're more apt to stay." She hugged him and suddenly she knew what she wanted to say to him. Maybe it was too soon. But she'd learned that you didn't get anywhere if you didn't take chances. "Thank you, Aaron. I l—"

Her words were cut off as Mattie, Lily and Sophie walked in together, kids and husbands in tow. They were the first of a stream of people who were anxious to see Boyd's and Josie's reaction to the house.

She might have been frustrated about not finishing what she was going to say to Aaron, but she realized she had all the time in the world.

They had all the time in the world.

She'd been the one to invite everyone here. They'd all agreed that a houseful of people would lend credence to their story that this was the house Santa was visiting in Valley Ridge.

Aaron pulled up his beard before the kids spotted him and went to sit in the big armchair between the tree and fireplace. Mattie and Finn's kids were the first to sit on his lap. Aaron had a huge stack of presents at his side, and more stuffed into his sack. When Maeve had asked about them, he'd hemmed and hawed, and never answered her question.

Now, he searched through the sack and selected a gift for each child. The kids squealed with joy upon opening their presents. These gifts weren't simple coloring books or candy canes, instead, there was a doll camper for Abbey, a remote-control car for Mickey, and an iPod dock for Zoe.

More people arrived. Her mom and Herm. Vera and Hank. Mayor Tuznik. The small house was soon crowded with people who'd come to witness Josie's and Boyd's reaction.

Sophie put baby Ben in Santa's arms and snapped a picture. Watching Aaron pose with the tiny baby, cradling him close, Maeve's heart melted.

Joe and his sisters were next. After the little girls sat on Santa's lap, Aaron slipped something to Joe.

Maeve wanted to ask what it was, but Tori arrived just then. She stood in the doorway for a moment and then made a beeline to Maeve. "The house looks so awesome," she said.

Santa called out to her. "Tori, come over here and see good old Santa. He's got a little something for you in his bag."

Tori laughed and went over to see Aaron, then the doorbell rang, and a hush came over the room. Boyd poked his head inside. Carl was on his hip and Josie was behind him.

"Come on in," Maeve said. The crowd parted, leaving the Myers family a clear path to Santa.

"Ho ho ho, Merry Christmas!" Aaron bellowed.

Carl spotted Santa and ran over to him. "Hello, Carl," Aaron said. "I have a present for you." He handed the little boy a gift. Carl crawled off his lap, sat on the floor and began to shred the wrapping paper in earnest.

"And, Boyd, Santa has a present for you, too. I'm sorry, but despite my best attempts, the elves couldn't figure out how to wrap this one. You see, it's come to my attention that Valley Ridge Farm and House Supplies has experienced some major changes. First of all, it has a new owner—" Aaron pointed to himself "—a brilliant, insightful comedian who's almost ready for prime time."

Maeve chuckled, which made Aaron smile beneath his white beard and mustache. "He has renamed it VR Supplies. I know, it's not overly inventive, but at least it's much shorter."

"Congratulations," Boyd said.

"And secondly, before the sale even went through, my uncle's manager, Tom, put in his two weeks' notice. He's accepted a new position at a store in Erie. That means we have an opening. And rumor has it that you have managerial experience. VR Supplies would be honored if you'd agree to take a full-time position with us."

Josie started to cry. Great, heaving sobs as she hugged her huge stomach.

"I think there's a chance Santa has one more present for you," Maeve whispered to her friend. "Hold it together for another minute."

As if on cue, Santa handed Josie a small box. "There's one last gift for all three of you...well, three and a half. There's a certain movie from years ago where a newspaper editor tells a little girl named Virginia that Santa does, in fact, exist. Well, that newspaper editor was right. Santa exists here in Valley Ridge. And it's Santa and the community of Valley Ridge who are giving you this gift."

Josie was still sobbing as she unwrapped the small box and removed the single key.

Maeve almost laughed through her own tears when she saw that Aaron had found a keychain with a bell to hang the key from.

It tinkled softly as Josie lifted the key.

Josie held the key out for Boyd to see, then turned to Aaron. "I don't understand."

"I think Maeve should explain," he said quietly.

"This house," Maeve said. "It's for you, Boyd and Carl if you want it. The entire town worked to get it ready."

Josie didn't say a word. She sank down on the couch and stared at the key.

Boyd shook his head. "That's wonderful, but even with the new job, we can't pull together a down payment, much less monthly payments."

Aaron shrugged. "That's something that we can work out. The house is owned by the Valley Ridge Home For Christmas Foundation and it's been set up to make the houses affordable. All you need to know is if you want it, it's yours. You can pull the RV over tonight and unpack. Carl could wake up here Christmas morning. Everything else will get sorted."

Boyd looked to Josie who nodded.

He turned to Aaron. "I'd say we'd pay you back, and we will pay back the money, but the rest of it? There's no way to pay you back for that. I don't know what to say, how to thank you." He extended his hand.

Aaron stood and shook it. "You should know this was all Maeve."

Boyd laughed, tears running down his face. "Of course it was."

Everyone else in the room cheered and clapped.

Maeve protested, "It wasn't all me. It was everyone. The tree came from Colton's farm, the butcher block in the kitchen came from Gabriel—but you know that because you found it when you cleaned out the garage, Boyd. Practically the whole town was here, putting up drywall, painting, fixing the porch or the roof. Mrs. Keith and Ray installed the tile backsplash in the kitchen. This house wasn't all me. It was all of us, and a lot of people who aren't here. They donated time, or items..."

Carl was sitting by the Christmas tree playing with his Noah's Ark. He took a wooden elephant and whacked at a branch, which sent a bell ringing.

Quietly, Boyd said, "Josie told me that everything happens for a reason. Now, Maeve Buchanan, you can protest, but I'm sure that if I asked anyone here who should get the credit, they'd all say you. And while I'm a proud man, I'm not too proud to say thank-you." He turned and nodded at the group. "Thank you, to each of you. Thank you for making us a part of the community. I can't think of a better place for us to live and raise our children."

Josie hadn't said a word until now. But once Boyd finished, she clambered to her feet and pulled Maeve into her arms and hugged her. "Thank you. I don't know what I ever did to deserve a friend like you, but I'm so grateful."

When Josie finally let go of Maeve, Boyd said, "Why don't you give us the tour of our new home?"

* * *

AARON WAS CERTAIN he wasn't the only one with a tear in his eye as he watched the Myers family accept the house. Maeve led the new home owners to the coat closet. "This is where the tour starts. Of everything in the house, this is my favorite part." She opened the door. "Everyone who worked on or donated to the house signed here on the inside. We wanted some way to remind you of all the people who care. This is Valley Ridge, New York. We're a community, but more than that, we're a family. And you all have a home here, and with us."

Josie traced some of the letters and studied the names, as if hoping to memorize each one. "It's amazing."

Aaron followed as Maeve escorted them from room to room. She didn't just show them the rooms, she introduced them to the people who'd worked on them. "...Mayor Tuznik donated and hung the new light, and Mrs. Esterly sanded all the baseboards.... Pete at the grocery store stocked the pantry and fridge. JoAnn, from the bed-and-breakfast, donated the bedding. Her mother made the quilt on your bed.... Hank gave you that big cast-iron pan. It's a Griswold. They used to make them in Erie, which is about a half hour away....Gabriel, Geoff and Colton are all local vintners and they stocked the wine rack. They said you should toast the new house, after the baby comes of course. Vera made all the doilies...."

Each item, each project. She remembered who was responsible and made sure she gave them the credit.

She didn't take any credit for herself, but Aaron could see from everyone's expressions that they all knew who was responsible for it all coming together.

Aaron now knew without a doubt that Maeve's motivation for everything she did was her beautiful heart. She'd believed the saying on the wall hanging in her kitchen 100 percent. *I can't save the world, but I can try.*

She enjoyed every moment of showing off the house. He could see how happy she was with this gift. The girl who'd once been homeless was giving someone else a home.

He could only imagine how much that meant to her.

She was on the other side of the room, standing with her mother, stepfather and Hank—the man who'd given Maeve and Renie a hand when they'd needed it the most. The three newly married Valley Ridge couples were in another corner, talking and laughing.

The whole room was filled with people in small, intimate groups and Aaron felt out of place.

"Santa, will you come sit with me a moment?" Josie called when the tour had wound down.

He smiled at Valley Ridge's newest resident. "It would be my pleasure."

"I have a couple of things I need to say to you. The first one is thank you. Thank you for Boyd's job."

"He's earned it. He's already an asset. And I have to have someone I can trust to take care of the day-to-day business. I've got my own work and while I want to be involved in the store, I can't really run it."

"And thank you for the house," Josie continued. "Maeve told me you're the one who bought it and then donated it to the foundation."

315

"I bet she didn't tell you that I actually screwed up her plans. She was prepared to buy it with her own money."

Josie looked at Maeve and shook her head. "You're right, she didn't."

"I'm not sure I'll ever really understand Maeve, but I plan to stick around and try to, even if it takes the rest of my life."

She patted his knee in a motherly way. "It took you long enough to figure that out. I knew as soon as I saw you both together."

He laughed. "And I'm willing to wait for her to figure it out, as well."

"I don't think it's going to take her very long, but you may need to help convince her." Josie grinned. "You know I'm cheering you on."

"Thanks," Aaron said, grinning back "I'll need all the support I can get."

* * *

Once The impromptu party had wound down. Aaron offered to drive the RV over to the house for the Myers.

He parked the RV and handed the keys to Boyd, his new employee.

"I'm going to miss seeing that from my kitchen window and knowing you were only steps away," Maeve said.

"Valley Ridge is small enough I don't think it will take that many more steps to come over. And you know you're welcome at ours anytime," Boyd said.

"Merry Christmas. I hope this is only the first of many happy ones. And you're still invited to dinner tomorrow at Mom's," Maeve told them.

"We wouldn't miss it," Josie promised.

Maeve wished them good-night and insisted they get indoors before Josie caught a chill. Maeve took Aaron's hand and they strolled down the front walk. She turned around and looked back at the bright house, the tree merrily lit in the front window. "I can't believe we got it done."

"You're the only one who can't. Everyone else knew that if you set your mind to it, it would get done one way or another."

"I didn't only do it for them. I did it for me, too." She knew she'd changed, but it wasn't the house that was the catalyst. It was Aaron. "Will you spend Christmas Eve with me?" she asked. She couldn't think of anything she wanted more than to wake up on Christmas morning with Aaron at her side.

"I thought you'd never ask."

They cut through the parking lot. She glanced at the store—at Aaron's store. "VR Supplies, huh?"

"It's easier to fit on shirts."

He took her hand and they walked home without saying another word. Simply holding his hand and walking in the light snow was perfect.

Once they were at her place, she plugged in her tree lights and scanned the pile of DVDs. "How about *A Christmas Carol*—"

Aaron laughed. "Is this the last one?"

"There are a couple more. This is the '04 musical version."

He wasn't nearly the Christmas movie connoisseur that Maeve was, but he knew this one. "Jesse L. Martin's in it, right? My sisters made me watch it."

She flipped the case and stared at the credits. "I'm not sure."

Aaron didn't want to watch the movie. He wanted to talk to Maeve. He wanted to tell her why he was staying. He wanted to tell her what he was feeling. He wanted to be with her for all her Christmases. He had told himself he'd be patient. Hell, he'd told Josie that he was going to be patient. But his patience was at an end before the movie was.

As he watched Ebenezer yet again, he had an epiphany.

He grabbed the remote control and hit Pause. He turned to Maeve. "I just realized, I've been living one of your holiday movies."

"Nestor, the Long-Eared Christmas Donkey?" she teased.

He shook his head. "I'm Ebenezer freakin' Scrooge. And you're the ghost of Christmas present."

She sat a little straighter and turned to face him. "I'm a ghost?"

He nodded. "And Boyd, Josie and Carl? They're the ghosts of Christmas future. Because of you, I helped them and that means I changed their future."

She frowned. "I don't think you're hitting the mark on this comparison."

"Close enough. You get the point."

"So, if that's the case, who's Christmas past?"

"My ex. Signing the divorce papers wasn't enough. I needed to talk to her, to resolve things between us. I was so bitter. I thought it was about the money. To be honest, I wanted it to be about the money. That would have absolved me from any fault. If she was a coldhearted money-grubbing ex, then it would be all on her."

"But that wasn't the case?" Maeve asked.

"No. No, it wasn't. Tracey did get a share of the money I made from my program in the settlement, but she was more than entitled to it. Obviously she didn't write the code, but she put up with me while I did. She was my sounding board. She took care of everything else—she took care of me—in order to let me concentrate on my work.

"I became so obsessed with my work that I forgot what mattered. I'm embarrassed to say that she spent more holidays with my family than I did. I didn't even notice she'd gone back to school. What she asked for in the divorce wasn't anything more than what she deserved, because what she asked for in our marriage, I couldn't—wouldn't—give her."

"And blaming her was easier than dealing with yourself?" Maeve asked, though it was more of a statement than a question.

"Yes. I've had my three visits this holiday season. I've seen what I've done wrong, and I'm being offered a chance to do better." He held her hands. "And I want to do better. I want you, Maeve. I love you. I know it's happened fast. But I can't control it. And nothing will change how I feel. I love you."

She was quiet for a long time before she said, "Ever since I lost my father, I've felt homeless. When I bought this place, I thought I'd found it. Somewhere I could put down roots. Somewhere that was mine. Somewhere I would always belong. But Josie showed me that home isn't a place. It's not a roof over your head, or the walls that surround you. It's a person. Or a family. I'm beginning to believe that my home is with you."

He kissed her. "I don't want to rush this. I want to do normal things—I want to date you. I want to go out to dinners, watch the sun set together. I want to take you to the movies, and go to book club with you. I want to see where it leads, but I think I already know."

She quoted the inscription in the book he'd given her, with a few changes. "Aaron, May you treasure the memories of our Christmases past. May you relish each moment of our Christmas present. And may we have many, many Christmases future to explore. All my love, Maeve." She smiled and added, "Merry Christmas, Aaron. I love you."

"Merry Christmas, Maeve. I love you, too."

EPILOGUE

Boyd held the door open with one hand, and secured Carl on his hip with the other. The bell on the door jingled merrily. "Happy New Year and welcome home, Mrs. Myers."

Josie stepped into her house, the newborn in her arms. She smelled the Christmas tree and felt a special warmth that had nothing to do with the heating. It had more to do with the bell that Boyd had given her for Christmas—a bell he once thought they'd put on a house in North Dakota—and more to do with the lights, which Boyd must have switched on. The feeling came from the fact that she was home.

"Welcome home, Maggie," she whispered to her daughter as they stood in the entryway.

Boyd set Carl down and took off his coat. "Josie, go and rest. Carl and I have everything under control." He held out his arms for Maggie to allow Josie to take off her own coat. She hung it on the peg.

"Now, relax," Boyd commanded.

Normally Josie didn't take orders well. Who was she kidding? She didn't take them at all. But today, she wanted to do nothing more than sit in her own home and rock her daughter while her husband and son took care of things. She kissed Boyd's cheek as she took the baby from him. "I don't mind if I do."

The rocker sat in the corner. She rocked Maggie as Boyd built a fire with Carl's "help."

Home.

Josie was home.

As if on cue, the doorbell rang. She knew she had a certain redheaded angel to thank for setting this all in motion.

"That must be dinner," Boyd said with a smile. She marveled that he seemed so at ease with the idea of someone making them supper and delivering it, too.

She knew that he hadn't permanently put away his pride. It was that he had faith in a future here— he had faith that he'd find a way to pay back any kindnesses anyone did for him.

She could hear Maeve arguing at the door about not wanting to disturb anyone, but Boyd insisted she and Aaron come in.

Maeve was right, Josie wasn't up for company, but Maeve wasn't that. Maeve could never be company. She was family.

"Come in, please?" she called. "If you don't, I'll have to get up and come see you."

That did it. Maeve and Aaron both walked into the living room. "I'd like to introduce you all. Maeve and Aaron, meet Margaret *Maeve* Myers. Maggie, actually."

"Oh," Maeve said and she quietly stepped forward.

"Would you like to hold your goddaughter—that is, if you agree to be her godmother?" Josie asked.

Boyd chuckled and she realized that her husband was back to being the lighthearted man she'd married. Thanks to Aaron and Maeve, his spirits had been lifted. If for nothing else, she'd owe them her eternal gratitude.

"That was my wife asking if you and Aaron would consider being Maggie's godparents," he clarified.

"Oh, Josie, you know we will." Maeve stood with the baby in her arms, swaying side to side. And Aaron looked at her with such love in his eyes that Josie knew that he and Maeve were going to make it.

"You seem like a pro, Maeve," Josie said.

Carl ran over to Aaron, and he picked up the child. Josie sat in her rocker, in her living room, with the glow from the tree and the fireplace bathing the room. She watched her two friends hold her children with clear affection.

"We're not going to stay. You all need to settle in," Maeve said, handing the baby over. "But if there's anything, anything at all we can do, call us. We can be here in minutes. And thank you for naming her after me. I'm so proud to be her godmother."

Boyd showed them out, the bell on the door ringing as he shut it.

Josie whispered to her daughter, "You're a very lucky girl, Maggie, to have people like that looking out for you."

Boyd stood in the doorway, Carl once again on his hip. He was smiling at her.

In his smile, she saw so much love. She remembered the young, awkward boy who'd asked her to the school dance. She could still see that boy in Boyd's smile.

"It's my guess that Valley Ridge will have another big wedding sooner than later. Maybe even this spring? Spring weddings are so beautiful. If not, then summer." She could see Maeve, flowers in her hair, looking radiant as she walked down the aisle toward Aaron.

Boyd laughed again. The sound delighted her.

"You always were the optimist," he said. "Do you remember when we got here in the middle of—"

"Snowmageddon."

"Yes, Snowmageddon. You told me that everything happened for a reason. That Plattsburgh wasn't our real home and that we had to leave in order to find it."

"And I was right." She tried to keep the smugness out of her voice, but she feared she wasn't quite able to manage it. "I thought we'd have to travel farther to find it, but it was right here, in Valley Ridge. In this house our friends built for us."

"You're wrong. My real home is wherever you and the kids are. I had it all along." He came over and kissed her forehead. "Thank you for being the eternal optimist. Thank you for everything."

"Happy New Year, Boyd Myers. Welcome home."

~~~

Dear Reader,

Thank you for picking up *A Hometown Christmas*, the eighth book in my *Hometown Hearts* series. I hope you enjoyed the story. If you did, please leave a review at your favorite online book store. It's the best way to help new readers discover my books.

Keep an eye out for the first book in my new series, *A View to a Kiln: A Harry's Pottery Mystery.*
Happy "Holly"days!

Holly Jacobs

Hometown Hearts

1. Crib Notes
2. A Special Kind of Different
3. Homecoming
4. Suddenly a Father
A Hometown Hearts Wedding

5. Something Borrowed

6. Something Blue

7. Something Perfect

8. A Hometown Christmas

ABOUT THE AUTHOR

Award-winning author Holly Jacobs has over three million books in print worldwide. The first novel in her Everything But... series, *Everything But a Groom*, was named one of 2008's Best Romances by Booklist, and her books have been honored with many other accolades. She lives in Erie, Pennsylvania, with her family. You can visit her at ***www.HollyJacobs.com***.

www.ingramcontent.com/pod-product-compliance
Lightning Source LLC
Chambersburg PA
CBHW051938220626
47052CB00004B/696